HARLEQUIN *Super*ROMANCE®

936
SEP

NEW YORK TIMES BESTSELLING AUTHOR

DEBBIE MACOMBER

Judith Bowen
Janice Kay Johnson

D0034447

BORN IN A
SMALL TOWN

$4.50 U.S./$5.25 CAN.

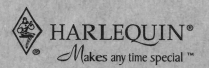

HARLEQUIN®

Makes any time special ™

ISBN 0-373-70936-6

9 780373 709366

50450

HARLEQUIN SUPERROMANCE
Celebrates its 20ᵗʰ Anniversary

Two decades of bringing you the very best in romance reading.

To recognize this important milestone, we've invited six very special authors—whose names you're sure to recognize—to tell us how they feel about Superromance. Each title this month has a foreword by one of these authors.

New York Times bestselling author Debbie Macomber says "Happy Birthday, Superromance. You're not getting older, you just keep getting better and better." Debbie says she's thrilled to be part of *Born in a Small Town*. And we're honored to have her novella, "Midnight Sons and Daughters," in this special Superromance anniversary volume—together with "The Glory Girl" by Judith Bowen and "Promise Me Picket Fences" by Janice Kay Johnson.

Born in a small town, always from a small town...

These stories bring you home to the small towns created by three popular authors:

Debbie Macomber's Hard Luck, Alaska
Judith Bowen's Glory, Alberta and
Janice Kay Johnson's Elk Springs, Oregon

It's time for a visit!

ABOUT THE AUTHORS

For many readers, **Debbie Macomber** needs no introduction. She is now a *New York Times* bestselling author who also makes regular appearances on the *USA Today* booklist. Debbie, who was first published in 1982, has written series romance fiction for both Harlequin and Silhouette, and has been writing for MIRA Books since 1997. There are more than forty-five million copies of her books in print. Debbie's story in this collection, "Midnight Sons and Daughters," introduces characters who first appeared in her MIDNIGHT SONS series. You can reach Debbie at P.O. Box 1458, Port Orchard, Washington 98366 or through her Web site at www.debbiemacomber.com.

Judith Bowen is a popular writer whose seventh MEN OF GLORY book (and fourteenth novel), *A Home of His Own,* is coming from Superromance in November of this year. Judith is familiar with the background portrayed in her books, since she grew up in Alberta and knows country life well. She has won several writing awards, including the Readers' Choice, and has taught a number of writing courses. You can access her Web site at www.judithbowen.com.

The author of close to forty books, **Janice Kay Johnson** has written for adults, children and young adults. When not writing or researching her books, Janice quilts, grows antique roses, chauffeurs her two daughters to soccer and play rehearsals, takes care of her cats (too many to itemize!) and volunteers at a no-kill cat shelter. Janice has twice been a finalist in the Romance Writers of America's prestigious RITA Awards. In October watch for Janice's newest Superromance, *The Daughter Merger.* You can reach her through www.superauthors.com.

DEBBIE MACOMBER

Judith Bowen ~~Page 109 Henry Sid~~

Janice Kay Johnson ~~page 285~~

Promise me Picket Fences

BORN IN A
SMALL TOWN

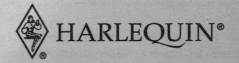

HARLEQUIN®

TORONTO • NEW YORK • LONDON
AMSTERDAM • PARIS • SYDNEY • HAMBURG
STOCKHOLM • ATHENS • TOKYO • MILAN • MADRID
PRAGUE • WARSAW • BUDAPEST • AUCKLAND

ISBN 0-373-70936-6

BORN IN A SMALL TOWN

Copyright © 2000 by Harlequin Books S.A.

The publisher acknowledges the copyright holders of the individual works as follows:

MIDNIGHT SONS AND DAUGHTERS
Copyright © 2000 by Debbie Macomber.

THE GLORY GIRL
Copyright © 2000 by J. E. Corser.

PROMISE ME PICKET FENCES
Copyright © 2000 by Janice Kay Johnson.

FOREWORD BY DEBBIE MACOMBER

Twenty years ago, when I was a struggling unpublished writer, Harlequin announced the launch of Superromance, a line of longer, more complex romance novels. This new market was exciting and welcome news to those of us yearning to sell our stories.

I remember how eagerly I pored over each book. I was introduced to some wonderful stories by wonderful new writers: *End of Innocence* by Abra Taylor, *Captive of Desire* by Alexandra Sellers, books by Margaret Chittenden, Linda Ward and others. Their novels opened up a whole new world of romance to me, both as a writer and a reader. As always, the love stories thrilled me, but it was the addition of subplots and significant secondary characters that I found especially gripping. These were stories that touched my heart, enlightened and intrigued me. LaVyrle Spencer's *The Hellion* and Sandra Canfield's *Voices on the Wind* remain on my shelf to this day.

As the years progressed, Superromance evolved along with its writers. We were introduced to a wide range of talented new authors—writers like Judith Bowen, Margot Early, Tara Taylor Quinn, Janice Kay Johnson and many more. Their stories, published by a series that benefits from the firm foundation of a twenty-year history, have been greeted by an enthusiastic and waiting audience.

Through the years, the traditions of love, courage, honor and dignity have remained the very heart of Superromance. The books so often have a depth, an added texture, an emotional maturity. Superromance has gained a reputation for stories that reach out and grab the reader by the heart and never let go.

For the past fourteen years, I've had the privilege of working with the Senior Editor of Superromance, Paula Eykelhof. When she asked me to be part of this anthology, I remembered how excited I was the day I first heard about the launch of this line. I remember wishing that someday I could write for it, too. It only took me twenty years—but it was worth the wait!

I'm thrilled to be part of *Born in a Small Town*, with two wonderful writers I'm honored to call friends. Happy Birthday, Superromance! You're not getting older, you just keep getting better and better....

Debbie Macomber

Midnight Sons and Daughters
Debbie Macomber

HARD LUCK, ALASKA

Hard Luck is a fictional town situated fifty miles north of the Arctic Circle, near the Brooks Mountain Range. It was introduced in Debbie Macomber's MIDNIGHT SONS series (*Brides for Brothers, The Marriage Risk, Daddy's Little Helper, Because of the Baby, Falling for Him* and *Ending in Marriage*—first published in 1995 and 1996 and reprinted in three volumes in 2000).

The town was founded in 1931 by Adam O'Halloran and his wife, Anna. By the time of the Second World War, its population was fifty or sixty people, all told. During the war, the O'Halloran sons, Charles and David, joined the armed services. Charles was killed; only David came home—with a young English war bride, Ellen Sawyer.

After the war, David qualified as a bush pilot. He then built some small cabins to attract the sport fishermen and hunters who were starting to come to Alaska. Eventually, he built a lodge to replace the cabins—a lodge that later burned.

David and Ellen had three sons born fairly late in their marriage—Charles (named after David's brother), Sawyer and Christian.

Hard Luck had been growing all this time, and by 1970 was home to just over a hundred people. These were the years of the oil boom, when the school and community center were built by the state. After Vietnam, ex-serviceman Ben Hamilton came to live here and opened the Hard Luck Café, which became the social focus for the town.

In the 1980s, the three O'Halloran brothers formed a partnership, creating MIDNIGHT SONS, a bush pilot service. When the original series started, the O'Hallorans were losing qualified pilots at an alarming rate—because there were no women in town! So, the brothers came up with a plan: Offer jobs and land to women willing to move to Alaska...

"Midnight Sons and Daughters" takes place almost twenty years later. Scott O'Halloran, stepson of Sawyer, and Chrissie Harris, daughter of Mitch, are keeping the great tradition of Alaskan romance alive!

BORN IN A SMALL TOWN
Midnight Sons and Daughters

Cast of Major Characters (introduced in the MIDNIGHT SONS series). The stories in which they play a central role are indicated in parentheses.

Matt Caldwell: Brother of Lanni (Caldwell) O'Halloran; married to **Karen.** Co-owners of Hard Luck Lodge, built on the site of the original lodge *(Because of the Baby)*

Ben Hamilton: Owner of Hard Luck Café; Bethany's natural father

Mitch Harris: Public Safety Officer (equivalent of sheriff or police); married to **Bethany** (Ross) Harris; father of **Chrissie** *(Daddy's Little Helper)*

Charles O'Halloran: oldest brother; geologist and silent partner in Midnight Sons; married to **Lanni** (Caldwell) O'Halloran, editor of the local paper *(The Marriage Risk)*

Christian O'Halloran: youngest brother, pilot; married to **Mariah** (Douglas) O'Halloran, who runs the Midnight Sons office *(Falling for Him)*

Sawyer O'Halloran: middle brother, pilot; married to **Abbey** (Sutherland) O'Halloran, a librarian; stepfather of **Scott** and **Susan** *(Brides for Brothers)*

Duke Porter: bush pilot employed by Midnight Sons; married to **Tracy** (Santiago) Porter *(Ending in Marriage)*

CHAPTER ONE

THE FIRST THING Chrissie Harris intended to do when she saw Scott O'Halloran was slap his face—hard. And she might have the opportunity today, she thought, reluctant to get out of bed on this clear August morning. The man had broken her heart, not once but twice—and she'd *let* him!

The first time she'd been seventeen, and she'd stood at the Midnight Sons airstrip one frigid winter morning and watched him fly out of Hard Luck, Alaska. Unable to get along with his mother and stepfather, Scott had enlisted in the army. Chrissie had thought her whole world would cave in without Scott. She'd been crazy about him from the time she was in grade school, when his mother had moved him to Hard Luck with him and his sister and married Sawyer O'Halloran. In third grade Chrissie had decided that as soon as they were grown-ups, she'd marry Scott; she'd believed he loved her, too—a belief she'd maintained for the next decade.

She'd been wrong.

Two years out of high school he'd clashed with his stepfather and promptly volunteered three years of his life to Uncle Sam. Chrissie had moped around for weeks, missing him dreadfully but pretending otherwise. In retrospect she realized she hadn't fooled anyone. Least of all Susan, her best friend and Scott's sister.

Every afternoon Chrissie had beaten a path to the post office, eager for a letter. Every night she'd poured out her heart to him in long missives. In the beginning Scott did write. Boot camp was hell, he'd told her. Following graduation he volunteered for Airborne Ranger School in Fort Benning, Georgia. Eventually his letters became less and less frequent. Finally they stopped altogether.

What hurt most was that Scott had asked his *sister* to break the news. As gently as possible, Susan let Chrissie know that Scott had met someone else.

That was the first time he'd broken her heart.

The next time happened five years later, the year Chrissie and Susan graduated from college. The two families had thrown a huge celebration party in Hard Luck, which half the town attended. Who should unexpectedly show up but Scott O'Halloran? He'd occasionally come home during the intervening years, but Chrissie had always avoided him. After the heartless way he'd dumped her, it was what he deserved. But at twenty-two she was older, more mature. Smart, too. She hadn't graduated magna cum laude for nothing.

Only, Chrissie wasn't nearly as savvy as she'd assumed. It took Scott less than a week to maneuver himself back into her life. He told her how much he'd missed her, how he regretted the way he'd treated her. He'd gone on to claim that every woman he'd met since paled compared to her. Blah, blah, blah.

Chrissie had swallowed his lies, every one of

them. She was so in love with him her brain had virtually ceased to function. Then Farrah Warner had arrived and declared herself Scott's fiancée. Scott had tried to explain, to apologize, but Chrissie had refused to listen. Before another day had passed, Scott and Farrah had flown out of Hard Luck, leaving everyone, including his own family, upset and confused.

Chrissie vowed that was the second and *last* time he'd ever break her heart.

Recently she'd heard that Scott was returning to Hard Luck permanently as a partner in Midnight Sons, the bush plane service owned by his father and his uncle Christian. Chrissie swore she wouldn't allow Scott O'Halloran to come anywhere near her. She would not give him the opportunity to break her heart a third time.

That determined, she rolled over and turned off her clock radio before the alarm could buzz. Sitting up, she rubbed the sleep—what little she'd managed to catch—from her eyes. She'd spent most of the night reviewing her history with Scott, going over and over his betrayals, hardening her resolve. At twenty-six, she wasn't a schoolgirl any longer. The law degree hanging in the office she shared with Tracy Santiago Porter said as much.

When the phone pealed at five minutes after seven, it jolted Chrissie so badly she nearly fell off the bed.

"Yes," she snapped.

"Scott's flight is due in at ten," Susan cheerfully informed her. Despite everything, her best friend continued to believe that Scott and Chrissie were meant to be together. As far as Chrissie was concerned, it wouldn't happen in this or any other life-time.

"Oh, Scott's coming home?" Chrissie asked, hoping she sounded bored and uninterested. "Is that today?"

"You know it is."

"Yes," Chrissie said, faking a yawn. "I suppose I did."

"This time it's for good. My brother's here to stay."

"Really?" Chrissie feigned a second yawn as if she couldn't care less. She cared, all right, but only because she wanted to tell him he was lower than a tundra rat—and then follow that with a resounding slap to his face.

"Mom and Dad are thrilled."

Chrissie tensed, struggling to hide her reaction.

"He's going to be flying for Midnight Sons. Mom and Dad have been wanting this for years. With Anna and Ryan older now, Dad's hoping to cut back his hours and… Oh, Chrissie, this is what we've *all* wanted!"

Chrissie knew that, but she wasn't sure Hard Luck was big enough for the both of them. All right, fine, she could deal with Scott living in Hard Luck. It wasn't as though her world revolved around him. Not anymore. Whether he stayed or moved on didn't make one iota of difference to her.

She could certainly be civil if she ran into him, although that wasn't likely to happen often. Hard Luck wasn't as small a town as it had once been. Twenty years ago the population was around fifty— mostly cantankerous men in need of women. The

O'Halloran brothers hadn't been able to hold on to their staff of professional pilots and were losing them at an alarming rate to other commuter-airline companies in Fairbanks and Anchorage. Something had to be done, and quickly. The best way to keep their pilots, the O'Halloran brothers had decided, was to lure women north.

Their plan worked, too. Surprisingly well. Abbey, Scott and Susan's mother, was the first woman to arrive, and a number of others had followed soon after. In the years since, Hard Luck had expanded, and its population had reached a robust six hundred. More families moved in every year.

Susan's husband, Ron Gold, and his partner, Matt Caldwell, did a booming winter tourist business, which involved dogsledding, camping and more. Midnight Sons flew in the adventure-seeking sightseers. That was only part of their business; they also functioned as a commuter line and a courier company. Actually the airline had a corner on the market, because the only way to reach Hard Luck was by plane.

It wouldn't be long now before the next group of visitors showed up. The last days of summer lingered on, but in early September the weather would start to turn chilly; snow would come by October—and with it, the winter tourists. ·

"Chrissie, Chrissie. Have you heard *anything* I said?"

"Sorry," Chrissie muttered. "I let my thoughts wander."

"I want you to be pleased Scott's moving home,"

Susan insisted. "You two make such a perfect couple."

Chrissie snickered. She couldn't help herself. She and Scott? Not anymore. She didn't trust him, couldn't make her heart vulnerable to him a third time. The first two times had hurt too damn much. No, she was a sensible attorney now, a woman who wouldn't be swayed by a glib tongue and a pair of bright baby blues, even if they did belong to the one and only man she'd ever truly loved.

"Scott could move next door and it wouldn't make any difference to me," Chrissie said in as matter-of-fact a tone as she could muster.

"You sure about that?"

"Positive." Leave it to Susan and her romantic inclinations. But then, Chrissie supposed Susan was entitled to feel optimistic on that score; the year she graduated from college, she'd married the boy she'd loved half her life. "Listen, I've still got to shower," Chrissie said. Knowing Susan wouldn't be satisfied until she had her way, she added, "When you see Scott, tell him hello for me." As soon as the words left her lips, she realized her mistake. Scott might consider that an invitation to look her up, and there was nothing she wanted less. Quickly she said, "No, don't. In fact, I'd rather you didn't mention my name at all."

"You know Scott's going to ask about you."

"Well, if he does, tell him I'm perfectly content without him in my life."

Susan laughed outright. "That sounds like a crock to me."

"Well, it isn't," Chrissie said, praying she wasn't

giving herself away. Hiding her true feelings from her best friend was something she found difficult. But the truth was, she fully intended to keep her distance from Scott.

Resolved to push all thoughts of him from her mind, Chrissie slammed into the office early. She refused to look at her clock, refused to remember that at ten that very morning, Scott O'Halloran was flying back into Hard Luck—and into her well-ordered life.

At eleven-thirty, just as she was about to break for lunch, Kate, the secretary she shared with Tracy, buzzed her. "Scott O'Halloran is here to see you. Shall I send him in?"

Already? Chrissie's heart began to race, pounding so hard she had to catch her breath. Scott was here? Now?

"Ms. Harris?"

Forcing her heart to slow down, Chrissie leaned over and pressed the intercom button. "Send him in," she said as evenly as her shallow breath would allow.

A moment later Scott strolled into her small office. He hadn't changed. He was still better-looking than any man had a right to be. He'd always had a real presence—a confident quality and a sense of life that invariably attracted people. Especially women. Chrissie made herself stand and meet him eye to eye. For one wild moment all she could do was stare. Furious at her reaction, she let her hands fall onto her desk for support.

"Hello, Scott," she managed to say, proud of revealing a complete lack of emotion. To all appearances, he might have been a stranger.

"Chrissie." He beamed her a smile bright enough to rival the sun.

She inhaled and held her breath. With hardly any effort, he was tearing down her defenses. And, no doubt, he knew exactly the effect he had on her, hide it though she might.

"You're looking good," he murmured with a nod of approval.

"Yes, I know," she said in blithe tones, wanting him to realize she wouldn't be won over by a bit of flattery and some practiced charm. Not this time. He could fall at her feet and beg her forgiveness, and she'd look down at him and feel nothing but contempt.

"Do you have a few minutes?" he asked.

"Actually I don't." Striking a casual pose, she crossed her arms. How *dared* he assume he could saunter into her office and pretend nothing had happened? He had nerve, she'd say that for him. Well, dammit, so did she. "Perhaps it'd be best if we cleared the air now," she said aggressively.

"Cleared the air?"

"If you think you can walk back into my life again, you're wrong. I'm older now. Wiser, too. The first time, shame on you, the second time shame on me. There simply isn't gong to be a third time."

Scott's lips quivered with a smile.

"You find this amusing?"

"If you'd give me a chance to explain…" he began.

She laughed lightly, breezily, as if to suggest she'd be a fool to listen to anything he had to say. "Explain *what?* You're the one who claimed to be in love with me—and all the while you were engaged to another woman! Frankly, I'm not interested in hearing any explanations. That's all water under the bridge.'' With great aplomb, she walked around her desk to her chair. Sitting down, her back very straight, she reached for her pen and glanced casually upward. ''I think you should leave now.''

''Well, the truth is, Chrissie, I didn't stop by to rehash old times. I was planning to hire you to draw up some legal papers, since I'm becoming a full partner in Midnight Sons.''

''Oh.'' Mortified beyond words, Chrissie fought to keep from crawling beneath her desk.

''But that's okay. I'll make an appointment with Tracy.''

''Ah…'' she blubbered, then nodded, implying she thought this was probably the best idea.

''Good to see you again,'' he said on his way out the door, closing it behind him.

Chrissie dropped her forehead to her desk. What was it about Scott O'Halloran that turned her into a complete idiot every time she saw him?

CHAPTER TWO

ABBEY O'HALLORAN'S HEART was full. As she shelved books at the Hard Luck lending library, she reflected on the reason for her happiness. She'd been waiting for this day a very long time. Her son was home. Years ago, divorced and raising two children alone, she'd moved to Hard Luck and, after a few weeks and a whirlwind courtship, had married Sawyer O'Halloran. They had a good marriage and had added Anna and Ryan, now seventeen and nineteen respectively, to their family. As soon as he could, Sawyer had adopted Scott and Susan, and loved and nurtured her children as his own. Scott, however, had gone through a difficult period of teenage rebellion that had left Abbey and Sawyer at a loss as to how to deal with him.

It'd all started his last year of high school, when he had a couple of minor run-ins with Mitch Harris, the sheriff and Chrissie's father. Mitch assured Sawyer and Abbey that Scott wasn't a bad boy and the pranks he'd pulled were typical of many teenagers. Skipping school and painting graffiti on the community-center wall were small infractions, ones Abbey had been willing to overlook. What she couldn't excuse was Scott's lack of respect for Sawyer. Her husband had been nothing but warm and loving to both Scott and Susan. Scott, though, had become an increasingly angry young man, and he'd vented that anger against Sawyer. Abbey had never completely understood why her son seemed so resentful, why he'd felt such rage. His unpleasant behavior had escalated during his high-school years and later, too, when Scott had briefly worked for Midnight Sons. Although Sawyer had never complained, Abbey knew he'd been deeply hurt by the things Scott had said and done.

Then one day, without a word to anyone, Scott had enlisted in the army. Not that Abbey or Sawyer would have objected. By this point it was obvious that Scott had problems he needed to resolve. As his mother, she'd longed to help him deal with his past, yearned to answer his doubts, but she couldn't help what she didn't understand. Watching Scott fly out of Hard Luck for boot camp was, without question, one of the most difficult moments she'd ever experienced.

She'd known someday he'd return. She just hadn't known when that day would come. She certainly hadn't expected it to be nearly ten years later.

The library door opened and Sawyer walked in. Even after all these years of marriage, she felt a rush of joy at the sight of him. His hair was almost completely gray now. The laugh lines around his eyes were more pronounced but he was as handsome and vital as when they'd first met.

"What are you doing here?" she asked, surprised to see him.

"Hey, I've got a library card."

His eyes held a warm teasing light and she smiled

in response. She'd loved this man for twenty years and borne him two children. They'd made a good life together in Hard Luck and looked forward to the time they could officially retire and travel, the way they'd planned. As Sawyer often reminded her, there was an entire world for them to explore. But no matter where they went, Alaska would always be home.

"I thought you were with Scott." She placed the latest Janet Evanovich mystery back on the shelf, then turned and kissed her husband, catching him by surprise.

"Hey, what's that for?"

"I'm just so happy I can barely hold it all inside. Scott's home! And this time it's for good."

Sawyer grinned with equal delight. "He's grown up, Abbey."

"I know."

"The years away have served him well. He's lost all that anger. He's made peace with himself and he's ready to step into the business." Sawyer moved toward her desk and perched on the corner. "Did you hear he's found a place to rent?"

"Already?" Abbey couldn't help being disappointed. She'd hoped for a chance to fuss over her son for the first couple of weeks.

"He wants to make his own way, and I can't say I blame him," Sawyer said in Scott's defense. "Matt and Karen are renting him one of the cabins they renovated this summer." Their good friends, the Caldwells, had owned and operated Hard Luck Lodge for the past twenty years and had always been fond of Scott. Their primary business was providing accommodations for the tourists who flew in with

Arctic Experiences, the tour company run by Matt and their son-in-law, Ron Gold.

Now that Abbey thought about it, one of those cabins was ideal. There was also a touch of irony attached to it. She'd come here in response to an advertisement offering jobs to women willing to move to Hard Luck, fifty miles from the Arctic Circle. To attract qualified job applicants, Midnight Sons had included a cabin and twenty acres of land for each. What the brothers hadn't bothered to disclose was that the cabins were dilapidated one-room shacks, desperately in need of repair. If *that* wasn't insult enough, the twenty acres they'd so generously thrown in were nowhere near Hard Luck or the cabins. For the most part they were only accessible by air.

"Matt's done a good job with those cabins," Sawyer remarked.

Abbey agreed. The original shacks had been torn down years ago and larger, better-equipped cabins built. The Caldwells had recently begun an extensive process of renovation and Scott would be renting one of the newly upgraded cabins.

"Scott's had a busy afternoon," Sawyer continued. "He was in to see Tracy about having the papers drawn up."

"Not Chrissie?" Abbey asked.

Sawyer shook his head. "Apparently not. My guess is, he knows he's got some amends to make."

Abbey nodded slowly. As Scott's mother she could think of no better wife for her son than Chrissie Harris. Although Scott had never discussed his feelings for Chrissie, Abbey knew he'd loved her as a teenager, and Abbey strongly suspected he loved her still.

That morning when he'd arrived, Abbey noticed the way Scott's gaze had moved over the crowd who'd gathered to greet him. He'd been searching for Chrissie; she was sure of it. And practically the first stop he'd made in town was the attorneys' office. Yes, there were some legal papers to be drawn up, but that certainly didn't need to be done the first day he was back.

"Abbey?"

She glanced up to find her husband watching her.

"You've got that look in your eye."

Abbey played dumb. "What look?"

"The one that tells me you're up to no good."

She frowned with indignation. "You haven't got a clue what I'm thinking, Sawyer O'Halloran."

"That's where you're wrong," her husband challenged, leaving her desk to sink into an overstuffed chair. Abbey sat on the chair arm beside him. "I do know what you're thinking," he told her. "Your eyes give you away. You're thinking about Scott and Chrissie."

Abbey considered arguing with him, but he was right and he knew it. "Don't you remember how badly Scott wanted us to get married?" she asked, the years rolling away with the memory. Sawyer had originally proposed for what Abbey believed to be all the wrong reasons. It'd nearly broken her heart to turn him down, but with one failed marriage behind her, she couldn't afford to make a second mistake. She'd already fallen in love with him, but his proposal had been motivated more by his fear that someone else might ask her first. Or so it had seemed to her. Loving him the way she did, afraid he didn't really love her, she'd believed that the only sensible option was to protect her family—and her vulnerable emotions. She'd decided to leave Hard Luck. Then Scott and Susan had disappeared. Abbey had never known such panic as she'd felt that night.

Her husband reached for her hand, gently squeezing her fingers. "If not for Scott and Susan running away, I might have lost you. I was crazy about you then and I'm even crazier about you now."

Abbey pressed her head to his shoulder, savoring the feel of his arms around her.

"Only, back then I didn't know how to tell you," Sawyer said, the frustration and anguish of that night evident even after all these years. "I didn't know how to persuade you to stay."

Abbey kept her head against her husband's shoulder. "Now Scott needs our help," she whispered.

"With Chrissie?"

Abbey nodded. "I'm afraid he's more like you than you realize. He loves Chrissie, but he's not sure how to proceed."

"Are you suggesting I give him advice?" Sawyer asked, looking aghast at the prospect.

Abbey giggled. "Hardly. The situation calls for diplomacy."

Her husband's frown cut deep grooves in his forehead. "Like what?" he asked warily. "And please note that I'm ignoring the slur on my diplomatic abilities."

Abbey smiled. "I think we should hold a welcome-home party for him. We have a lot to celebrate, don't you think?''

"We do indeed." Sawyer's face relaxed. "And there's someone you're going to invite, isn't there?''

"Shh." Abbey brought her index finger to her lips. "I don't want to be obvious about it.''

"Right," Sawyer said, sounding amused. "We wouldn't want to be obvious.''

"We'll make it a surprise party.''

"A surprise party?" Sawyer echoed. "But who do you intend to surprise? Scott or Chrissie?''

IT WAS ALMOST FOUR-THIRTY when Scott walked into the Hard Luck Café—too early for the dinner crowd. The restaurant hadn't changed much over the years, and neither had Ben. To Scott's eyes, Ben Hamilton had aged barely a year in the past ten. He was in his sixties now, his hair a little thinner on top but his welcoming smile as warm and wide as always.

"Scott!" Ben greeted him with unconcealed delight. "Hey, boy, you're a sight for sore eyes.''

The two men exchanged hearty handshakes and then impulsively hugged.

"So you're moving back to Hard Luck?" Ben asked.

"I am," Scott confirmed, and slid onto a stool at the counter. He picked up a menu, although he wasn't planning to order a meal. The menu was a lot more professional-looking than it used to be with its smudged type and cracked plastic coating. But fancy menus or not, the Hard Luck Café had been his favorite restaurant for years, and in his time away he hadn't found any better.

"We got salmon on special. Mary poaches it in a lemon sauce that's out of this world." Ben extravagantly kissed his fingertips as he spoke.

In the old days, Ben had served everything loaded down with fat and extra calories. No more; his wife, Mary, had seen to that. Healthy food choices had started appearing on the menu when Ben married her, although the changes had been fairly subtle.

"Salmon sounds good, but Mom's cooking me a feast. I'd better not disappoint her." He closed the menu and tucked it behind the sugar canister. Ben automatically poured him a mug of coffee.

"So I hear you're going to be flying with your dad and Christian."

"I am." His hands cupped the mug. Scott had earned his pilot's license when he was sixteen. Whereas most teens hungered for their driver's license, Scott had been far more interested in learning to fly. After his stint in the army, he'd worked for a flight service out of Utah, flying tourists over the Canyonlands. He'd been content during those years, enjoying his freedom and earning decent money. He'd had friends, lots of them, and a number of women he saw on a regular basis—but these relationships were all casual, without depth or commitment. He'd also been engaged once, but that had turned into a spectacular mess, and he hadn't repeated the experience. Then, a month ago, he'd suddenly realized he'd been running away from what he wanted most, and that was his home and his family. He missed Alaska, regretted the anger of his youth and the pain he'd brought his parents. It was time to make amends. In fact, it was long past time.

And then there was Chrissie.

He smiled just thinking about their encounter that morning. When he announced that he'd merely come for legal advice, she'd looked like she wanted to crawl into a hole and die. He'd managed not to laugh then but he couldn't restrain his amusement now. He chuckled, replaying the scene in his mind.

"Did I miss something funny?" Ben asked, sidling up to the counter and leaning against it just as he had for more years than Scott could remember.

"Not really," Scott told him, suppressing his mirth. "Just something that happened this morning, soon after I got here."

"Oh."

Scott had stopped by Chrissie's office on business, but he was willing to admit there was more to it than that. He'd wanted to see her and, in fact, had been anticipating their meeting for weeks.

Chrissie was one of the reasons he'd stayed away from Hard Luck and one of the reasons he'd come home.

"Seems just like the old days seeing you again," Ben said.

"The old days," Scott repeated. Back then, the Hard Luck Café had been the gathering place for the entire community. Men, in particular, used to meet at Ben's the way some might socialize in a tavern. Not only that, many people in the community, if not most, had come to Ben at one time or another to talk through their troubles. Scott suspected they continued to do so.

"Do you still have that Frequent Eater program?" Scott asked.

"Nah," Ben answered with a grin. "Don't need it. These days I got more business than I know what to do with."

Scott nodded; he wasn't surprised that Ben's remained popular. He knew that over the years a couple of other restaurants had opened, but the Hard Luck Café was—and deserved to be—everyone's favorite. Ben was officially retired; however, he couldn't quite keep his hands out of the business.

"I remember you as a youngster, sitting on one of those stools," Ben said with genuine fondness. "Only seems right to see you here now."

"It used to be I could talk to you about anything," Scott recalled.

"Still can, if you've got a hankering," Ben assured him.

Scott was tempted. Many a time he'd talked out his problems with Ben Hamilton. Many a time he'd felt as if the world was against him. Few people knew it, but Ben was the one who'd suggested Scott consider enlisting in the military. A former navy man, he'd been disappointed when Scott chose the army. But not as disappointed as Sawyer that he hadn't decided on the air force.

Back then, Scott had been downright contrary. Angry, too, only he didn't know why or at what. Eventually he'd recognized that it wasn't Sawyer he hated or even his biological father, a man who'd rejected his own wife and children. He knew now that he'd been old enough at the time of his parents' separation to be aware of his father's rejection and to be seriously hurt by it, to wonder if he was somehow to blame. The teen years had become increasingly difficult, and then Eagle Catcher, his husky, had died. The grief he'd felt over the loss of his dog—a grief he couldn't share—had turned to anger. Hardly understanding himself, he'd lashed out at those he loved most. The things he'd said and done deeply embarrassed him now.

"Anything you want to discuss?" Ben asked, sounding eager. "It stays right here. Nothing you tell me goes any further."

Scott hesitated, then decided to ask about Chrissie. Really, there wasn't anyone else he could ask. Not Susan, who was guaranteed to run to her friend and repeat every word. Not the other pilots, either, or his uncles or aunts. No one in his extended family, that was for sure.

"Is Chrissie seeing anyone special?" he blurted out before he could stop to ponder the wisdom of showing his hand like this.

"Chrissie Harris?" Ben asked as if there were two Chrissies in Hard Luck. He averted his gaze. "As a matter of fact, she is."

"I see." So Chrissie *was* involved. It made sense that she would be; he knew she hadn't married. Ridiculous though it was, considering their history, he'd hoped she'd be as interested in renewing their relationship as he was.

"I've never met him, mind you," Ben continued.

"He's in Fairbanks?"

"So I understand."

"You hear anything else?"

"Some." Ben was less forthcoming than usual. Scott waited patiently.

"I don't know who he is. I'm probably speaking out of turn by telling you anything."

"I'd like to know," Scott insisted. "I *need* to know," he thought to himself.

"She visits Joel every second weekend. That's all I know—Joel, Fairbanks, twice a month. Okay?"

"Does Joel have a last name?" Not that it mattered, but Scott was curious.

"Must have, but no one's ever told me."

There'd been a Joel Higgins a year behind him in school—a good athlete, well liked and well adjusted. Needless to say, Scott hadn't cared for him and dismissed him as a male Goody Two-shoes.

"Every other Saturday morning Chrissie flies into Fairbanks and doesn't return until Sunday afternoon. Generally she comes in here for a bite to eat before heading home. Once in a while she mentions Joel, but she's pretty closemouthed about him. Let me add one thing, though," he said, and paused, frowning heavily. "By the time she steps off that plane, she's really dragging."

Scott didn't need Ben to say another word; he got the picture. Chrissie spent weekends with Joel and arrived in Hard Luck exhausted. He didn't need to guess the reason, either. No wonder his sister hadn't mentioned Chrissie's involvement with someone else.

Sure as anything she knew, but she hadn't so much as dropped a hint—because his finding out would ruin everything. Susan, the hopeless romantic, refused to let go of the idea that Scott and Chrissie belonged together.

"Ask her," Ben advised.

"Ask *Chrissie?* You have to be kidding!"

"Why not?" Ben demanded. "Nothing works better than the direct approach. According to Mary, that's what women want these days. None of this second-guessing stuff. That went out with the seventies. If nothing else, Chrissie will respect you for being forthright enough to ask."

Ben's idea was worthy of consideration. "I'll think about it," he said.

Scott finished his coffee, but when he went to pay for it, Ben told him it was on the house. His old friend's generosity hadn't changed. In addition to a good cup of coffee, he'd given Scott something to think about.

The next few days passed quickly. Thursday afternoon Scott had an appointment at the law office. He was in the waiting room when Chrissie walked into the reception area. She halted midstep the instant she saw him.

"Hello, Scott," she said, her voice remarkably cool and even.

"Chrissie." He nodded. Then, feeling the need to explain the purpose of his visit, he added, "I have an appointment with Tracy."

"Yes, I know." She held a folder pressed flat against her stomach and wore a slightly puzzled expression, as if she'd forgotten why she'd come out of her office. "I, uh, gather everything's going very well for you at Midnight Sons."

"I'm enjoying myself."

"Everyone's pleased to have you home."

"Everyone?" he asked, wondering if she included herself.

"Your family, certainly." This came after a slight hesitation.

"I had coffee at Ben's the other day," he said casually, hoping to ease into a more comfortable conversation. "It's amazing. I swear he hasn't changed at all."

"He's wonderful. So is Mary."

A short silence followed, which Chrissie broke. "I understand Matt and Karen rented you one of the renovated cabins."

So she'd been checking up on him. That was encouraging. Maybe, just maybe, she still cared. That thought gave him the courage to ask her out. "I was thinking you and I might have a drink one afternoon," he suggested.

Her eyes widened and her arms tightened around the folder.

"A drink," she repeated slowly. "At Ben's?"

He nodded. "Or dinner, if you prefer."

She squared her shoulders and chewed her lower lip before answering. "I don't think so."

He shrugged, as if her refusal was of little consequence to him. "That's too bad. I had a few things I wanted to discuss with you."

Chrissie's expressive eyes had always told him what she was thinking before she uttered a word. He'd wondered if this would be a detriment to her as an attorney, but apparently that wasn't the case.

"You had something you wanted to talk to me about?" she finally said.

"Yeah."

She worried her lower lip further. "Maybe..." She hesitated, then seemed to regain her resolve. "I don't think so, Scott. Thanks, anyway.'' She turned away to enter her office.

"How long do you intend to avoid me?" he called after her.

At his question, she turned back. "Avoid you? Don't flatter yourself. What I *intend* to do is live my life just the way I am now."

"You obviously have every intention of avoiding me."

"I have *every intention* of not seeking you out. That's not the same thing."

"I see."

"Apparently you don't," she returned in her best lawyer voice. "You're out of my life, Scott. That was your choice, not mine."

"People change, Chrissie. They—"

"Oh, no, you don't," she interrupted, waving her finger at him. "You're not going to do this to me. Not again."

"I asked you out for a drink. I wasn't proposing we move in together."

"Oh, sure, a drink—for old times' sake."

"No," he corrected. "A drink to clear the air. I deserve that much, don't I?"

Her eyes flared with outrage. "What you deserve, Scott O'Halloran, is a slap across the face." She raised her chin so high she threatened to put her neck out of joint. "All right," she said abruptly. "Fine. As a matter of fairness I'll have a drink with you."

Scott experienced a surge of hope. "When?"

"Friday night at the party."

Scott frowned. "What party?"

"The party your parents are—" She bit off the rest of the sentence.

"Chrissie?"

Squeezing her eyes shut, she slowly exhaled. "Oh, damn, it's supposed to be a surprise."

CHAPTER THREE

THURSDAY MORNING Karen Caldwell poured her husband a second cup of coffee, then joined him in the massive kitchen at Hard Luck Lodge. Working as a team, they'd built the lodge into one of the most popular tourist destinations in the state. It'd taken almost twenty years of blood, sweat and tears, but they were equal partners, not only in their business, but in life.

During those years they'd also had three children and managed to create a warm nurturing home for their family.

Clay, their eldest, had been the best surprise of their lives, conceived while they were divorced and living apart. The pregnancy was what had brought them back to their senses. Clay was at UCLA now, studying chemistry. The girls, Jill and Emily, were sixteen and fourteen respectively and attended the local high school.

"You're looking thoughtful," Matt said when Karen sat down across from him at the table. In a flurry of activity and near-panic, the girls had flown out the door for classes. After the long summer break they were having trouble resuming the discipline of waking up early for school. Only a few moments ago, Jill had been searching for her misplaced gym uniform. While her sister dashed frantically about, Emily had slapped together lunch for both of them. Now, with the girls gone, blessed silence enveloped the kitchen.

"You're worrying about Clay again, aren't you?" Matt's tone held a slight accusation.

Karen hadn't found it easy sending their son off to college a few weeks earlier, especially a college so far from home. Still, she knew that Clay was a lot like her—steady and capable. Jill and Emily were more like Matt—creative but a bit unfocused. The focus part would come in time, the way it had with their father, Karen believed.

"Actually I was thinking about Scott O'Halloran," she told him.

"It's good to see him again, isn't it?"

Karen knew Matt was pleased to rent out one of the cabins on a long-term basis, especially to Scott, whom they both liked. "He's still hung up on Chrissie, isn't he?" Karen asked, knowing her husband had talked to Scott a number of times.

Matt shrugged, and Karen rolled her eyes. In her opinion, most men were hopeless when it came to romance; Matt was no exception. And Scott—well, as a kid he'd had delusions of romantic expertise.

"Don't you remember what Scott told us just before Clay was born?" she asked her husband.

Matt chuckled. "Sweetheart, that was a lot of years ago."

Karen's memory was good, and this particular incident had stayed with her. She smiled, recalling the day the young boy had stood resolutely before her. "He claimed that he was responsible for bringing the two of us back together. In fact, he felt we owed our reconciliation to him.''

Matt burst out laughing. ''Scott's the one who said I should take you camping.''

''In order to wine and dine me, right?'' Karen muttered. Scott's idea of creating a romantic mood was that Matt should drag her and all the necessary and assorted gear to his favorite fishing place. Apparently Scott believed that sleeping on the ground, battling off mosquito attacks, plus catching, cleaning and cooking all their meals would rekindle their love. All this when Karen was several months pregnant with Clay. What a disaster that had been.

For one thing, fishing had never been her forte, and Matt had been furious when she'd nearly lost his favorite rod and pole. Then she'd fallen in the river and gotten drenched from head to toe. Matt had managed to catch fish after fish, and all she'd caught was a miserable cold, as if pregnancy hadn't made her uncomfortable enough. By the time she returned to Hard Luck, it was a miracle they were even speaking to each other.

''Scott used to see himself as quite the matchmaker, didn't he?''

They exchanged smiles across the table, smiles that quickly turned into laughter as the memories continued to surface.

''You know what I think?'' Karen said, reaching for her coffee. She held the mug in front of her lips as she mulled over her idea. ''Turnabout is fair play.''

Matt stared at her. ''Oh, I don't know about

that…. Anyway, this is none of our business. They—''

Karen went on as though he hadn't spoken. ''We could arrange for Scott to take Chrissie somewhere he once considered wildly romantic…like, I don't know, the garbage dump? I remember you once suggested we go out there and watch the bears.''

Matt chuckled. ''*Scott* will think that's fun, but I'm not so sure about Chrissie.''

''True,'' Karen agreed, still thinking. ''Hmm. All we need to do is figure how to get the two of them alone. Given a little time, I'm sure they'd work everything out.''

''At the garbage dump?''

Karen rolled her eyes again. ''Someplace else. You come up with a spot. You're the creative one in the family.''

''Sweetheart, be sensible. First of all, you don't have any real evidence that Chrissie still feels the same way about Scott.''

''She does,'' Karen said. ''I'm positive.''

''Okay, so they went together for a while, but that was ages ago.''

''Chrissie's loved Scott from the time she was eight.''

Matt seemed to require a moment to think that through. ''All right, Chrissie loves Scott. But how will Mitch feel about all this? I didn't get the impression he's too thrilled to have Scott back in town.''

Her husband had a point. Mitch Harris was Chrissie's father and represented the law in Hard Luck. Scott wasn't really a bad kid, but Mitch and Scott had clashed a number of times. Not that Scott's misdemeanors were anything new in Hard Luck; other teens were guilty of similar behavior. The difference was Chrissie's involvement with him. Father and daughter had argued over Scott more than once. Mitch had refused to make allowances for his daughter's boyfriend, regardless of her desperate pleas. Karen knew the sheriff had breathed a sigh of relief when Scott left Hard Luck, despite Chrissie's broken heart.

"Mitch never disliked Scott," Matt said. "If anything, he was doing him a favor by making him accountable for his actions."

"I know, but..."

Studying her, Matt set his mug aside. "What's gotten into you? I've never known you to meddle in anyone's love life before. Why now?"

Karen sighed and realized her husband was right; this wasn't her usual style. Still, what happened between Scott and Chrissie bothered her for some reason, bothered her a lot, and she felt a mother's urge to fix things, to repair the situation. Maybe she was being fanciful, but Karen saw in Chrissie the same kind of pain she herself had once felt.

"If Scott and Chrissie are meant to be together," Matt said, relaxing against the back of his chair, "then it'll happen without any interference from us."

"Don't be so sure."

"Karen!"

"I can't help myself," she protested. "I've seen the look that comes over Chrissie's face when anyone mentions Scott's name. And the same is true of Scott. I know what it's like to love someone so much that the hurt only seems to get worse. When we got divorced, it just about killed me.''

''Me, too,'' Matt said quietly, his gaze sobering.

''We were both stubborn and afraid and in such pain.'' Those weren't times Karen ever wanted to relive. Pregnant and alone in California, afraid to tell Matt about the baby, afraid not to.

''And both of us so damn much in love.''

''Not that it helped us communicate any better.'' They'd been defensive and bitter. In those days it'd been impossible to talk without their discussions erupting into arguments.

Matt reached across the table and squeezed her hand. ''The part about me loving you hasn't changed. All these years together proves it.''

On rare occasions, her husband could actually be romantic. And it was more meaningful because Karen knew it was genuine, heart-deep, and never a mere gesture.

''So you want to help Scott get back together with Chrissie?'' he asked in a satisfied tone.

''If we can,'' she said. ''But we can't tell anyone.'' Whatever they did would have to be on the sly. Maybe a private conversation between Matt and Scott? Or a little confidential ''girls' talk''? They'd have to figure out the best approach.

''It'll be our secret,'' Matt agreed.

They emptied their leftover coffee into the sink and then, with a quick kiss, went about their busy days.

CHRISSIE ARRIVED at Scott's ''surprise party'' early Friday evening. His mother opened the door, and

Chrissie instantly lowered her gaze, feeling dreadful that she'd been the one to spoil the surprise. Almost immediately following her second run-in with Scott, Chrissie had called Abbey and confessed her faux pas. As always, Abbey had been gracious and immediately forgiven her mistake.

"Chrissie, would you stop?" Abbey said now, leading her into the large family home. "A surprise party was a ridiculous idea, anyway. I'm glad Scott knows, because it took away the pressure. Come inside and make yourself comfortable."

Chrissie didn't think that was possible. If not for Susan, she'd have found a convenient excuse to miss this party. Susan, however, wouldn't have let her live it down.

Neither would Scott.

She'd say one thing about Scott O'Halloran—he was determined. That morning, when she got to work, she'd found a lovely bouquet of roses. Not just any roses, but red ones—a dozen perfectly formed buds. The card had read simply *Scott*.

Chrissie suspected he'd purchased them in Fairbanks the day before. Not that she was about to let a few beautiful roses sway her decision—although they must have cost him the earth.

It would take more than flowers. A lot more! As soon as the thought went through her mind, Chrissie tensed. No. She refused to even *consider* any kind of reconciliation. She refused to give Scott the power—or the opportunity—to hurt her again. He wasn't going to find himself back in her good graces. No, sir! She'd be civil, but that was it. He was part of her past, not her future, and she fully intended to keep it that way.

With a quick detour to exchange hugs with Christian and Mariah O'Halloran, Chrissie headed straight for Susan, who was in the kitchen fussing with a variety of hors d'oeuvres. She slid them, hot from the oven, onto large ceramic platters. "Chrissie!" she cried when she saw her. "I *knew* you'd come."

Grumbling, Chrissie reached for a green olive and munched on that, rather than argue. There was no point in explaining that she was here only under protest.

"Have you seen Scott?" Susan asked.

"No." As much as possible, Chrissie planned to spend the night avoiding him—which was exactly what he'd accused her of. Too bad, she told herself firmly. She had no choice. Anyway, his opinion of her behavior was irrelevant.

"He's the guest of honor, you know."

Chrissie tossed her friend a dirty look and Susan laughed good-naturedly. Susan was pregnant and although the apron barely fit around her extended belly, she looked beautiful and healthy—and very happy. Ron was in the family room, chatting with friends. Chrissie caught a glimpse of him as he glanced at his wife. A pang of envy shot through her at the love, the adoration, she saw in his eyes.

"Let me take those mushrooms out for you," Chrissie offered, and Susan handed her the oven mitts. Staying busy was the key, she decided. Standing around making idle chatter, wondering where Scott was—and how to stay out of his vicinity— would quickly drive her insane. She had to ignore the fact that he was somewhere in this crowded room…and probably watching her.

Picking up the large platter required two hands. A moment later, she was walking into the family room, balancing it carefully, when without warning Scott appeared directly in front of her.

Chrissie couldn't think of a thing to say. Not a single thing. She stood there, doing an excellent imitation of an ice sculpture—cold and unmoving.

"Did you like the roses?" he asked.

"They were very nice." She kept her voice expressionless.

"Thoughtful, too, don't you think?" He turned toward his sister and winked.

Obviously the flowers had been Susan's idea. Chrissie should have known her friend had put him up to this.

She purposely hardened her heart and stared at him, her composure intact. "I'm afraid you wasted your money." Then she sidestepped him and marched into the other room, her tray of mushrooms aloft.

This wasn't the first time Scott had sought her out at a party; the last occasion had been five years earlier, following her college graduation. He'd managed to pull her aside and hand her a batch of lies about missing her and wanting her back in his life. At the time she'd been so much in love with him she'd cherished every word. The memory chilled her blood. She'd been gullible and naive, but she wasn't now.

The O'Halloran home was crowded, and Chrissie wove her way in and out, smiling, chatting, offering hors d'oeuvres to the guests while Abbey welcomed late arrivals. These included Chrissie's dad, Mitch Harris, and her stepmother, Bethany. She paused, still holding her tray, and kissed both of them in greeting. She and Bethany chatted for a few minutes as Mitch moved toward Sawyer, then Chrissie resumed her duties. It might have been her imagination, but she sensed that everyone was watching her. She had the definite suspicion that all the interest she was generating had nothing to do with the crab-stuffed mushroom caps.

She was about to return to the kitchen when Scott sneaked up behind her. "We were going to have a talk, remember?"

"No, I don't remember! I didn't agree to that," she informed him stiffly. "As far as I'm concerned, there's nothing to discuss."

"I want to clear the air," Scott persisted.

"The air's as clear as it's going to get." She edged away.

Scott followed. "Not from where I'm standing."

He was making this awfully hard. Chrissie could feel herself weakening; she couldn't allow that to happen.

"Could I have everyone's attention?" Sawyer called as he stepped into the center of the room. He held a bottle of champagne in one hand and a flute glass in the other. Anna, Ryan and several others appeared with champagne bottles and trays of glasses, pouring drinks for all the guests.

"We'll continue this conversation later," Scott said in a low voice.

"I told you before—there's nothing to discuss," Chrissie insisted, her voice carrying farther than she would have liked. Several people turned to look in their direction.

"Our son is home to stay," Abbey said, tears of happiness brightening her eyes.

Sawyer slipped his arm around Abbey's waist. "And he's now a full partner in Midnight Sons." He raised his champagne glass. "I'd like to propose a toast. To Scott. Welcome home, son."

"Hear, hear!" Matt Caldwell yelled, and his words echoed around the room as glasses were lifted in Scott's honor.

"Speech, speech," Ryan, Scott's seventeen-year-old half brother, shouted.

Scott groaned, but his objections were quickly overruled when his family and friends took up the cry. He moved closer to his parents and grabbed Ryan by the shoulders, squeezing hard. "Thanks a lot, little brother," he muttered.

Everyone laughed. Scott looked a bit uncomfortable and needed a moment to gather his thoughts. "I'd like to thank everyone for this wonderful *surprise* party," he began.

The entire room erupted into laughter, and several people grinned at Chrissie. If it hadn't been in poor taste, she would have left right then and there. Scott had knowingly set out to embarrass her. She fumed and said nothing, refusing to acknowledge his statement.

"If I've learned anything from this experience, it's that we all make mistakes, say and do things we later regret. I've certainly committed my share of those, and will probably be guilty of more before my life is over."

"As will we all," Mitch Harris inserted. Bethany stood beside him, smiling; she sought out her step-daughter, who tried to look away.

From across the room her father's eyes connected with Chrissie's, too, as though to remind her that he was willing to let matters rest between him and Scott—and so should she. Chrissie broke eye contact.

"As most of you know," Scott continued, "I had something of a...rebellious youth."

Sheriff Harris saluted the comment with a raised champagne glass, and a few guests chuckled.

"I said and did things that caused grief for those I love. I know I've hurt my family, but despite everything, they never lost faith in me."

"Not once," Sawyer said in agreement.

"My family and friends have put up with a great deal," Scott added, and glanced toward Chrissie. Almost immediately he turned back to his parents. "It's good to be home, Mom and Dad."

A chorus of "Welcome Home," followed from everyone in the room, and again, the family and friends of Scott O'Halloran toasted his return.

There was a surge of chatter then, and Chrissie went to the kitchen to assemble another platter of hors d'oeuvres. Susan came in shortly afterward and stared at Chrissie, obviously waiting for her to say something.

"What?" she snapped, glaring at her friend.

"Scott was talking to *you* just now."

"I know. He was talking to you, too. He was talking to everybody."

"Doesn't that mean anything? What he said about past mistakes and regrets and all?"

Chrissie was saved from having to answer when Abbey walked in. Grateful for the escape, Chrissie edged her way out of the kitchen. Her relief was short-lived, however. No sooner had she entered the family room then Scott joined her.

"We were having a discussion…"

"Yes," she said with an exasperated sigh. "As I recall, it was about air quality."

Scott grinned, which made his classic features even handsomer and more appealing. Chrissie doubted hers was the only heart he'd broken since leaving Hard Luck.

His eyes grew solemn. "I meant what I just said. I made a lot of mistakes, and I want you to know I'm sorry for the pain I caused you."

Chrissie dropped her own eyes, rather than let him see how deeply his words affected her. She'd never expected Scott to apologize, and it took her a moment to absorb. "Apology accepted," she whispered.

"Can you really forgive me?" He clasped her shoulders and compelled her to look at him.

Chrissie knew what he was asking, but she wasn't sure she could say what he wanted her to. "I *have* forgiven you. I put everything behind me years ago, Scott."

He expelled an enormous sigh as if he'd been waiting a long time to hear that. For an uncomfortable moment he gazed into her fate. Then he said, "I'd like to see you again."

"See me?"

"Go out with you," he corrected. "As in date. I'd like us to start again."

Oh, Lord, she was tempted. Where she found the

courage to refuse him, Chrissie would never know. Slowly she shook her head.

"I did say I'd forgiven you, Scott," she said. "But there are consequences to one's actions. Nothing you can say now will ever undo the past. I wish you well, Scott, I really do, but I'm not going to risk letting you hurt me again."

He didn't say anything for a few seconds, then finally let his hands fall. "I can understand that," he said quietly.

He turned away, and she didn't stop him.

CHAPTER FOUR

BETHANY HARRIS sat cross-legged on the bed, impatiently waiting for her husband to return from his final rounds. Her thoughts had been confused all evening, and she wanted to discuss the O'Halloran party with him. When they'd left, Mitch had dropped her off at the house, then stopped at the station to check with the night dispatcher, a habit he'd developed during his twenty-five years in law enforcement. He wouldn't be long, she knew, but she was eager to talk about the events of the evening. Especially the exchange she'd witnessed between Chrissie and Scott.

The sound of the door closing propelled Bethany off the bed. "I'm glad you're back," she said, greeting her husband in the kitchen. She was barefoot, her eyelet cotton gown reaching nearly to the floor.

"Is Jack in?" he asked.

"Present and accounted for," she assured him. Jack, their youngest, was a high-school student. Their older son, Jeremy, attended classes at the University of Washington in Seattle. "Did you notice Chrissie tonight?" she asked right away.

"She was helping serve, remember?" Mitch reminded his wife absently. He moved into the living room, unbuttoning his shirt as he walked.

"What Chrissie was doing," Bethany told him, "was avoiding Scott." She knew her stepdaughter well enough to recognize that Chrissie was keeping herself occupied all evening in an effort to elude Scott—not that her plan had worked.

Mitch frowned and sank into his favorite chair in front of the television. "I thought she was over Scott. I assumed she was willing to forgive him and ready to move on."

"I'm sure she *has* forgiven him, but..." Sitting on the arm of his chair, Bethany shook her head. "As for being over him, forget it." Half the night she'd had to resist the urge to throw her arms around her stepdaughter and comfort her. How well she understood the doubts and uncertainties Chrissie felt; it was like seeing history repeat itself.

"I'd better have a talk with her," Mitch said, still frowning. "Someone has to tell her."

"Tell her *what?*" Bethany demanded, wondering if her husband knew something she didn't. When it came to police matters, Mitch was closemouthed. As he should be. Bethany respected his discretion. But her husband sometimes kept private fears and concerns to himself, too. If he had information regarding Scott and Chrissie, she wanted to hear it.

Mitch's gaze clouded with indecision. "I'm not keeping any deep, dark secrets, if that's what you're thinking. It's just—" He abruptly changed his mind about whatever he'd planned to say. "Actually, Chrissie may want to talk to me about Scott, and I was hoping you'd give me a few suggestions—unless, of course, *you'd* prefer to talk to her."

"I'd gladly talk to Chrissie," Bethany told him quietly, "if I knew what to say."

They were both silent for a moment. "I think very highly of Scott for publicly apologizing to his family," Mitch said. "That couldn't have been easy."

"It was a kind and generous thing to do," Bethany agreed. Scott's admission of his faults had taken maturity and inner strength; so had his decision to seek his family's forgiveness, especially in a roomful of people. Part of his speech, Bethany realized, had been directed at Chrissie.

Her stepdaughter was a warmhearted woman who'd already forgiven Scott—that much Bethany was certain of. But apparently forgiveness didn't extend to resuming their relationship.

Bethany had seen Chrissie leave the party soon after Scott's speech, unable to hide her misery; Bethany had desperately wanted to follow her out. She sensed that Chrissie loved Scott yet despite her feelings refused to take another risk on the man who'd hurt her twice.

"There's something I never told you." Her husband's eyes sparked with hidden laughter. "Just before our wedding, Scott came to talk to me, man to man."

"*Scott* did? He was what—eight? Nine?"

"Nine, I think, and sincere as can be."

Bethany could only imagine what the boy had had to say.

Mitch rubbed the side of his jaw. "Scott felt I needed to know you were in love with me long before I ever noticed."

Bethany, who'd moved to sit across from her husband, knees tucked beneath her chin, lifted her head. "He didn't!"

Mitch raised his hand. "I swear it's true. Scott said he recognized the *look*. According to him, Abbey looked at Sawyer the same way you looked at me. He asked me if love made people act dumb because that was how his mother and Sawyer behaved. He wondered if that would happen to us."

Pressing her forehead against her knees, Bethany couldn't suppress a laugh.

"Apparently he didn't approve of what his sister and Chrissie had done in order to get us together, either."

"I don't believe this."

"Then he recommended I marry you in spite of Chrissie and Susan's matchmaking, and congratulated me for seeing through their ploys." Her husband's smile was delighted as he reminisced. "I could talk to Scott," he finally suggested. "Man to man, the way he spoke to me."

Bethany considered that, but instinctively knew Chrissie would resent her family's intrusion. "You've already had a number of talks with Scott."

Mitch's smile disappeared and he slowly nodded. "He was an angry teenager, but nothing I said helped him."

"Don't be so sure."

Mitch leaned forward. "I've seen other kids like Scott. He was never vicious or even all that bad. First there was the pain of losing his dog and then…well, this is what I started to tell you. He contacted his father when he was fifteen. He never told Abbey and Sawyer."

"But *Sawyer's* his father."

"By adoption, true, but Scott had things to resolve with his birth father—and it didn't really happen. The bastard out-and-out rejected him. His own kid!"

"You never told me this before."

Mitch's eyes avoided hers. "I know. He asked me to keep it confidential. But I tried to help him as best I could."

"I think you did help him, although Chrissie didn't realize it at the time."

"Well, she did later," Mitch murmured. He shook his head. "Scott hurt her the same way he hurt himself. Now he's back and she doesn't trust him, and really, can you blame her?"

"No..." Still, Bethany wished a reconciliation was possible.

"Maybe you *should* talk to Chrissie." Mitch glanced hopefully in her direction. "Maybe that would be the best approach, after all."

"And say what?" Bethany asked.

Her husband hesitated. "I don't know. Something inspiring. Hey—you could always ask Ben for advice. Seems to me he has a knack for knowing the right thing to say."

In theory Mitch's idea sounded good, but this was a delicate situation that required sensitive handling. Chrissie might take offense at her family's meddling in her affairs. In fact, Bethany could amost guarantee it. Besides, knowing Ben, his solution would likely to be to hog-tie Chrissie and Scott and refuse to release them until they'd sorted everything out.

On second thought...

"You think we *should* ask Ben for help?" Mitch murmured.

Bethany gave a thoughtful shrug and laughed softly at the thought of leaving her stepdaughter's love life in the hands of crusty, outspoken Ben—the man who also happened to be Bethany's birth father and the reason she'd moved to Hard Luck in the first place. "I think we should let Chrissie make her own decisions. Although, I suppose, if the right opportunity presents itself…"

Mitch took a moment to mull that over. Then he nodded. "You're right. And you never know—one of them might actually *ask* for our advice. In which case, we'll be happy to give it. Come on," he said, stretching his arm toward her. "It's past my bedtime."

CHRISSIE AROSE early Saturday morning and dressed warmly for her bimonthly flight into Fairbanks. As she ate some toast, she filled her backpack for the weekend, then walked to the Midnight Sons landing strip. Duke Porter, her law partner's husband, generally flew her into town. They'd gotten to be good friends over the past few months, since she'd started the mentoring program arranged through a Fairbanks social-service agency. Joelle Harmon was a twelve-year-old foster child at risk. Abandoned by her mother, father unknown, Joelle had been in six foster homes in four months, until she was accepted into the experimental group home. Chrissie had spent months building a strong relationship with the girl.

Her breath formed small clouds as she hurried toward the Midnight Sons office to check in for the normally scheduled flight. It would turn bitterly cold soon enough. Within the month, snow would fall and winter would set in with such ferocity that just the thought of it sent shivers down her spine. Despite that, Chrissie loved Alaska; she'd lived here almost her entire life and couldn't imagine settling anywhere else.

Opening the door, she stepped into the office. "Duke, I—" She stopped as soon as she realized it wasn't Duke standing there, but Scott O'Halloran.

"Morning," he greeted her cheerfully. He was pouring himself a cup of coffee and didn't bother to look up.

Her smile quickly faded. "Where's Duke?"

"Sleeping in, I assume." Scott finally glanced up. "I'm taking the morning flight."

Chrissie hesitated, unsure what to do.

He reached for a clipboard and headed out the door. He paused when she didn't follow. "You coming or not?" he asked, as if it was of little concern to him. "I'm leaving now. I have some deliveries to make in Fairbanks."

Chrissie figured she didn't have any choice. She might as well get used to being around Scott, no matter how uncomfortable she felt.

Climbing into the plane, she was relieved when Scott immediately placed a pair of headphones over his ears. Making polite conversation with him would have been difficult, and at least he'd circumvented any requirement to do so. He ran through a flight-check list before starting the engine of the Lake LA4 amphibious plane. He could have been flying alone for all the attention he paid her.

Frankly, that was the way Chrissie wanted it. Yet when they soared into the endless blue skies toward Fairbanks, she found herself wishing circumstances could've been different. This wasn't the first time she'd flown with Scott; she'd been in the air with him dozens of times. In Hard Luck planes were equivalent to cars anywhere else. More than one summer's afternoon had been spent flying to nearby lakes for a refreshing swim.

The first time he'd ever kissed her had been underwater. They'd done plenty of kissing above water, too. Chrissie closed her eyes, not wanting to remember.

At the first sign of Fairbanks, she relaxed, grateful to be close to her destination and away from the confines of the plane. Away from Scott. His landing was smooth, a greaser as the pilots called it, and the aircraft came down gently, touching the tarmac with barely a jolt.

"Nice landing," Chrissie said when Scott removed the headphones.

"Thanks."

"Will you be flying me back tomorrow afternoon?" Not that it mattered, but she wanted to know.

"My name's on the schedule." He unlatched the door and climbed out, his jaw noticeably tight—as though her question had angered her.

Refusing to allow his mood to intimidate her, Chrissie opened her own door and climbed down the wing, rejecting Scott's offer of assistance. Once firmly on the ground, she slipped her backpack over her shoulders and straightened. "I'll see you tomorrow, then."

He nodded curtly.

Without another word, Chrissie turned and started toward the terminal.

"Have fun with your boyfriend," he called after her, his voice dripping with sarcasm.

Boyfriend? She couldn't imagine where he got that idea. Chrissie thought about explaining that she was mentoring a twelve-year-old girl, then changed her mind. Perhaps it was for the best if Scott believed she was involved with another man. Not many people knew about her work with the experimental foster-care program. Her parents, of course, and Tracy. She'd briefly mentioned it to Ben's wife, too, but none of the details; she'd only referred to visiting Joelle on a particular weekend.

Joelle's group home was a foster-care program being tested by the state. School-age children were placed in a situation similar to a boarding-school facility. Each student was assigned a volunteer mentor from the community, who spent time with the child, encouraging and listening.

Chrissie had been working with Joelle for two years and had grown to love the quiet soft-spoken child. At first it was all Chrissie could do to get the painfully shy girl to speak above a whisper. Gradually, over time, thanks to the support of the group home and the trust Chrissie had built, Joelle grew more confident. Chrissie could hardly recognize the child she'd first met in the smiling chattering girl Joelle had become.

"I leave at four o'clock sharp," Scott shouted.

"I'll be on time," Chrissie responded, tossing the words over her shoulder.

"See that you are," he snapped, "or I'll leave without you."

His parting shot annoyed her, and she jerked open the heavy glass door leading to the terminal. Her frown quickly changed to a smile as Joelle raced toward her. "Chrissie, Chrissie!" the girl shouted. "Guess what? I got an A on my essay for English!"

Chrissie enveloped the girl in a hug as a surge of joy and triumph rushed through her. Joelle had come so far, and Chrissie couldn't help feeling a personal pride in the progress she'd made. Every accomplishment was significant, Chrissie knew; every accomplishment took her farther from her disadvantaged past and toward a hopeful future.

"Oh, Joelle, I'm *so* proud of you." Simple words, spoken with heartfelt sincerity, and it was a wonder to see the smile on the girl's face.

"I've got a busy weekend planned for us," Chrissie told her.

Joelle wrapped an arm around Chrissie's waist. "I brought my paper if you want to read it."

"You bet I do," she told her, and they walked out of the terminal together.

Four o'clock Sunday afternoon, as promised, Chrissie was back at the airport. Two days with Joelle, and she was exhausted. A friend who worked as a flight attendant for one of the airlines let Chrissie use her apartment. The arrangement worked well for them both. Jackie usually had weekend assignments, and whenever she was on duty, Chrissie watered her plants and brought in her mail.

Scott was waiting for her. "We may have trouble with the weather," he said by way of greeting.

"What kind of trouble?"

He stared at her. "A storm front's headed toward us. Would you understand the meteorological details if I explained them?"

"Probably, but I'll just take your word for it," she said. "Are we stuck in Fairbanks?"

"Not if I can help it. I've been on the phone for the last thirty minutes. If we leave now, we can squeak through. Ready to go?"

"Of course."

"Then let's get this show on the road." He led her to the plane and Chrissie dutifully followed him and climbed inside, fastening the seat belt. Although she knew they were in a hurry, she was reassured that Scott took the time to go over the preflight checklist thoroughly.

It was nearly dusk when they soared into the sky, which was clear and cloudless. Those conditions, however, didn't last. About halfway between Fairbanks and Hard Luck, they hit thick cloud cover and heavy winds, and the plane pitched and heaved. Rain and sleet lashed them from all directions, and ice started to build up on the wings. Chrissie didn't need to be a pilot to know how dangerous that was.

Although she'd flown in every type of weather, the rough-and-tumble ride unsettled her. During one particularly bad stretch, she closed her eyes and bit her lower lip.

"You okay?" Scott asked.

"Uh-huh."

Talking into his headset, Scott was busy for several minutes. "We're going down," he suddenly announced, his voice emotionless.

Adrenaline bolted through her. "We're landing? Where?" It was nearly nightfall and raining. She could barely make out the landscape below.

Scott, however, was concentrating on the radio, reporting the details of where they were, and he didn't answer her.

Chrissie clenched her hands tightly as he circled the area and slowly made his descent. By the time the lake came into view, her nerves were shot. Just as flawlessly as he'd landed the day before, Scott guided the plane onto the water's surface and cut the engine, gliding it toward shore.

"Where are we?" she asked once her heart had stopped pounding.

Scott heaved a sigh as he took off his headphones. "Lake Abbey. We'll wait out the storm here."

Terrific, just terrific; he'd chosen the very lake where he'd first kissed her. The lake Sawyer O'Halloran had named after his wife.

CHAPTER FIVE

SCOTT MANEUVERED the plane as close to shore as possible, all the while feeling Chrissie's glare. The woman was in a rage, which was ridiculous. It wasn't as though he'd invented this storm or conjured it up, although to tell the truth, he wasn't really complaining. It gave him the opportunity to talk to Chrissie without her dashing off the way she usually did whenever he was in the vicinity.

"You did this on purpose," she accused him.

"If you want something to blame, I suggest you look at the weather," Scott replied.

"The storm's only an excuse, and you know it. We never should've left Fairbanks."

She had him there, but he'd honestly believed they could slide in before the cold front hit. Rather than argue with her, he said calmly, "My family built a cabin here." He cringed at how damned convenient that sounded; not only did it seem like a setup, but she already knew about the cabin. So she probably figured he'd planned this all along.

"I suppose you're going to suggest we wait out the storm there," she said scathingly.

"Well, yes..." No wonder she doubted him, but as God was his witness, he *hadn't* planned it.

"I'm well aware of your parents' cabin," Chrissie returned defiantly, crossing her arms.

"You're welcome to spend the night in the plane," he said nonchalantly. She couldn't—he wouldn't allow it—but she didn't know that. He'd make his way to the cabin, build a fire, and if she hadn't shown up by the time he finished, he'd go back for her.

"That's exactly what I intend to do."

Scott should have suspected as much. He didn't remember Chrissie being this obstinate, but then, he hadn't been around her for a number of years.

"I'm going to the cabin," he told her, opening the aircraft's door. A bone-chilling blast of Arctic wind shook him, and he gasped at the shock of it.

"I have plenty of blankets here," she told him, sounding less sure of herself now.

"If you need anything, just holler." He closed the door, wondering if he should drag her out of the plane right then and there. Damn her pride, she was being ridiculous—again. But he quickly realized that after Chrissie had spent thirty minutes sitting in the frigid cold, her attitude would soften.

Edging along the pontoon, Scott leaped from the plane onto the shore. Luckily his boots protected his feet from the icy water. A flashlight led him toward the cabin through a night as black as he'd ever seen. Moon and stars were hidden by dark clouds, and there was no snow to provide even a tiny bit of reflection. The rain still pelted down.

He reached the cabin without incident. Scott's parents, Sawyer and Abbey, had built the log structure about fifteen years earlier, with plenty of help from family and friends. It'd been quite a feat and required nearly three years of planning. Naturally the cabin had no modern conveniences, but it'd served as a family vacation home ever since.

As soon as he was inside, Scott lit the lantern and set it in the window, making sure the light was visible for Chrissie, should she change her mind. He couldn't keep from looking out, although it was difficult to see anything more than the faintest silhouette of the plane.

His next challenge was to get a fire going. Luckily everything he needed—logs, kindling and matches— had been left within easy access for just such an emergency. Once he had the wood burning, Scott checked the cupboards. Again, his family had provided an adequate supply of canned goods. He and Chrissie shouldn't be trapped here long, four or five hours at most. The worst of the storm would pass by then, and they'd be able to land safely in Hard Luck early tomorrow morning.

He had the coffeepot brewing on the old stove when he thought he heard a noise outside. It was probably just the wind, but in case it was Chrissie, he wanted to appear as relaxed as possible. If she happened to peek inside, he wanted her to think he didn't have a care in the world. Throwing himself down on the big chair, he leaned back his head and closed his eyes.

Ten minutes later his patience was gone, vanished along with the pretense. Chrissie was an idiot if she thought he was going to leave her to wait out the storm in the plane while he sat, warm and cozy, inside the cabin. He grabbed his coat, determined to trudge back to the lake.

The wind was now mixed with ice and snow, and it stung his face when he opened the door. He shone the beam of light on the narrow footpath leading to the water's edge. Shoulders hunched against the wind and rain, he kept his gaze down. The flashlight guided his steps, illuminating the walkway a few feet at a time. Scott paused when the light fell on a pair of wet boots. Chrissie.

"I...I changed my mind," she announced.

Scott bit off any chastisement, although he had plenty he wanted to say. Instead, he held out his hand. "I'll help you."

She hesitated before slipping her gloved hand in his. "Thank you."

She moved close to his side, and his arm went about her waist as he helped her to the cabin. With the wind at their backs, propelling them forward, they were at the door within minutes.

The cabin was warm, comfortable and surprisingly intimate, despite its size. At first Chrissie stayed near the door, as if she feared what might happen if she advanced completely into the large open room.

"How about a cup of coffee?" Scott asked, his back to her.

"Please."

He dared not turn around for fear she'd see the amusement in his eyes. Judging by the way she maintained her distance, she apparently expected him to ravish her at any minute.

"You were able to let someone know where we are?" she asked, rubbing her hands together as she stood in front of the fire, which was now burning well. The wood crackled and flames leaped merrily, casting warmth throughout the room.

"Duke took the message." Her lack of trust distressed him, and the situation no longer seemed amusing.

"Good," she said briskly.

He poured them each a steaming cup of fresh coffee. He found sugar but no cream; there was, however, a bottle of whiskey, and he doctored his coffee with that. Might as well get comfort where he could. She declined.

Making himself comfortable, Scott sat in the big overstuffed chair Sawyer favored. If Chrissie wanted to act like a piece of cardboard, that was fine by him, but *he* intended to relax. Despite the impression he'd given, landing the plane during the storm had been a stressful experience. "I haven't been here in years," he said, glancing around, seeing the cabin with new eyes.

"Me...too."

"The last time—" He stopped abruptly the second he realized exactly when that last time was. Five years ago. He'd been with his sister and Chrissie; it was the summer they graduated from college.

"The last time you were here was with me, wasn't it?" Chrissie asked. She sat on the sofa across from him, huddled over her cup as though it was something that required her protection. Her boots and socks were off and drying by the fireplace. She sat with her bare feet tucked beneath her.

"Seems like a lifetime ago," he said, his voice a little hoarse. He'd watched Chrissie that day and he'd remembered everything he'd spent the past few years trying to forget. Even after he'd hurt her, she'd been trusting and sweet. The teenage girl he'd left behind had matured into a woman. That afternoon had been one of the most wonderful of his life; it'd opened his eyes to what he really wanted. All this time he'd been running away—from his family, his town, the people he'd known—and until that afternoon he hadn't realized how much he missed Chrissie, how much he needed her.

His original plan had been to fly into Hard Luck, attend the graduation party, then head out immediately afterward. His relationship with his mother and Sawyer was strained, and he hadn't wanted to overstay his welcome. During his years away, he'd made a new life for himself, first in the military and after that, in Utah. He'd hurt his parents, embarrassed them. It seemed better for everyone involved if he kept out of their lives.

To his surprise, Sawyer and his mother had been genuinely delighted to see him, and willing to put the past behind them. He'd loved spending time with Susan, Anna and Ryan, and he'd remained in Hard Luck for ten days. His reluctance to leave, however, was due to more than his family. Scott had lingered in town because of Chrissie.

With Sawyer's permission, he'd borrowed the Cessna, had Ben pack him a lunch and then taken off with his high-school sweetheart for an afternoon of swimming and fun. As soon as he could manage it, Scott had Chrissie back in his arms again.

The minute they'd kissed, those five years had dissolved and it was as if he'd never left. Every time they kissed, he had another reason to stay. Every time they touched, he felt a sense of rightness. This was home. This was Chrissie, the first girl he'd ever loved, the only girl he'd ever loved....

"Are you tired?" he asked, wanting to cut off his memories before they took him into territory best left undisturbed.

"Exhausted," Chrissie admitted, sounding more relaxed now that she'd had a warm drink.

"I'll scrounge up some blankets from the loft." He was anxious to do something, preferably something that required movement. Sitting around reminiscing about the one summer afternoon he most wanted to forget wouldn't help matters. Unfortunately it was the same summer afternoon he most wanted to remember.

He straightened the ladder that led to the loft. His parents used the upper area for storage in case bears broke into the cabin. Climbing up, he discovered that his mother had packed everything neatly away for the winter, but it didn't take him long to find extra bedding.

Grabbing several blankets, he carried them down for Chrissie. She'd finished her coffee and placed her mug in the sink.

"If you want, you can sleep down here on the sofa close to the fire," he suggested.

She nodded.

"I'll take the loft."

She nodded again.

"Good night, Chrissie."

"Night," she muttered, her voice suspiciously low.

Scott started up the ladder, then stopped. "Chrissie?" he asked, uncertain what had changed. Clearly something had. He heard it in her voice, although she kept her head averted and he couldn't see her expression.

"Yes?" She sounded cheerful again.

He stepped off the rung and moved toward her. "Is everything...all right?"

Turning to face him, still in the shadows, she said, "Listen, I know I was out of line earlier. I'm sorry for what I said."

"That's okay."

"You can't control the weather." They stood no more than a few feet apart, tension electrifying the air between them. Scott didn't know what to make of it. Part of him wanted to shout that it was time to put aside the hurts of the past and talk honestly. He opened his mouth to say as much but saw her stiffen and knew it was useless. She wouldn't lower the emotional barricades she'd erected against him. Nor could he forget that there was another man in her life now. A man she visited in Fairbanks at least twice a month.

"Good night," he said again, unnecessarily. After he'd stacked extra wood by the fireplace, he climbed the ladder to the loft.

He made up his bed, and when he lay down, he could see Chrissie below. She'd piled blankets on the sofa, then turned off the lantern. The only light in the cabin came from the flames dancing in the fireplace, throwing shadows about the room. The wind moaned outside the door. Another time the low whistle might have lulled him to sleep, but not tonight.

Not with Chrissie only a few feet below, snuggling on the sofa, warm and sweet.

Closing his eyes, he was beseiged by the memory of her kisses—the taste of her mouth against his, her eager response to him, the need she created in him with a single touch.

"Scott?"

Her soft voice startled him and he opened his eyes. "Yeah?"

"Are you asleep yet?"

"No."

"Do you mind if I ask you something?"

Anything would be better than this stilted politeness. "Sure, ask away."

"Do you remember that last summer we were here?"

He almost groaned aloud. "I'm not likely to forget."

"I wondered..." Her voice broke.

"What did you wonder, Chrissie?" he encouraged.

"I need to know if what Farrah said was true. Back then. *Were* you engaged to marry her?" She paused, then added, "Was it true?"

He'd been lying on his stomach, his head resting on his folded arms. He rolled onto his back and stared blankly at the ceiling. He opened his mouth to tell her, to explain it all away—but he couldn't. Yes, he had excuses and justifications for that day they'd spent on the lake, when he had, in fact, been engaged to another woman. He could tell Chrissie how he'd finally understood that Hard Luck was his home, that she held his heart. He'd *wanted* to tell her, but his

hands had been tied. It would have been grossly un-
fair to Farrah, and he owed her that one kindness
before he broke off the engagement.

"Your silence is answer enough."

"I don't have any excuses, but—"

"There's always a but, isn't there?" Her voice had
an edge that he'd never heard before.

"Chrissie—"

"No, listen, it's all right, really. I shouldn't have
asked. I knew, but I needed to hear you say it."

At that moment he would have given anything for
the ability to lie to her. Still, he couldn't make himself do it. "I didn't marry her."

"I noticed," she said sarcastically. "She dumped
you, huh? I don't blame her. No woman in her right
mind would marry a man who—" She choked off
the rest, took a moment to compose herself, then continued. "A man doesn't give a woman an engagement ring and then get involved with a high-school
flame. You deserved what you got."

Scott could hardly keep himself from saying that
not marrying Farrah was *his* decision—and the
smartest move he'd ever made. He thanked God that
he'd come to his senses in time to save them both
untold heartache. They'd fallen conveniently in love,
and getting married had seemed the inevitable next
step. Farrah was a looker, and they got along fairly
well. Not until he'd seen Chrissie again did he realize
his mistake.

He'd wanted to tell her the truth about Farrah that
summer day. He'd intended to break off the engagement once he returned to Utah and then, as soon as
he was free, come back to Hard Luck and plead with

Chrissie to marry him. So much for the best-laid plans. The matter of his engagement had blown up in his face when Farrah unexpectedly flew up to see him; she'd arrived with great fanfare and announced to everyone within earshot that she was his fiancée. Scott had seen the look his parents exchanged. His mother had been confused, especially after all the time he'd spent with Chrissie. Sawyer had been angry and they'd argued. Soon afterward, without a word to Chrissie, Scott had left Hard Luck, feeling lower than a snake.

He owed her an apology, and more. "I know it comes five years too late," he ventured, "but I am genuinely sorry."

His words appeared to fall on deaf ears. Then, "Is the apology meant for me or Farrah?" she asked.

"Both."

"It must've given your ego a real thrill to have two women in love with you at the same time."

He let the comment slide. "I'd settle for just one," he said quietly.

The fire popped, then briefly flamed, spreading a warm glow arouhnd the room. Scott watched as Chrissie threw aside the blankets and leaped to her feet. "Oh, no, you don't!"

"Don't what?" he asked, sitting up. He couldn't imagine what he'd said that she found so offensive.

"Let's get something straight. You think you can bring me back to Lake Abbey, stir up a few old memories and then weasel your way back into my life. Well, I'm here to tell you it isn't going to happen."

"Chrissie—"

She covered both ears and started to hum Christmas carols. "I'm not listening. I'm not listening. Nothing you say will make one bit of difference."

If she didn't look and sound so silly, Scott might have let the moment simply pass. Not now. Climbing down the ladder, he marched over and sat on the sofa next to her.

Gripping her shoulders, Scott looked her directly in the eyes. "Nothing I can say will make any difference?" he questioned. "Then try this one on for size. I love you, Chrissie Harris. I've loved you half my life."

CHAPTER SIX

DUKE PORTER waited until he knew Scott and Chrissie had landed safely on Lake Abbey before he left the Midnight Sons office. As he walked through his front door, taking off his wet jacket, he inhaled deeply. The scent of sage and his favorite chicken dish filled the house. He could hear sounds of laughter from his youngest daughter, Sarah Lynn.

"Are Scott and Chrissie okay?" Tracy asked, carrying a chicken casserole to the dining-room table.

"Yes and no," Duke told her, helping himself to a black olive.

"Daddy!" Sarah playfully slapped his hand. "You're supposed to wait for dinner."

"Sorry, I forgot," he said, and winked at his middle daughter who stood a short distance away, a frown of disgust on her face. Shortly after turning fourteen, Leah had, without any warning, completely lost her sense of humor. Almost overnight, his fun-loving outgoing daughter had turned into a morose and sullen teenager. From experience, he knew it was a stage. His oldest daughter, Shannon, had forged a path through the troubled teen years, so he knew what to expect. Or so he liked to believe.

"What do you mean Scott did and didn't land safely?" Tracy demanded.

"He landed," Duke explained, "only it wasn't in Hard Luck."

"He's all right, isn't he?" Leah asked, her brown eyes wide with concern.

His fourteen-year-old had a major crush on Scott O'Halloran. "I presume so. He thought he could beat the storm system coming our way, but he couldn't. So he decided that, rather than risk it, he'd touch down on Lake Abbey."

"All alone?"

"Chrissie's with him."

Leah slouched in the kitchen chair and pouted. "Some women have all the luck."

Tracy returned to the dining room with a pitcher of water and placed it in the center of the table. When she looked up, her eyes connected with Duke's. "How long will they hole up there?"

"Overnight, I suspect, perhaps longer. Depends on the weather."

Tracy's bold smile triggered a responding one from Duke.

"What?" Leah asked, glancing first at her mother and then her father.

"Nothing," Tracy muttered.

"Never mind," Duke said.

"Oh, puh-leeze," Leah groaned, and rolled her eyes. She nudged her younger sister. "Cover your eyes. Mom and Dad are going mushy on us."

"Shannon! Dinner's ready." Tracy called their oldest daughter, a high-school junior, from her room.

Shannon appeared, looking so much like Tracy that even now it took Duke by surprise. When he'd married Tracy, he'd envisioned a houseful of rough-

and-rowdy sons; instead, he had three beautiful daughters. Not once, not for a single second, had he been disappointed. His life was full and he deeply loved his wife. In fact, marriage was the best thing that had ever happened to him.

They all sat down together and joined hands for grace. Before the completion of the "amen," Duke had reached for the serving spoon and leaned toward the casserole. His wife cast him a disapproving glance, which he ignored.

"Did I hear someone mention Scott and Chrissie?" Shannon asked.

"He's stranded with Chrissie up at Lake Abbey," Leah complained. "Can you imagine getting stuck in a storm with a hunk like that? Why can't it happen to me?" Still bemoaning her sorry lot in life, she stretched across the table for the plate of biscuits and helped herself to one.

Duke quickly grabbed a biscuit before he got shortchanged; it'd been known to occur. To his surprise, Tracy had turned out to be a excellent cook. He'd had his doubts when he first married her, and with good reason. Once, during their brief courtship, he'd visited her in Seattle and she'd insisted on making dinner. The meal had damn near killed him. But soon after they were married, she'd taken cooking lessons from Mary Hamilton and proved to be an apt pupil.

Duke had to give all due credit: His wife was a marvel. She'd gone into this marriage convinced she could do it all and have it all. She'd claimed she could maintain her career as an attorney and keep up with the ever-increasing demands of being a wife and mother. And for the most part, she had. They'd planned the first two additions to their family. It wasn't until Sarah Lynn was born that Tracy took a leave of absence from the law firm. With infinite wisdom—and with advancing age—she'd declared that yes, she *could* have it all, just not at the same time. When Sarah Lynn started kindergarten, Tracy put on her attorney's suit again. Three years ago Chrissie Harris had joined the law office and was working out well.

Within ten minutes, all three girls had eaten and vanished. Duke and Tracy lingered over the last of their coffee.

"So…Scott and Chrissie are stuck up at Lake Abbey," Tracy said, bracing her elbows on the table and holding her coffee cup in both hands.

"Stir any memories?" Duke teased.

She smiled. Twenty years earlier Duke and Tracy had been involved in a fairly serious airplane crash. Tracy had been living in Seattle at the time, and she'd flown up to Hard Luck to attend a friend's wedding. Duke had been scheduled to fly her into Fairbanks for her connecting flight to Seattle. The two of them had clashed from the moment they'd met, a couple of years before. Tracy Santiago was everything Duke disliked in a woman; he found her bossy, independent and headstrong. He'd derived real pleasure from baiting her and soon discovered she could more than hold her own. Tracy had viewed him as an unreasonable male chauvinist pig—one of the few men who truly fit that now-dated expression. Their arguments and dislike of each other had been legendary.

Then the plane had gone down, and Duke was badly hurt. He'd broken his arm and sustained internal injuries. During the long hours before the rescue team arrived, Tracy had shown herself to be both capable and compassionate. While she confidently dealt with the crisis at hand, caring for him and guiding the rescue party to the downed plane, Duke realized he'd done something very foolish. He'd gone and fallen in love with her.

Tracy loved him, too, and had the wisdom to recognize that although they were vastly different, they had everything necessary to make a good life together. Duke had just needed some time and distance to appreciate what Tracy already knew.

He'd claimed, in the days before Tracy, that he wanted a conventional wife. One who'd stay home with the children, bake cookies and do other wifely things. None of that interested Tracy. He'd married her, convinced he'd survive on frozen dinners the rest of his life, but by then he'd loved her too damn much to care. Over the years there'd been some bad meals, but more than enough fabulous ones to maintain the balance. Some of the inedible dinners he'd cooked himself. Tracy wasn't the only one who'd changed; he'd done his fair share, too.

Twenty years and three daughters later, he was more than willing to admit how right she'd been. Not that their years together had been easy. On plenty of occasions he'd been convinced they'd made a big mistake, but he refused to give up on their marriage. And she felt the same way. What mattered most was the love and the commitment they shared. The fact that they were both hardheaded, stubborn fools had turned out to be an advantage.

"Are you remembering the crash?" Tracy asked.

Duke nodded. "I think it's poetic justice that Scott and Chrissie are stuck up there together. He loves her."

Tracy didn't immediately agree.

"You don't think so?" Duke asked.

"I don't know about Scott," Tracy said with a thoughtful look, "but I certainly know how Chrissie feels."

So the two women had talked about Chrissie's relationship with Scott. It shouldn't surprise him, seeing that they worked together. "When did Chrissie mention Scott? What did she have to say?" Duke pried.

"Actually she didn't say a word," his wife told him, standing. "We don't generally discuss our personal lives at the office."

"But you just said..." Duke trailed her into the kitchen. "How do you know about Chrissie's feelings if she didn't mention Scott?"

"The way I always know," Tracy said casually, putting the butter dish back in the refrigerator. "It's what people *don't* say that's more informative."

"Girls!" Duke shouted to his three daughters. "Dishes."

His order was followed by a chorus of protesting groans, all coming from different parts of the house. Duke ignored them, as did his wife.

Tracy retired to the living room and reached for the mystery novel she was currently reading. Normally Duke would turn on the television, but he left it off this evening.

"I hope Scott and Chrissie can work it out," he said, relaxing in his comfortable chair.

Tracy glanced up. "So do I."

"Anything interesting on television tonight?"

Tracy continued to read. "There's a documentary on Discovery I was hoping to catch. Something about frogs."

"It's not on too late, is it?"

"Why?" She raised her eyes to meet his.

"I was thinking of making an early night of it."

Tracy returned to her book. "Any particular reason?"

"Yes." It was a test of his determination not to laugh. Tracy knew full well what he had in mind. After being married to him all these years, how could she *not* know?

"You coming to bed early or not?" he asked.

"Oh, I'll be there," she said, the corner of her mouth quivering. "I wouldn't miss it for the world."

THE CABIN HAD BEEN quiet for more than a hour, and Chrissie was convinced Scott had gone to sleep. His breathing was regular and even. She wished the sound of it would lull her to sleep, as well, but so far it hadn't. She envied his ability to drift off like this, especially after their heated discussion.

Scott had claimed he loved her—and she'd laughed at him. That probably wasn't the most tactful response, but she couldn't help herself. He didn't honestly expect her to believe him, did he?

No man in his right mind treated a woman the way

Scott O'Halloran had treated her. They'd both said some things tonight that would've been better left unsaid, and then he'd stalked away, climbed into the loft and promptly fallen asleep.

His ability to put their discussion behind him so quickly only went to prove that she was right. Otherwise how could he possibly sleep now? It made no sense. Not when she worried and fretted, rehashing their argument, the anger and resentment churning inside her. If he *did* love her as he'd said, then he should be upset, too; he should care. Clearly he didn't.

Their argument, however, was only part of what was keeping Chrissie awake. Hunger contributed its own pangs to her sleepless state. She and Joelle had eaten a late breakfast, but that was almost twelve hours ago. If she read her watch right, it was now 10:00 p.m. She squinted down at her wrist, trying to make out the miniature numbers on her uselessly elegant watch. Maybe it was only nine, she thought; nevertheless, she was famished.

The way she figured, she had two options. She could stay up, seethe with resentment toward Scott and listen to her stomach growl, or she could be angry with Scott and quietly investigate the canned goods in the kitchen.

The second option held more appeal. As silently as possible, she threw aside the quilts and tiptoed toward the kitchen. The latch on the cupboard door was tricky and she couldn't see to get it open, no matter what she tried. She felt so frustrated she wanted to slam her fist against it.

"You have to be smarter than a bear," Scott said from behind her.

Chrissie whirled around. "I thought you were asleep!"

"I wasn't."

"Oh." She sighed heavily, wanting to avoid another confrontation with him—although she wouldn't back down if he started one. Gone was the shy teenage girl he'd jilted and the young college graduate whose heart he'd broken. She was a woman now, and perfectly able to deal with the likes of him.

"You're hungry."

Chrissie's nod was stiff, distrustful.

"Breakfast in bed, was it?" he asked in a sarcastic tone.

At first Chrissie was going to disabuse him of that idea, then decided she should let him believe what he wanted. He didn't know her, and time had proved he never *had* known her. Not really. "Something like that." She said the words flippantly.

He reached behind her, his hand grazing her ear, and twisted the cupboard knob. The door instantly sprang open. The top of her ear, where his finger had inadvertently touched, burned hotly. She didn't want his touch to affect her like this.

"You can leave now, thank you very much," she muttered fiercely.

"I'm hungry, too," he said. Leaning forward, he grabbed a can from the shelf. Wanting to avoid any further chance of contact with him, Chrissie stepped to one side, but all she managed to do was position herself more securely in his arms.

His ability to fluster her only irritated her more.

She stiffened, and Scott's brows arched when he noticed her reaction.

"I'll get out of your way," she offered, eager to escape the circle of his arms.

He didn't respond, nor did he move.

She watched as his eyes narrowed. Wondering how much he could see in the firelight, she prayed that not a hint of what she really felt was reflected on her face. Her heartbeat was out of control, and her mouth had gone completely dry. She didn't dare moisten her lips for fear he'd read that as an invitation to kiss her.

"Scott...let me go." She waited for him to release her.

He did so with obvious reluctance, dropping his arms to his sides. He stepped away, and she saw his eyes harden—and then he did something so unexpected, so underhanded, that for one shocking moment, Chrissie couldn't believe it.

He kissed her.

Not in the gentle sweet way she remembered. Not the cherished kisses of their youth, the memory of which she'd carried with her all these years. Instead, his mouth was hard on hers, the kiss wild and dangerous, stealing the very breath from her lungs.

Chrissie gasped and would have protested further if Scott had allowed it. Pinned against the cupboard, Chrissie had no means of escape. She tried to break it off, tried not to enjoy the familiar taste of him. It'd been five years since he'd last kissed her. She shouldn't remember, shouldn't savor his touch. She was strong and capable. Yes, she was. But one kiss and already she could feel herself weakening. He'd hurt her deeply, but she found herself thinking there was probably a legitimate reason for the things he'd done. Already she was making excuses for him!

"No!" She wrenched away.

He hesitated, eyes puzzled. "Why did you...?"

Oh, what the hell. But if he was going to kiss her, it would be on her terms, not his. Grabbing him by the shirt collar, she jerked his face toward hers. If he wanted to kiss, then it would be a kiss he wouldn't soon forget.

Scott gave a deep growl and half lifted her from the floor. Her feet dangled several inches off the ground, but by this point Chrissie wasn't about to let a little thing like suspended animation distract her. The kiss was unrestrained, intense, and she let it continue, wanting to make sure he knew she hadn't been lying home at nights wondering about him.

When he ended it, his breathing was ragged. Hers, too. Chrissie pressed the back of her hand to her lips and boldly met his look.

"I hope that answers your questions," she said as pleasantly as she could.

"Well...not really."

He reached for her, but she was quick enough to sidestep him. "No, that was a mistake, and one that won't happen again."

"Or what?" he demanded. "You'll take me to court?" Scott returned to the main part of the cabin, dropped into the chair, then leaned forward and ran his fingers through his hair. "Tell me about him," he said.

"Who?"

"Joel."

Chrissie could hardly believe her ears. "Joel! You want to hear about Joel?"

His response was to glare at her from across the room.

Outraged, Chrissie glared right back. "Is that why you kissed me, because you couldn't bear the thought of me being with another man?" Whatever appetite she'd experienced earlier faded away, and she merely felt hollow, not hungry. Her legs weren't all that steady, either. Shocked and a little disoriented, she sank onto the far end of the sofa.

This explained everything. He was jealous. Everything he'd said and done had been prompted by his fear that she was involved with someone else. The minute he learned Joel was really Joelle, his interest would wane. It was all a game to him.

A game Chrissie refused to play any longer. "For your information, it isn't Joel I go to see, it's Joelle."

Frowning, he looked up. "Joelle?"

"She's twelve, and I'm her mentor."

"Are you saying—" he spoke slowly, deliberately "—it isn't a *man* you fly out to spend time with every other weekend?"

"That's exactly what I'm saying. Not a man. A twelve-year-old girl."

"But you said—"

"I said nothing. All right," she added, wanting to be as fair as possible, "I might have let you believe it was a man, but you were the one who suggested it in the first place. I don't know who gave you that impression, but—"

"Ben," he muttered, his frown deepening.

Chrissie closed her eyes and shook her head. She'd

mentioned Joelle once to Mary, who must have told Ben. Clearly he'd either misheard or jumped to the wrong conclusion or both.

"You talked to Ben about me?" she asked suddenly. She didn't like the idea of Scott discussing her—with Ben or anyone else. That thought angered her even more. "You have some nerve, I'll say that for you."

"Chrissie—"

"Don't Chrissie me. I'm not a naive sixteen-year-old, nor do I have stars in my eyes. I know exactly the kind of man you are."

He stared at her. "You *don't* know me," he snapped. "If you did—"

"I know all I want to know."

"Fine."

Refusing to give him the last word, she muttered, "Fine with me, too."

It seemed a sad way to end their conversation, if indeed it could be considered a conversation. Scott returned to the loft with an opened can of beans and a fork; she jerked the blankets over her shoulders. Wordlessly she sat and guarded the fire, trying to forget Scott's kisses.

CHAPTER SEVEN

"WELL?" MARIAH O'HALLORAN glanced up from the secretary's desk where she filled in one day a week at the Midnight Sons office. Years earlier she'd been one of the first women to respond to the O'Hallorans' advertisement; she'd accepted the position of secretary and ended up marrying her boss.

Christian gently closed the door and slumped into the chair nearest her desk. Her husband wore a strange look, and Mariah didn't know what to think. "Scott and Chrissie are back, aren't they?"

"They're back."

"And?" She hated it when Christian made her dig for every little detail. He knew that she and half the residents of Hard Luck were dying to hear what had happened between Scott and Chrissie. Everyone had hoped the two of them would mend their differences while stranded on Lake Abbey.

In her eyes the situation was ideal. The two of them alone together while the storm raged outside. Christian claimed she was an incurable romantic, but if that was true, then so was almost everyone in Hard Luck. "I want to know about Scott and Chrissie."

"You and the rest of the town. There must've been a hundred people at the airfield this morning when they landed."

Mariah leaned forward. "Did it look like everything's okay with them?" she asked.

"Hardly," Christian said with a shake of his head. "The minute the engine stopped, Chrissie had the door open and was scrambling out. Seemed to me she was in an awful rush."

"Oh." This wasn't encouraging news. "What about Scott? Did he go after Chrissie?"

"No." Christian frowned. "He took off in the opposite direction. Now that I think about it, he seemed to be in a rush himself."

"Oh, dear."

"It's too bad, isn't it?"

Her husband's comment surprised her, since he rarely showed any interest in other people's romantic problems.

"I think the world of Scott," Christian went on to say.

"I know you do," Mariah said.

"He's a good guy—turned out well. I know he had a few problems as a teenager, but lots of boys do. I certainly don't hold it against him. Hey—remember when he read Susan's diary and wrote comments in the margins?"

"I sure do," Mariah said, grinning. She agreed that Scott had turned out well. In more than one sense. He was a fine-looking man. Mariah had watched him, Susan and Chrissie mature into young adults. From the time Scott and Chrissie were in high school, she'd known they shared a special bond. Like almost everyone in Hard Luck, she'd assumed that one day they'd marry. Only, she'd apparently assumed wrong, and that saddened her.

"Years ago," Christian said, stretching out his legs, "before we got married, Scott and I had a talk...about women."

Mariah managed to hold back a smile. She didn't even want to *think* what a nine-year-old boy had to say on that subject.

"Scott offered me some advice," Christian said, grinning broadly, "having to do with romance and the two of us."

"Don't you dare tell me after all these years that you married me on the advice of a fifth-grade boy!"

Christian's eyes avoided hers. "I guess it wasn't exactly *advice*."

"You'd better tell me the worst."

"Well, Scott bragged about the help he'd given others—like Sawyer and Matt Caldwell and even Mitch Harris—when it came to love and marriage." Christian shook his head, a half-amused grimace on his face. "He suggested he could help us, too"

"Did he now?"

"He did, but I would've come to the right conclusion—eventually." He paused. "You'd decided to leave Hard Luck, and I was pretty down in the mouth about it."

In Mariah's opinion, Christian's memory was a bit flawed. "You fired me, if I remember correctly."

"Yeah, but that's because I was crazy about you. I thought if you were gone, then— But I don't want to get sidetracked here. All I can remember is how bad I felt when I realized you were actually going to leave. Nothing was working out the way I thought it would." His eyes held hers for an extra-long moment. "The fact is, I'm as crazy about you now as I was then."

Mariah resisted the urge to walk around her desk and kiss her husband—but only because she wanted to hear the rest of his story.

"You remember what it was like back then, don't you?"

"I'm not likely to forget." She wouldn't, either. Christian claimed he'd been down in the mouth, but it didn't compare to how she'd felt. The weeks after she'd left her position at Midnight Sons had been some of the bleakest of her life. To this day, Mariah didn't know what she would have done without her friends. Matt and Karen had provided housing and encouragement. Abbey, Lanni O'Halloran, Bethany—they'd all rallied around, offering comfort and advice when all she'd wanted, all she'd ever wanted, was for Christian to love her.

"It seems odd to remember a conversation I had with a kid almost twenty years ago," Christian admitted, smiling wryly, "but in some ways, it's as if it took place yesterday. That's how clearly I remember Scott giving me his advice to the lovelorn—and talking about Chrissie."

"What did he say about her?"

"He told me that one day he was going to marry her, freckles and all."

Mariah smiled. "That boy had sense even then."

"Unfortunately he appears to have lost it," Christian murmured. He glanced at his watch, and looked surprised when he noted the time. Leaping to his feet, he said, "Gotta go. Are you picking up the boys from soccer practice this afternoon or am I?"

"I'll do it," she said, and smiled at his look of relief. Both their sons were enthusiastic about indoor soccer.

"I'll be glad when they can drive themselves," he said on his way out the door.

"Me, too," she agreed. Their two boys, born thirteen months apart, were in their mid-teens. The fun years, as Bethany Harris and Tracy Porter were quick to tell her. They were wonderful kids, and Mariah didn't expect any trouble with them. Both were crazy about sports. The oldest, Tyler, loved to fly and often accompanied Christian on his scheduled flights. He was a sociable, gregarious boy. The younger, Travis, while as athletic as his brother, was more of an introvert.

"See you tonight, then," Christian called.

Mariah went over to the door and watched her husband leave. She hadn't quite made it back to her desk when the door opened a second time, and to her astonishment Scott O'Halloran walked in. He looked none too pleased.

"Christian here?"

"He just left," Mariah told him. "If you hurry, you can catch him."

"That's okay, thanks." Scott began to head out the door. "I'll see him later."

"We were just talking about you," Mariah said, and regretted it the instant the words were out of her mouth.

"Me?" Scott hesitated at the door.

"Christian was remembering some advice you once gave him about romance."

Scott seemed puzzled. "I gave Christian advice?"

"It isn't any surprise you don't remember," she said, making light of it, "especially since you were only a kid at the time."

"What did I say?"

She thought for a moment, then decided it wouldn't do any harm for him to know. "You were quite the matchmaker in those days."

"Not me," he said, grinning for the first time. "I left that to Susan and Chrissie."

"That's not the way I remember it," Mariah said.

"Those really were the good old days," he muttered. "Now that I think about it, maybe you're right. When I was twelve or so, I toyed with the idea of writing an advice column. I even talked to Lanni about putting it in her newspaper."

"Pretty enterprising of you."

"Especially when you consider what a hopeless mess my own love life is."

"Scott, that's not true." Mariah felt sorry for him. "I'm sure things aren't hopeless."

"It is true," Scott countered.

He seemed utterly defeated, and Mariah suddenly wanted to throw her arms around him, as though he were one of her sons. "Christian seemed to think you got *him* thinking in the right direction," she said bracingly.

Scott's expression was incredulous.

"Whatever you told Christian worked. We have a long-standing marriage to prove it." She had his interest now. "If you love Chrissie—"

"Mariah, let me stop you here. It's over. Chrissie isn't interested."

"Don't you believe it."

He shook his head. "I'm afraid you're wrong. She as much as told me so this weekend. And I think it's probably for the best."

THE ENTIRE OFFICE fell quiet when Chrissie entered. Everyone stared at her as she walked in. The secretary, Kate, jumped up from her desk immediately, clutching a handful of files, and followed her down the short hallway.

"We were all worried when we heard you'd been held up by the storm," Kate told her.

"There was nothing to worry about," Chrissie muttered, wanting to avoid the subject. She reached for the stack of mail on her desk, shuffling through it.

"I have your appointment calendar for the day."

"You can leave it with me," Chrissie instructed. In other circumstances, she would have headed directly home, soaked in a hot tub and slept through the day. Mondays, however, were often hectic. She had appointments all morning, and it was too late to reschedule them now.

No sooner had she sat down behind her desk than there was a polite knock at her door.

"Come in."

"Hi." Tracy stuck her head in. "Glad you got here safe and sound."

"Thanks."

"Everything go all right?"

Chrissie wasn't sure how to answer. "Reasonably well, I guess."

The worst of the storm hadn't passed until daylight, and by the time she and Scott returned, the

entire town of Hard Luck had heard about their pre-
dicament. If that wasn't bad enough, their families,
friends and neighbors had all rushed to the airstrip,
eager to welcome them back. Unfortunately, at that
stage, Chrissie and Scott were barely on speaking
terms.

Everyone, her parents included, had stared at them
with great anticipation, obviously expecting their engagement to be announced on the spot.

"Are you sure you're all right?" Tracy asked.

"I'm fine, really. Just tired."

"If you need anything, let me know."

"I will," Chrissie promised. "Listen...there's
something I want to talk over with you later."

Tracy frowned.

"I'd explain it now, but there isn't time. My first
appointment is due in ten minutes and I have to read
through his file. Can we talk this afternoon?"

Tracy nodded. "Of course. Whatever you need."

Her partner's words touched her. "Thanks,"
Chrissie whispered as Tracy quietly closed the door.

Chrissie buried her face in her hands. It didn't help
that she was exhausted, not having slept the entire
night. How could she, with Scott only a few feet
away? She doubted he'd gotten any more sleep than
she had.

Scott had left the cabin well before dawn and gone
to the plane. At first she'd panicked, fearing he'd fly
off without her, but then reason had reasserted itself,
and she'd acknowledged that, for all his faults, he
wouldn't abandon her. Apparently he'd made radio
contact and received the latest weather information.

In thirty minutes or so, he returned and told her they could leave at first light.

During the trip back she might as well have been sitting next to a robot. He didn't speak to her. For that matter, she didn't have anything to say to him, either. The situation was dreadful and destined to grow worse. Until this weekend misadventure, they'd at least been cordial with each other. Now even that was gone.

It was clear to her, if not to him, that they couldn't both stay in Hard Luck. One of them had to leave. Leaning back in her chair, Chrissie tried to think rationally about it. Since he'd only recently returned and was now a partner in the family business, it didn't seem right that Scott should leave.

She was the one who'd have to go. Tears threatened again, but she refused to give in to self-pity. She'd move to Fairbanks, she decided. Get out of Scott's way.

That decision made, there was only one thing left to do.

Tell Tracy, and then Scott.

CHAPTER EIGHT

SCOTT HADN'T SLEPT all night, and he suspected Chrissie hadn't, either. He was bushed. After a visit to the office to drop off his flight bag and chat briefly with Mariah, he headed home. He genuinely sympathized with Chrissie, having to work all day. But the sad fact was, she didn't want his sympathy or, unfortunately, anything else to do with him.

When he made a quick stop at the Hard Luck Lodge, Matt and Karen were openly curious about what had happened between him and Chrissie, but they accepted his vague explanation. Once in his cabin, he stood under a long hot shower and then collapsed on his bed, falling instantly asleep.

A pounding on his door woke him. Light bore into the bedroom's one window and he glanced at his clock radio, astonished to see that it was already mid-afternoon.

"Just a minute," he growled. Grabbing a pair of jeans, he hurriedly pulled them on, along with a sweatshirt. He padded barefoot to the door, yawning as he went.

Finding Chrissie on the other side was a shock. He froze, his yawn half-completed.

"Do you have a minute?" she asked stiffly.

"Sure," he said, and stepped aside. From the tight

lines about her eyes and mouth, he could tell she hadn't had a good day. There were dark shadows beneath her eyes, and she looked in desperate need of sleep. He wondered what was so important that it couldn't wait.

Chrissie peered inside the small cabin and shook her head. "Not here."

"Where, then?" he asked, not quite concealing his irritation.

"Can you meet me at the Hard Luck Café in fifteen minutes?"

He hesitated, thinking this probably wasn't the best time for them to discuss anything. Not with her so tired she could barely keep her eyes open and with him feeling so on edge. Despite that, he was curious. "I'll be there," he said briskly.

"I'll get us a booth."

He closed the door, then rubbed his face. Something was up, and he was about to learn what. It took him the full fifteen minutes to find his shoes, socks and gather his scattered wits.

The September wind cut into him as he hurried toward the café. As promised, Chrissie was sitting in a corner booth, her hands clutching a mug. The lunch crowd had disappeared, with only one or two stragglers. Ben and Mary stared at him, their curiosity as keen as his own.

"She's been here all of five minutes," Ben whispered when Scott stopped to collect his own coffee.

"Looking at her watch every few seconds," Mary added.

"She wants to talk to me," Scott muttered.

"We'll see that you have as much privacy as you need," Mary assured him.

"You settle this matter once and for all," Ben said. "You're both miserable, and the whole damn town with you."

Scott had to grin. "I'll do my best."

He carried his coffee to the booth and slid in across from Chrissie. "You have something to say?"

"I do." Her back was ramrod-straight, her arms unbending as she held her coffee away from her, both hands clamped around the mug.

Scott waited for several minutes, his patience wearing thin when she still didn't speak.

"Are you aware," she finally said, keeping her gaze focused on the tabletop, "that we have a problem?"

"What do you mean?" He wasn't being sarcastic, just inquisitive.

"Did you notice how everyone gathered at the airfield?"

He'd noticed, all right.

"How did that make you feel?" she asked.

He shrugged, wondering if there was a correct answer. "Uncomfortable, I guess."

"Embarrassed?"

"Yeah."

"Me, too." Her look softened perceptibly.

"Everyone was expecting something from us."

"They weren't interested in your American Express card," he said in a weak attempt at a joke.

"No," she told him, with not even a hint of humor. "What they were looking for was some *sign* from us."

"True," he admitted, refusing to sound defensive, "and we gave it to them, don't you think?"

"Oh, we sure did," she returned.

"So what's the problem?"

She glared at him as though he should have figured it out long ago. "The problem is, we've disappointed the whole town."

His friends and family weren't nearly as disappointed as Scott himself was, but he didn't mention that. In his view, he'd laid his heart on the line already. He'd told Chrissie he loved her and she'd laughed in his face. His pride had reached its quota for abuse, and he wasn't willing to accept more.

"I feel that we can no longer both remain in Hard Luck," she announced.

"What?"

"Just as I said. One of us has to leave."

So *this* was what her meeting was all about. She wanted him out of Hard Luck. Well, it wasn't going to happen. This was his home, his life, and he wasn't going to let Chrissie screw it up. Not when he'd done such a good job of that himself. He wasn't going anywhere; he'd only recently found his way back.

His face hardened right along with his heart. "You're asking me to leave."

Chrissie's eyes widened. "No!"

Her answer perplexed him. "What do you want, then?"

"I...I'd never ask that of you, Scott. I'll be the one to move. I've been thinking about it all day, and it makes perfect sense that I should leave town. I have connections in Fairbanks and then there's Joelle and..."

She rattled on, but the longer she spoke the more Scott realized how close she was to tears.

"Chrissie," he said, stopping her, "why are you doing this?"

She stopped abruptly. "Isn't it obvious?"

Tears glistened in her eyes now, and she blinked several times in an effort to hide them. Scott's frustration and anger melted away, and he resisted the impulse to reach across the table and touch her cheek, comfort her somehow. What prevented him was knowing she would resent any display of affection. He clenched his hands into fists and said, "You're not thinking straight. Listen, go home, get some sleep, and we can talk about this later."

"No. My mind's made up. One of us has to leave, and it has to be me."

"You're overreacting." After a good night's sleep she'd see that and regret this entire conversation. "This is an important decision. Let's sleep on it before you—or I—do something rash."

"No," she argued again, her voice gaining strength. "You don't understand."

"What I understand is that you've gone thirty hours without sleep, and now isn't the time to make a critical decision."

"But I know exactly what I'm doing," she insisted.

"Why should *you* be the one to move?" he demanded, completely losing his patience now. "You've lived here your entire life. This is your home. If anyone goes, it should be me."

Chrissie closed her eyes and shook her head. "I can't let you do that."

"Why not?"

"Because I love you," she whispered. "I refuse to let you leave."

Scott was sure he'd misunderstood her. "You... love me?"

Her eyes flared as though she didn't realize what she'd said. "You've just come back. It's been a long time, and...and you can't. You're a partner in Midnight Sons. The papers have already been drawn up and..." She shrugged. "It just makes sense that I be the one to go."

"What has any of that got to do with you loving me?" He wasn't about to let the subject drop, no matter how hard she tried to talk around it.

She ignored the question and continued. "I'm getting to the point in my career where my practice is growing. I fly into Fairbanks regularly on business. It's logical that I live there, so I'll go."

"You didn't answer my question."

"It...was a slip of the tongue," she said through gritted teeth. "I didn't mean it."

Scott relaxed against the vinyl cushion and then slowly smiled. "You never were much good at lying."

Her eyes grew wide and her face reddened as she sputtered, "But...but—"

"You love me, Chrissie. You've always loved me."

She shook her head, refusing to respond.

"I should have known it when I kissed you. I would have, too, if I hadn't been so caught up in what was happening. It was all I could do to keep from making love to you right then and there."

"As if I'd let you," she sniffed.

She seemed ready to slide out of the booth, and Scott reached across the table and grabbed her hand.

Chrissie's gaze shot to his.

"I have a better suggestion about how to settle this. A compromise." He had her attention now. "One in which neither of us has to move away from Hard Luck."

She didn't ask what he meant, but he sensed her interest. He hesitated, debating the wisdom of what he was about to do. Experience had taught him to be wary with Chrissie—but then, she had a right to mistrust him.

"Marry me," he said simply.

She didn't say anything right away. "Marry you?" she repeated at last.

"I love you." He wouldn't add any embellishments, nor would he offer her unnecessary compliments. If she couldn't already see that he was speaking from his heart, then anything else he had to say wouldn't help his cause.

"Scott...like you said, we need to sleep on it. We're both tired. It was an exhausting night—"

"I don't need to sleep on it. I love you, Chrissie. I want to make you my wife. I want us both to live right here in Hard Luck, to raise our children here, to grow old here. Together."

She swallowed hard.

"There's no one else waiting in the wings, either. Only you."

As though she didn't trust her voice, she shook her head again and slipped out of the booth. Without a word, she started to walk away.

So that was his answer. The burden of his disappointment seemed too much to bear. He propped his elbows on the table and covered his face with his hands.

"I'll pack up my things and be gone by morning," he told her, his voice raw.

She stood with her back to him, but at his words, she whirled around. "I told you I'll move."

"No, I said I'd go." He took his first and last sip of coffee, left the mug on the table and slid out of the booth, too. He hadn't gone more than a few feet when Chrissie stopped him.

"All right!" she cried. "All right."

Frowning, he faced her. "I'll be out of Hard Luck by morning."

"I...I wasn't agreeing to that. I meant, I'll marry you."

Mary stood in the background, both hands over her mouth as though to keep from shouting with glee. Scott cast her a warning glance, and her eyes twinkled with sheer delight.

"Why would you marry me?" he demanded. "Other than the fact that I asked you to."

"First..." She lowered her gaze to the floor. "I...love you. I've loved you for as long as I can remember."

"I want a woman's love and not a schoolgirl crush."

"Give me a chance, and you'll see how much of woman I am."

He grinned. "Any other reason?"

She nodded. "I couldn't stand to let you walk

away from me again. It nearly killed me the first two times.''

''It's not going to happen, sweetheart.'' He held open his arms, and not a moment passed before she was in them. His hold was so strong he practically lifted her from the floor, then her lips were on his. She kissed him in a way that left him in no doubt of her feelings. And in no doubt that she was every inch the woman she'd claimed.

''This is wonderful news!'' Mary cried from behind them.

Scott heard the honking sound of Ben blowing his nose and recognized that his friend was shedding a tear of shared happiness.

Scott broke off the kiss, afraid to believe Chrissie was actually in his arms. ''You aren't going to wake up tomorrow morning and change your mind, are you?''

Her smile told him there was no chance of that. Her expression sobered and she sighed. ''I promised myself I wouldn't let this happen, but, Scott, oh, Scott, I'm so happy it did. I've always loved you.''

Still he held her. ''Don't make any more promises to yourself, all right?''

Chrissie laughed softly. ''All right,'' she whispered. ''I won't.''

And then she kissed him again.

From the *Hard Luck Gazette*
By Lani O'Halloran, Editor

It's official! I don't suppose I'm the only one who's noticed that Chrissie Harris is sporting an engagement ring. I spoke with the soon-to-be-mother-of-the-bride, Bethany Harris, early this afternoon and Bethany confirmed that Scott O'Halloran and Chrissie have set the wedding date for New Year's Eve.

Bethany and Mitch proudly claim credit for having brought this couple together as a result of some timely advice to the bride to be. However, this conflicts with what Matt and Karen Caldwell recently told me, which suggests that *they* were the ones who'd played a major role in the wedding plans—although when pressed Matt insisted their part in furthering the romance would remain his and Karen's secret.

The new Mrs. O'Halloran will continue practicing law with Tracy Porter, while Scott's duties with Midnight Sons will expand, particulary since his father, Sawyer O'Halloran, intends to retire. Sawyer and Abbey have already booked a trip to New York and are looking forward to a second honeymoon.

As a "Welcome Back to Hard Luck" gift, Sawyer has given his son a purebred Alaskan husky, who is a direct descendant of Scott's beloved Eagle Catcher, whom many of our readers will remember. Scott and Chrissie have both expressed their delight.

A bridal shower will be hosted by Scott's sister, Susan Gold, and will be held at the Hard Luck Community Center the sixth of November. On the same night, Ben Hamilton will host a bachelor party at the Hard Luck Café.

As a wedding gift, my husband, Charles O'Halloran, and I, together with Mariah and Christian O'Halloran, as well as Scott's parents, have presented the engaged couple with twenty acres of land—and a cabin. Kind of goes full circle, doesn't it?

The Glory Girl
Judith Bowen

GLORY, ALBERTA

I've spent a lot of my life in towns, starting with twelve years of riding the school bus an hour each way to attend school in a small town in Alberta. I've lived in small towns all over Canada, from a remote coastal village in British Columbia, where I met my husband, to a farming and fishing village in Prince Edward Island, where my oldest child was born.

Today, I still live in a small town, this one on the banks of the Fraser River in B.C., with my family of five.

When I started writing romance novels, it made sense to write about the kind of life I knew best. Thus, the fictitious town of Glory was born, set in the beautiful Rocky Mountain ranch land and foothill country of southern Alberta. Glory is small enough for everyone who lives here to know everyone else, and big enough to supply the district's needs for groceries, doctors, lawyers and so on.

Over the past seven books, my readers have come to know Glory well. They've seen the same characters drift in and out of the novels and have seen children grow and the librarian retire. They've sympathized with the landlady who keeps losing her tenants to marriage and they've waited in the doctor's office with creaking oldsters and cranky youngsters.

I love small towns. Glory's a hometown like no other—and like all others. I hope you enjoy your stay!

Judith Bowen

Other Men of Glory books by Judith Bowen

HARLEQUIN SUPERROMANCE

CHAPTER ONE

"EVERYTHING?" THE BARBER paused in the act of retrieving a bowl of hot towels from the old microwave that sat on the shelf, along with the bay rum, the jar of licorice twists, the tin of humbugs and the black-plastic comb card. He caught Jack's eye in the spotty mirror. "Mustache?"

Jack raised both hands and felt his jaw and full luxuriant mustache, then relaxed and stretched his six-foot-plus frame under the cape. No regrets. He crossed his feet at the ankles on the chair's footrest. "Take it all off, Saul. I'm changing my image. Cleaning up."

Every time he came back to civilization, he treated himself to an old-fashioned shave and a haircut at Saul's Barber Emporium next to Calgary's St. Regis Hotel, a service only practitioners like Saul Crabbe still delivered. Steaming hot towels applied just so, a perfect shave with a straight razor honed on an old-fashioned leather strop, a scissor cut, plenty of bay rum splashed around afterward whether you wanted it or not.

Jack had had the mustache for years. His pride and joy. He'd always secretly believed it suited him— gave him a devil-may-care look. But he'd ruthlessly scrutinized his appearance and general air this time when he came out of the bush and had decided: The mustache had to go.

He smiled as Saul applied the towels, one by one. Wasn't this the life? Back in the city, rested up, pockets full of money, a little pampering at the hands of a master like Saul and then…maybe he'd head out to Glory once he'd seen his uncle again. He had plenty to attend to out there. Or he'd spend another night in town and drive out tomorrow. He wanted to buy some new clothes. And it was Halloween. There'd be a party somewhere. Then he reminded himself that he was finished with that kind of thing. It was time to get serious. Forget the party life.

"Cleaning up? What's the occasion, Jack, my boy?" The old man stared at his customer's reflection in the mirror as he critically combed through Jack's overlong hair. Black as the bottom of a well and past his collar. "New girlfriend, eh?"

Jack laughed. "I wish," he said, and shrugged slightly under the snowy white, carefully mended and patched linen barber's cape.

"Girls. Huh." Saul cleared his throat and spat expertly into the brass spittoon he kept a few feet from the barber's chair, just out of eyesight of his customers. Those who chewed knew where it was; those who didn't weren't interested in having it on display. Jack had never seen the barber without a plug in one cheek.

"Doesn't sound like you think much of the idea, Saul," Jack continued, closing his eyes. The warm waves of steam from the towels made him sleepy.

That and his reclining position in the old leather chair.

"Young ladies today!" Saul shook his head. "Bad news," he muttered, as if he'd had some experience in that department. Saul Crabbe was sixty-six years old, and Jack happened to know he'd been married for forty-two of those years to Sadie, who made the best blueberry pie east of the Rockies, according to her devoted husband.

The barber lifted the towels to inspect Jack's beard. "Mad Jack Gamble, isn't that what they call you up north?" Saul asked. "The ladies call you that, too?"

"None that I know of. Just buddies, here and there."

"Yeah, I know 'here and there.' You and that digging around looking for gold in the rocks. It's nuts. They're rocks, Jack, just rocks. You oughtta take up a real occupation. Some kind of business—like barbering. Or keeping store. Take a steam-fitting course, maybe."

Jack had heard the argument before. For twelve years he'd been prospecting on and off in Canada's far north. He'd had his run of luck. And when he was in the money, he spread it around. His friends didn't know whether he was plain generous or plain crazy. Thus the nickname. Maybe he *was* crazy. He hadn't saved much in all that time. Now, with Ira's farm falling on his shoulders, he wished he had.

There was silence in the barbershop for a few minutes. The barely audible sound of a baseball game on the radio, permanently tuned to a sports station, buzzed soothingly in the background.

"World Series?"

"Yeah. Those damn Braves," Saul growled as he snipped at the thickest parts of Jack's beard. Jack hadn't shaved in six months. "I hope they lose. I can't stand that hatchet song. Na-na-na-na. So, tell me, what's this about girls?"

"*Girl,* Saul." Jack emphasized the singular. "I'm going to find myself a nice quiet Glory girl and settle down. Get married. Have kids. The works."

"Settle down?" The barber laughed, then coughed. "You? Ha! Don't pull my leg, please. I'm an old man. My health's not so good anymore—"

"I'm serious. My prospecting days are over, Saul. I've done that. I'm taking up farming, didn't I tell you?"

"Farming?" The barber wheezed with laughter and pulled on a chunk of Jack's beard. Jack winced. "Oops, sorry, fella—but *farming?* Now I've heard everything!"

"Steady there with the scissors, Saul. You ever hear me mention my uncle? Ira Chesley?"

The barber shook his head.

"He's not really my uncle, but he's related to me some way or other. Don't know exactly how. I used to spend the summers at his farm—" Jack frowned, thinking back to those days "—when I was a kid, I mean."

He'd spent the winters at various relatives' houses, too, ever since his mother had died, when he was eight. There'd never been a father, not that he remembered, anyway, and whenever he asked, he was told to mind his p's and q's and not ask questions. Leave well enough alone, they always said. All of them, the variety of "aunts" and "uncles" and "cousins" who'd raised him. Ira Chesley had been one among many. He remembered staying with Ira's sister, too, in Saskatchewan somewhere. The Maple Creek area. But that hadn't been nearly as much fun. His aunt Minnie had made him wash and brush his hair before meals and go to church with her every Sunday.

"Ira's had a heart attack. He's not doing so well. He wants me to take over his farm."

"I see." Saul didn't sound convinced. Jack decided to shut up and let Saul shave him.

Ira Chesley had been one of the best. Jack believed that the old bachelor had actually loved him in his gruff offhand way. Ira had been kind to him, and now, when he was laid up and the doctors had said he'd never farm again, who had he asked for?

Jack Gamble. Little Jackie, Ira used to call him. And how could he refuse? Ira needed him. Ira, who'd always been there for him.

And, of course, the doctors were right. Ira Chesley had to be pushing seventy. Even without this bad-heart business, his working days were numbered. Last time Jack had seen him out at the farm, two or three years ago, the old man had been so crippled up with rheumatism he could hardly put his work boots on. Now he was a thin feeble old man lying in a hospital bed, worried sick about his pack of mangy dogs back at the farm. Jack had visited him that morning on the extended-care ward and had assured him his dogs were all right. The ward gave him the creeps. Old men with dull eyes and nicotine-stained fingers grasping at the bedclothes. The pink and yellow cotton blankets, washed too many times. The smell of disinfectant and the squeak of rubber-soled shoes on granite floors. He wanted to get his uncle out of there, but he had nowhere to take him. Not until he got himself fixed up at the farm.

When he'd first seen his uncle after coming out of the bush, Jack knew he'd made the right decision to trade in his pickax for a pair of overalls. In fact, he was looking forward to it. Farming was a crapshoot, the way finding something worthwhile in the rocks had always been. Prospecting was a fool's game, and so was farming. Jack knew he was up to the challenge.

Only, if he was settling down for good, he needed a wife. He wanted to do things properly. He'd thought it over and decided that the women he'd been involved with over the past few years were highly unsuitable. He'd always had a soft spot for the flashy babes, the party gals, the glamour chicks— when he had the money. Not one of them was the type he'd phone up to hold his hand when he had the flu.

If he was settling down and turning into a farmer, he needed a proper farmer's wife. Someone who knew how to care for kids and collect eggs, someone who knew how to put a decent meal on the table for a harvest crew, someone who could sew and bake and read stories to their children, when they came along. Help them with their homework when they were a little older. Jack wanted children, and to get children, he needed a wife. Heck, he *wanted* a wife. It was time.

"A Glory girl, huh?" Saul said, wiping away the traces of foam on Jack's face. "You figure?"

"That's right, Saul. Just like Sadie."

Saul snorted. "Ha! Good luck, pal. They don't make 'em like my Sadie anymore."

Jack grinned, eyes still closed. He knew better. Yes, a no-nonsense small-town girl was the girl for him. A Glory girl.

CHAPTER TWO

HMM. HOW MUCH soy flour could you put in oat-meal-raisin cookies without totally destroying the taste? After all, cookies weren't really *meant* to be nutritious.

Hannah put down the pumpkin she was mutilating in the name of Halloween and pulled the last pan of cookies from the oven, then transferred them to a wire rack. She took a sample from an earlier pan and thoughtfully broke it in two to inspect the middle. It looked good. She sniffed. Smelled good.

She chewed a piece and swallowed. With the double cinnamon and extra dollop of brown sugar she'd added, if she didn't know she'd substituted soy flour for a third of the regular flour, she wouldn't be able to tell. And Seth Wilbee certainly wasn't going to notice.

She took up her paring knife again and adjusted the pumpkin's eye. *Stab!* Nutrition was important. Hannah frequently brought baked items to Seth Wilbee, the town tramp—to put it kindly—who lived on the other side of the big culvert, near the bridge over the Horsethief River. Hannah was sure he didn't eat properly, had probably never heard of Canada's Food Rules. She had no idea what he ate, really, although she'd seen him fishing in the river and knew he had a small vegetable patch behind his shack.

Hannah passed his culvert every day as she walked to work at the library and had taken to stuffing nutritious goodies in his mailbox as she passed. She didn't know what the big galvanized mailbox was all about—she was pretty sure Seth Wilbee didn't get any mail—but she put her offerings in it, anyway, raising the red flag to let Seth know he'd received something.

She was planning to take him this jack-o'-lantern as a gift when she'd finished it. She'd helped Ella Searle with her first-grade class field trip out to Sanchez's Pumpkin Farm yesterday and had come home with two for herself, one of which already sat in her living-room window grinning at passersby on the street below.

She'd met Seth Wilbee several times since she'd started giving him baked goods and he was always gracious, if usually rather vague. He'd told her early on that he didn't care for nuts, so if it was no trouble to her, he'd appreciate it if she'd leave out the nuts. And once, he'd invited her to tea in his shack, which had been quite an experience. That was when she'd seen his garden patch.

Hannah stacked the cooled cookies in a tin she'd bought earlier that week at Ripley's Department Store. It had a witch and a black cat painted on the lid, and Seth would no doubt find a use for it after Halloween. Maybe he'd put the dried-out tea bags he collected from the town's restaurants in it. Or maybe straightened nails. Seth was a recycler of the first order.

Halloween tomorrow.

Hannah was torn. On the one hand, she wanted to be home in her warm comfortable two-bedroom apartment in case little trick-or-treaters came by. But there was always a problem with Joan, her parrot, who shrieked at the tiny hobgoblins, employing the dreadful vocabulary she'd picked up from a former owner. Hannah had seen little children burst into tears in her hallway.

On the other hand, her sister had invited her to the opening of a new nightclub in Calgary. Hannah was tired of Emily's efforts to marry her off. Her sister's regular annoying invitations, which she just as regularly turned down, were Emily's thinly disguised attempts to match her up with poor some unsuspecting man that she—Emily—deemed suitable. Suitable meant little more than single and employed. She supposed Emily's intentions were good.

The younger Parrish sister by four years, Emily was convinced Hannah would never meet anyone on her own. She was just too quiet, too staid, too sensible, too…well, Emily had even gone so far as to call her boring.

Maybe it was true. Maybe she *was* boring. But Hannah enjoyed her quiet life. She had friends, mainly women. She was a member of three clubs in town—Friends of the Library, the Glory Garden Club and a quilting group that met once a month. She read a lot. She enjoyed going out to the occasional movie or renting a video and watching it with her cat, Mr.

Spitz, and Joan. Sometimes she dated Bruce Twist, the insurance salesman from the farm-insurance agency on Main Street, but not often. Or Danny Philpot, a clerk at the county courthouse. She didn't want to mislead them, but she had no real romantic interest in either man. Oh, they were nice enough. She'd tried her best, but it just hadn't worked. So she usually turned them down. How could she explain that she was only interested in simple companionship? They'd be sure to think she was, well, odd.

Generally, very few trick-or-treaters made it up to her second-floor apartment. Still, she didn't know if she wanted to drive all the way to Calgary for a Halloween party at some new club next to the St. Regis. The club name alone—the Howlin' Tiger— was enough to make her shudder. Rap, probably. And techno-stuff.

The last time she'd gone out for Halloween, back in Tamarack, the small town where the Parrish girls had grown up, she'd been Cinderella. Her mother had said she was too old at twelve, nearly thirteen, but Hannah didn't want to miss out on all the candy. She'd never been so scared in her whole twelve years—or since—when she'd spotted that pig's head at the old witch Mrs. Birch's house.

She'd gone out with her best friend, Lorna Gagliardi and Emily. Her mother had insisted she and Lorna take Emily, who happened to be on the outs with her current friends and wanted to go trick-or-treating. Lorna had dared Hannah to go up to the witch's house. Everyone called it that. No one ever went there, especially on Halloween. It was too scary.

The house was ramshackle and unpainted and had been built at the back of the lot, well away from the street and the comfort of streetlights. Emily, she recalled, had jeered at Hannah's initial hesitation. Sometimes Emily could make her so mad. And so she'd told Lorna that she'd go if Lorna would.

Emily had screamed dramatically at their bravado and jumped up and down and said she was staying on the sidewalk and they weren't to be too long. Who was the scaredy-cat now? Hannah had declared with some satisfaction.

Clutching each other's hands, she and Lorna had made their way gingerly up the overgrown path to the porch, where a single low-wattage bulb burned over the door.

Her heart dropped when she pushed back the creaky screen door, the bottom half scuffed and worn. The porch was so full of stuff—junk—that it was no surprise they hadn't seen the head right away. Lorna knocked and Hannah stood right beside her, heart pounding, ears strained for sounds from within the dark cottage. They'd heard the shuffle of slow feet. Lorna had just turned to her and whispered, "Let's go," when her eyes widened at something behind Hannah. Hannah turned.

At first she couldn't grasp what she was seeing. Then she saw the sunken eye with pale bristly lashes, the gaping nostrils, the slack lower jaw with visible molars, oddly human. It was covered with a single layer of mosquito net or cheesecloth, maybe to keep the bugs off, although there were no bugs this late in the year. The cloth hid nothing.

Including the blood that pooled in the bottom of the big enamel pan.

Hannah and Lorna had grabbed at each other's shoulders and screamed, and then run out of the porch, all the way to the street where Emily waited. Branches scraped at their faces, brambles tore at their bare legs. Hannah lost her glittery Cinderella shawl.

They didn't stop at the sidewalk, and Emily ran, too, yelling at them to wait up. That had been Hannah's last—and final—experience with Halloween.

Later, many years later, Hannah realized that poor old Mrs. Birch had probably planned to boil up her hog's head next day with herbs and cornmeal for scrapple or headcheese, or some such rural delicacy. And, of course, she wasn't a witch at all. Just a lonely old woman who no doubt would've been pleased to have a visitor or two on Halloween.

Naturally, if Hannah went to the party in Calgary, there would be no need to dress up. Emily had made that clear. She'd said she and her friends weren't dressing up; they were just going out for a little dancing and fun.

Hannah sat on the Queen Anne hall chair that she'd recently recovered with a scrap of toile she'd found on sale and pulled on her boots. Then, on tiptoe, she went back to collect the cookie tin from the kitchen counter. Joan squawked her displeasure at seeing her mistress dressed to go out, and Hannah put her fingers to her lips to shush the bird.

The phone on the kitchen counter jangled and and

Hannah picked it up. Joan shrieked, "Blimey! Fiddlesticks! Take off, eh?!"

"Han? It's Em. About the party, you make up your mind yet?"

Hannah stood on one foot, annoyed at the interruption. Her boots were gritty and she'd just polished the hardwood hallway. "No."

"You mean you *might* come? Oh, that's terrific! There's a whole bunch of us going and—"

"'No' just means I haven't decided, Em. Look, I'm ready to go out. I have some errands to take care of—you're at work? Okay, I'll catch you at home tonight. 'Bye."

Hannah hung up and tiptoed back to the entry, carrying the carved pumpkin and the tin of cookies. Why was she even considering Emily's plan? They might be all grown-up, but sometimes Emily still felt like the taunting younger sister, now singing the refrain that Hannah didn't know how to have a good time, that she'd never meet a man and fall in love, that if she didn't *do* something exciting once in a while, nothing would *ever* happen.

She'd pointed out more than once that Hannah was the hideous age of twenty-eight and she'd never had a boyfriend, not a real one. Which was true. You couldn't count a few snatched kisses and a feel or two with Lennie Thompson backstage at the Christmas concert in grade eight. Or the occasional holiday romance, now that she was an adult. And worst of all, Emily would wail pitifully, Hannah would die an old maid if she wasn't careful, living alone with her cats and her birds. Like that creepy old Mrs. Birch! Was *that* what she wanted?

Of course not. But suffering through a few parties where she was sure to be bored silly certainly didn't guarantee that she would not. Hannah was happy to leave love to chance. After all, their mother had been nearly thirty-five before she'd met and married their father. Hannah wasn't worried. Things happened—good things—when you weren't looking for them.

And of course it would never occur to Emily that she might prefer her quiet weekends, Hannah reflected, carefully locking her apartment door behind her and nodding to Mrs. Putty, who lived two doors down and across the hall. "Good morning, Mrs. Putty!"

"Lovely day, isn't it, dear? I've just been to the Shop-Easy. Got a cake mix for a treat and a dozen eggs. Ooh, what a nice pumpkin you have there! I suppose you're getting all ready to go out to some fancy party tomorrow," Mrs. Putty wheezed, her eyes twinkling. "With some handsome young man. Oh, my. You youngsters have all the fun—"

"I don't know about that, Mrs. Putty," Hannah said with a smile that quickly faded as she headed down the stairs that Mrs. Putty had just lumbered up. *We youngsters have all the fun?* Still, the poor woman probably did wish she was thirty again.

Hannah delivered her cookies and put the red flag up. She set the pumpkin on top of the mailbox. Then she decided to continue walking on into town. It was her regular day off from the library—Friday—and she had three weeks' holidays starting next week.

Other years she'd gone somewhere, for at least a week of that time. Mexico once. San Francisco another time. This year she'd decided to stay home.

No reason. She just couldn't think of anywhere she'd rather be. And it was always a nuisance finding someone to take Joan and Mr. Spitz for a week or two.

She waved at several people she passed on Main Street—knowing everyone was part of what she loved about living in Glory—and popped into Foster's Drugs to pick up some dental floss. She paused at the long shelf of hair products, inspecting the pictures on the packages. Beautiful women, gorgeous hair. Her own was a plain serviceable brown, although Emily tried to convince her it was a glorious chestnut. Chestnut! Once in a while she'd flirted with the idea of trying a rinse. Even trying to straighten out its jumble of curls. She usually kept it tucked up in a neat twist. Maybe now that she had three weeks off…

Or maybe not. Hannah put the box back on the shelf and left the store.

She stopped at the delicatessen to pick up half a pound of fresh-ground coffee. Kenyan, her usual. On her way past Maude's Unique Boutique, she paused to study the window. Maude Bexley had outdone herself with bats and spiders and daring black-and-orange merry widows cinching up sexy lace stockings on the headless, armless mannequins. One had on a very short leather skirt, a nearly see-through tank top and a black boa. Grinning, winking, lighted pumpkins were positioned along the bottom of the window.

Emily had said you didn't have to dress up for this party at the Howlin' Tiger. The idea was to meet other people and have fun. Supposedly you could come in whatever you were wearing.

Hmm.

Suppose, just suppose, Hannah Parrish was the type to wear a short leather skirt and a boa?

CHAPTER THREE

JACK LISTENED to his buddy's phone ring for the tenth time and hung up. So much for that. He leaned on the small wooden shelf in front of the telephone in the hotel lobby, drumming his keys and considering who else he could call for companionship this evening when he suddenly realized he was eavesdropping on the conversation next to him.

"Sick? What do you mean—sick? You *can't* be sick. You were fine this afternoon when I talked to you, and now I've decided to come in for this…this stupid party and my car's in the garage, I can't even drive home and…and now you're telling me I'm the only one here. The what?"

Jack held his breath. The woman's voice was deliberately low, but he could hear the passion in it. The fury. The energy. He smiled, wondering idly what she looked like.

"Oh, I don't know," she began again irritably, "something to do with the starter or something, Em. Forget the car. Listen, I want to know if you're coming down here or not. You're not? And what about that guy you were meeting here? All the…the friends you said were coming?"

This was getting interesting.

There was a pause, broken by an exasperated sigh. "Oh, that's just great. He's over at your place, holding your hand and feeding you chicken soup. Wonderful. Just make sure he's gone before I get there, because I have to sleep on the couch." Pause. "He'll be...with you. Oh."

Then, in a painfully serious voice, she said, "What if *he* gets sick, Em? Whatever you've got? That wouldn't be fair. You'd better be careful. Okay, take care, Em." You could tell the woman was fond of this "Em." Her initial anger had melted away. Jack heard a thump as she hung up the phone.

"Damn! Blimey! Fiddlesticks!" *Blimey?* A few more unladylike sounds followed from the other phone carrel and then Jack realized that all kinds of small shiny things were rolling around his feet. She'd dropped her purse. He spotted coins, two lipsticks, a small bottle of aspirin, some keys, a half roll of Rum 'n' Butter Life Savers, a film canister, a package of tissues.... He backed out and bent to collect them.

"Ma'am?" He rose and held them out to her, hoping to mask the surprise that must be all over his face. She was gorgeous. About five and a half feet— or she would be without those incredible three-inch platform boots. She was wearing a minuscule black leather skirt, some kind of brief glittery top, weird earrings with feathers and gold hoops, and her hair— her hair was out of this world. Red, slinky, down past her shoulders. *Bare* shoulders.

Man, this was his lucky day.

"Oh, I'm so sorry," she said. Jack noticed that she was blushing. He didn't think women who looked like this ever blushed. She seemed totally thrown by the loss of half the contents of her bag. And, no doubt, by the conversation he'd overheard.

She'd picked up the spillage on her side and now held out her hand to take the things he'd collected. He gave them to her, wishing their fingers had touched. "Not at all. Glad to be of help." He glanced at her left hand—no ring. Not that it was of any consequence.

"Yes, well," she muttered, tossing the assortment of items back into her bag and zipping it shut with a ferocious yank. She flipped back her hair with her free hand. Her eyes were stormy, tawny, flecked with green. She was a knockout. "Well…" She hesitated and bit her lip, an anxious childish gesture that, like the blush, didn't go with the rest of her. She looked scared. "I'd better get moving. Thanks!"

Then she turned and stalked off toward the door leading to the new club, the Howlin' Tiger, that had just opened beside the hotel. She disappeared behind the glass-and-brass doors that led, twenty feet farther on, to the club. Jack knew, because he'd checked the place out earlier, just after he'd had his dinner. The setup on the bandstand and the general appearance wasn't what he'd expected. It was clearly aimed at a young crowd, and he wasn't in the mood for a lot of loud techno-rock.

He took the elevator back to his room and switched on the television. News, the World Series, a game show featuring couples who'd met in a supermarket, an English sitcom, *Buffy the Vampire Slayer,* a Disney movie… He settled down to watch something on ancient Egypt and realized twenty minutes later that his attention kept wandering away from the pharoahs.

To a certain green-eyed redhead. What was she doing in that club? Did "Em" ever show up? Was she with someone? No, she'd said she was alone. Her car was out of commission.

Jack made up his mind. He flicked off the television and took a quick shower. He found that he was actually humming as he pulled on a clean turtleneck sweater and refastened his old Rolex. He'd bought it at an auction. How many farmers wore a Rolex? A memento of one of his flusher periods. Easy come, easy go. But it was a damn fine timepiece, all the same.

He slipped on one of the new jackets he'd bought that day and slid his wallet into the inside pocket. Then he left the room. He pulled the door nearly shut, changed his mind and went back in to switch on a lamp beside the bed.

That was better—soft glow, nice and romantic. A king-size bed was a lot of room for one person. You never could tell. He might get lucky tonight.

HANNAH MADE HER WAY to a table and sat down. She was promptly joined by a young man in leathers and dreadlocks and covered with piercings. He had to be all of twenty. "Mind if I join you?" She hesitated, then shook her head.

"I'm waiting for some friends," she lied. Darn her sister, anyway! How sick could she be?

"Me, too," he said, setting down his pint of beer.

Some of the foam sloshed over the side and onto the fake marble tabletop. ''You want a drink? I could get you one.''

She felt rattled. The call to Emily and then dumping her purse like that. What a klutz. And in front of that man! Had he overheard her? A stockbroker or something. A lawyer, maybe. He looked very trim, very city, very…handsome.

''Oh, no thanks. I'm waiting until my friends come,'' she said. She didn't want a drink. She needed to figure out what she was going to do next—she needed to get out of here. She'd stay a little while, just to let Emily think she might've had a good time, then she'd take a cab to Emily's house. She didn't want to show up too soon, not when Steve or Nigel or whoever was there. Sick! Hannah didn't believe it for a moment. In fact, she wouldn't put it past Em to have planned the whole thing.

''I'm Phil. What's your name, babe?'' The man in leathers asked. He seemed friendly enough, although definitely not her type. Usually men didn't waltz up and talk to her. They sure didn't call her *babe*. Was it the crazy outfit she'd worn? The hair? It had come out a lot redder than it had looked on the package. Oh well, it was supposed to wash out in eight shampoos. She'd be back to her usual brown by the time she had to return to work.

''Name? Er, Annabel,'' she said; she had no idea why, except that she didn't want him to know her name. Besides, Hannah was kind of…old-fashioned. Annabel was so old it was new—chic, modern, trendy.

"Hey, Annabel!" he said, thankfully not extending his hand. "Cool club, eh?" He glanced around and so did Hannah. She'd like nothing better than to leave right now and drive back to Glory. This had been one of her really stupid ideas. She should have followed her instincts and turned Emily down flat and stayed home tonight for the trick-or-treaters.

Some trick she'd pulled on her sister! And Emily wasn't even here to find out that Hannah could dress up and have fun just like everyone else if she wanted to. It was just that she *didn't* really want to—she'd rather be home with Joan and Mr. Spitz.

Hannah narrowed her eyes. She was positive she'd spotted the man she'd seen in the hotel lobby, but when she stared toward the club entrance again, he wasn't there. *Wishful thinking, Hannah Parrish. Besides, no man like* that *would ever be interested in you.*

Just then a crowd of men in dreadlocks and leathers, and girls with various metal bits thrust through their lips, cheeks, eyebrows, ears, you-name-it, one wearing a lime-green fright wig, came up to the table. Hannah leaped to her feet.

"Here, you take my place," she offered, grabbing her purse, which she'd thrown over the back of the chair.

Phil protested.

"No, really! I'll find somewhere else to sit."

As she stumbled through clumps of people toward the door, the band started to play. Some horrifically loud crashing and screaming by the singers, and lights flashing everywhere. This was not her kind of place. If only she could get through the crowd that had materialized in the past fifteen minutes. The club's opening party was obviously a success.

"Looking for someone?" The voice was very close to her left ear. She raised her head. That man!

"Oh!" She didn't know what to say. She hadn't imagined him this time, he was here. "No, no—I'm just trying to get out so I can leave."

"Already?"

"I...um," Hannah paused and looked around again. People seemed to be enjoying themselves. Some were dancing. She saw the young man who'd been at her table moving toward her, yelling.

"Hey, Annabel! You left this—" He handed her the jacket she'd draped over her chair. "Whew! I see you found Annabel!" he shouted, addressing the man from the lobby. "Lucky thing, in this crowd." Then he turned and made his way back.

"Nice fellow. Friend of yours?"

"Not really. He was at my table."

"You alone?"

"Yes." It had just slipped out. She hadn't told the young man with dreadlocks that she was by herself. Why had she told this man?

"Here, let me take that." He slung her jacket over his shoulder and reached for her hand. Then he shouldered his way through the crowd, with her in his wake.

At the side of the club, near the mirrored wall, he smiled at her. "Well, you're not alone now, Annabel. I'm Jack." He held out his hand. "Jack Gamble."

He had a wonderful smile. Even white teeth. Dark eyes. A healthy tan.

"How do you do?" she murmured, taken aback. She shook his hand quickly. "I'm, er, not Annabel." She didn't think he'd heard her. Oh, well. What did it matter? It was Halloween; she could be whoever she wanted.

"Would you like a drink?" he asked, raising a hand to catch the attention of the waiter.

"No." She took a deep breath. "Thank you, anyway. I'm not going to stay."

"Why not?" He looked concerned. "You could keep me company. I'm here alone, too."

"Oh, I'm sure you'll be just fine," she returned dryly. She couldn't help smiling at him. What a line! "I...I've got to get back to my sister's place. She's sick."

"Is she the one who's, er, being fed chicken soup by a gentleman friend?" he asked, still smiling. "She sounds fairly well taken care of."

He'd heard! She felt her face go a furious red. "You heard me talking to her!"

He nodded, not abashed in the slightest.

"She was supposed to meet me here. She talked me into coming. I, uh...well, I'm sure you're not interested in the whole stupid story."

"I am, actually." He held up her jacket. "I'll check this at the lobby desk for you. Just take a sec. Then let's dance."

"S-sure," Hannah agreed, slipping her purse strap over her shoulder. The music didn't seem too bad anymore. Besides, wasn't that why she was here—

to have fun? To meet people? The best-looking guy in the place had just asked her to dance. Could you believe the luck? And no Emily to witness it!

NOW WHY HADN'T HE suggested they share a bottle of wine up in his room? Or at least invited her to accompany him to the piano bar on the tenth floor? It would be a lot quieter there. They could talk. Then, if it looked promising, they could go to his room....

But something didn't seem right to Jack. This woman wasn't as smooth or sophisticated as she appeared. Maybe she didn't get out much. She was ready to leave the club less than an hour after she'd arrived. She was alone. If he hadn't come across her, she'd probably be on the bus already, heading for her sister's place. *In long leather boots and a tank top.*

"Ready?" He reached for her hand again. She had a gorgeous smile. She'd actually looked relieved to see him when he'd met her in the club a few minutes ago, and that didn't feel too bad, either.

They danced all evening. They ducked out to the hotel bar for a quick glass of wine and a breather. That was when he found out her name was Hannah, not Annabel. She didn't explain the mix-up, nor did she seem inclined to talk much about herself. Then, instead of ending up in his room, as he'd hoped, they went back to the club and danced some more.

Just after eleven-thirty, Jack saw her checking her watch. "Turning into a pumpkin?"

She laughed, the delightful laugh that made bubbles fizz in his bloodstream. Like fireworks. Or good champagne. "It was the carriage that turned into a pumpkin, remember? Cinderella's supposed to lose her pretty ball gown and end up back in rags." She glanced down at her skimpy skirt, the slinky tank top that just brushed the swell of her breasts—Jack knew; he'd already taken a quick peek—and the long sexy boots. "This is hardly a ball gown."

"Nice substitute," he murmured, bending to brush her knuckles with his lips. "I prefer it, frankly."

They'd been like this all evening. Back and forth. Lighthearted. Having a good time. She seemed comfortable with him, as though she truly had no idea what he'd originally had in store for her. For her and him both, he decided firmly. Mutual pleasure. He was no predator. He was only willing if the lady was willing.

They'd danced a few close dances, and he liked the feel of her in his arms. Perfect. He'd been tempted to kiss her. Wanted to, badly. Something held him back. Honor? He must be getting foolish in his old age.

No, it had to do with intentions. He had no honorable intentions with regard to her—she was just a lucky pickup, or so he'd thought at the beginning of the evening. A good-time girl.

But it hadn't turned out like that, either. Beneath all that sexiness and sass and apparent sophistication was a sensitive vulnerable woman. Jack sensed that, and he realized, too, that he didn't want to be the one to hurt her. He got the feeling she could definitely be hurt.

But not by him. He no longer had time for these

kinds of games. Life had become serious for him the moment he'd heard his uncle was so sick. "Ready to go? I can drive you."

She blushed again. She did *that* delightfully. "I can get a cab."

"No way. I'll drive you. Where does your sister live?"

Hannah told him, then allowed him to help her on with her jacket at the desk. He had the hotel valet bring his car around, his old Mustang, the car he kept at a buddy's place in Calgary whenever he was out in the field. He'd already put an ad in the paper to sell it. A sporty muscle car was not suitable transport for a farmer, and it hadn't been much use for a prospector, either. He'd barely put ten thousand kilometers on it during the two years he'd owned it.

He handed her in on the passenger side and shut the door firmly. He gave the attendant a ten-dollar bill in return for his keys.

"Have a nice evening, sir," the valet said, with a grin and a wink.

Jack nodded and got into the driver's side. He checked the rearview mirror and the side mirrors and shifted into gear. The Mustang moved away from the curb like a tightly leashed panther. It was a beautiful machine. Harvesters were beautiful machines, too, he reminded himself. Harvesters, tractors, grain trucks.

"Snazzy car," she said, with a smile and one eyebrow raised. The low bucket seat brought her minuscule skirt even higher on her silk-clad thighs. Her knees were pressed together and turned demurely toward the door. With an effort, Jack wrenched his eyes back to the road.

"Yeah? What did you think I'd be driving?" he asked, rolling down his window for a breath of fresh air. "Too windy?"

"No," she said, tossing back her hair. "I thought you'd be driving more of a stockbroker's type of vehicle. You know, a BMW or a Mercedes or something."

"Me?" Jack laughed. "No way!"

"Is that what you are—a stockbroker? Lawyer?" she asked, adding quickly, "I'm just guessing."

"No." He considered. Did he really want to tell her he was a small-time farmer? Or about to become one? They hadn't had much chance to talk in the club or in the bar, which had been almost as noisy. "I'm a geologist by trade. Prospector."

"Really! Ever find anything exciting?"

"You mean like diamonds or gold? No." He shot her a look in the dark of the car, lit only by the instrument panel and the streetlights as they drove slowly up Edmonton Trail. He was in no hurry to get to the sister's, where she said she was staying. He had the impression she was just visiting Calgary, that she was from somewhere else. Edmonton?

"You ever find *anything?*"

"Oh, sure. Boring useful stuff like zinc and copper. Molybdenum."

"Hmm." She sounded dreamy, not really paying attention to him.

"Turn here?" He indicated the quiet residential

street that ran parallel to the Bow River valley at the top of the hill. She nodded.

"It's the house up there, the one with the van parked in the driveway."

Jack noticed the van had "Emily's Kitchen" painted on the side. Her sister. There was another vehicle beside it, a new Bronco.

He parked and got out of the Mustang, then walked around to her side, feeling real regret that the evening was over. He opened the door for her. "I'll walk you to the house."

"All right." She seemed at loose ends all of a sudden, the intimacy of the warm interior of the car shattered in the crisp night air. She shivered and drew her jacket closer, and Jack put his arm around her shoulders. She leaned into him for a few seconds, head bent. He squeezed her shoulders, then released her and reached for her hand. His heart was beating like crazy.

They walked quietly up the frosty sidewalk.

"Are you going to ring?" Jack asked, ready to push the doorbell with his thumb.

"No," she said, putting her hand on his arm. "I've got a key. Well—" she looked up at him "— thank you for everything, Jack. I had a wonderful—"

What the hell. He reached for her and lowered his mouth over hers, then wrapped his arms around her, pressing her tightly against him. Her mouth was soft and sweet. She'd long ago lost her vampy lipstick, and he liked that. He deepened the kiss, suddenly desperate to have her, all of her. It wasn't going to happen, not in a million years. She was clearly a city gal, and he was looking for a different kind of woman to share his life. Not that one chance encounter at a noisy club meant he was even thinking along those lines, at least as far as she was concerned.

But, man, she was luscious. And beautiful. And sexy. And...inexperienced. He could tell by the way she kissed. Awkward, yet intense. The very sense he had of her vulnerability had him pulling away from her.

"Hannah?" He tilted her chin up. "I had a great time tonight. You're one terrific lady. I won't forget you."

He took the key from her, inserted it in the lock and held the door open as she stumbled inside. She looked as shaken as he felt. "Good night, Cinderella."

She lifted her hand in a feeble wave, and he closed the door and tore off down the sidewalk, cursing how quickly good luck could turn to bad.

Still, in his business, wasn't he used to that?

CHAPTER FOUR

HANNAH MADE HER WAY quietly into Emily's small living room. Sheets and blankets were piled on the arm of the sofa bed. A light on the end table was the only illumination in the otherwise dark room. Hannah hoped she hadn't disturbed Emily and her... visitor, coming in late like this.

She bent down to unzip her boots and kicked them off. Then she sank onto the soft chenille upholstery of the sofa and stretched and sighed.

Jack had kissed her. He'd actually kissed her! He'd seemed to *mean* it. To really, truly *want* to kiss her. Hannah put her hands to her cheeks, still flushed and hot. What a night!

And then a thought struck—it wasn't *her* he'd kissed. He'd kissed the person she'd pretended to be, all dressed up in sexy clothes and hair dyed red. The makeup, the earrings, the—

"Steve!" came a frightened yelp from the hallway that led to Emily's bedroom, as well as the extra bedroom she used as a home office for her catering business, and the bathroom.

"Em?"

Hannah was bewildered. Her sister had appeared briefly at the end of the hall, in slippers and bathrobe, then turned and streaked back down the hallway. She could hear a furious low-pitched discussion, a man's deep voice and then Emily appeared at the corner of the hallway again, just peeking into the living room.

"Emily, for heaven's sake, what's wrong?" Hannah smiled. Her sister was incorrigibly dramatic.

"Hannah! Omigod, I didn't recognize you! I thought it was someone else in my house. A burglar or something. Steve!" she yelled over her shoulder. "You can come out now—it's my sister!" She came over to Hannah, shaking her head. "That guy! I swear he grabbed his cell phone and dived under the bed…"

She came closer and did an exaggerated double take. "Look at *you!*" She grabbed Hannah's shoulders. "What happened? What did you do to your hair? It looks fabulous. You look terrific. Are those your boots? Omigod—*Prada?*"

Hannah shot her a wry glance. "A knockoff."

"Wow, you could be straight out of *Vogue*. What's got *into* you?" Her sister stood up and switched on another table lamp.

"You," Hannah said wryly. She tossed her new jacket onto the arm of the sofa, revealing the glittery tank top in all its sexy splendor. It had cost a ridiculous amount of money. So had the boots, a knockoff or not. She was freezing. "Oh, Em. You're always telling me I'm so dull. I just wanted to prove to you for once that I was capable of dressing up—and then you don't show."

Emily looked guilty, but not as guilty *or* as sick as Hannah had expected.

"You didn't plan it this way, did you?" she asked suspiciously. "Throw the boring big sister out of the nest to see if she can wobble along on her own?"

"No, definitely not!" Emily sniffed and sat down again. She did sound a little congested. "Was the club nice? I hear that band's really hot. You have a good time?"

Hannah threw her a superior look. She was enjoying this. "Oh, excellent."

"Uh, meet any guys?" Now her sister was getting to the main point—at least the point that interested her the most.

"A few." She paused for effect. "One very nice man, in particular. He drove me home."

"He did?" Eyes alight, Emily moved closer to her on the sofa. She plucked at the soft leather of Hannah's skirt. This foray into chic had cost Hannah a month's wages. "Very cool. You get that in Glory?"

Hannah nodded. "Maude's." She reached for the overnight bag she'd left at Emily's earlier, when she'd come into town. Emily had been at work. She pulled out a nightgown, her usual rose-sprigged cotton flannel, and made a silent gesture toward the hall and mouthed, "Steve?"

"Never mind him. Here, I'll make up your bed while you go change."

"I'll do it, Em," Hannah said firmly, her hand on her sister's arm. "You're sick—remember?"

She shooed her sister away and padded down the hall to the small, old-fashioned bathroom with her nightie and her toiletries bag. Back to being plain old Hannah Parrish. The car would be ready at noon. The adventure was over. It'd been a lot of fun, she had to admit. But she wasn't going to make a habit of this kind of thing.

She folded her new clothes carefully and stacked them in a little pile on Emily's laundry hamper to repack. Back to sweaters and skirts. And comfortable shoes. And cotton underwear. She carefully peeled off the false eyelashes. *Ouch!* Back to no makeup—moisturizer and maybe lip gloss. The fake fingernails could stay for now. She'd paid forty bucks; she might as well enjoy them. She'd work on removing them when she got home. But what if she had to live with acrylic talons? Maybe they wouldn't come off.

I'll never forget you. Had he really meant it? she wondered sadly, wiping off her eyeshadow. She'd never forget him, either, but that was irrelevant. The ball was over. The prince was still a prince—somewhere—but Cinderella would be back to her old life in the morning.

HANNAH WENT to church with Mrs. Putty on Sunday, something she often did. The old lady was always so grateful to have company on the short walk to the church. Hannah didn't care much about the sermon, but she liked the singing.

The next day she did laundry and thoroughly cleaned her apartment, which barely needed cleaning. One person, especially a careful orderly person like Hannah, didn't make much mess. She turned up the heat and gave Joan a bath. The parrot adored water and created such havoc in Hannah's bathroom that she kept the bird's bathing down to once a week, mostly in the summer because she worried about Joan's catching cold. It wasn't summer now, so this was a special treat. "Atta girl! Blimey! Atta girl! Take off, eh?" Joan squawked over and over, letting Hannah know the bath was appreciated.

After her bath, Joan would spend the rest of the day quietly grooming herself, so it was worth the chaos in order to get the peace and quiet of a contented parrot.

Mr. Spitz, who was black with a white spot on his head, was no trouble. He was getting on—Hannah had no idea how old he was, since she'd gotten him from the High River pound—and spent most of the day sleeping on top of the refrigerator or in Hannah's bay-window seat.

She washed her hair before she went to bed, the fifth shampoo since she'd tinted it. She was getting a little worried. Her hair didn't show the slightest sign of fading back to its regular brown, and the tint was supposed to come out in eight washings. Good thing she still had her whole vacation ahead of her.

That was Monday.

Tuesday, she went shopping and restocked all her cupboards and made Seth Wilbee a pound cake. She put soy flour in it, too, and wondered if he'd notice. She could hardly cover up the flavor with spices, not in a pound cake. At the last minute she threw in a few handfuls of raisins. Now it was a raisin cake. Extra nutrition, she told herself.

That evening she started a new needlepoint project—a bellpull she wanted to give to the senior librarian, who was retiring this year, as a Christmas gift—and watched something on public television. Beginning a new needlework project, usually a source of great satisfaction to Hannah, just didn't hold her interest, and after half an hour, she put it away. Even the television bored her, and by half-past nine, she was in bed reading, hair damp from the sixth washing. But she couldn't keep her mind on the story. All she saw on the page was a redheaded woman dancing with a mysterious stranger.

Wednesday, Hannah wrapped up the cake and took it over to Seth. This time, she decided to walk under the bridge and along the overgrown path that led to his house and deliver it in person. She realized she hadn't spoken to a soul except Joan—did talking to a parrot count?—since she'd gone to church on Sunday with Mrs. Putty. Seth Wilbee was working in his garden, an interesting hodgepodge of unrecognizable vegetables and weeds.

"Hello there, miss," he said, leaning on his spade. "Mighty fine cookies those were last week. Mi-ighty fine. I'm very partial to raisins."

"I brought you a cake today," Hannah said, handing him the foil-wrapped loaf. Lucky about the raisins, she thought. "What are you digging up? I thought your garden would be done by now."

"Oh, a little bit of this, a little bit of that," the tramp said. "Two or three parsnips for my supper and a bit of celery. Parsnips don't mind the weather, you know."

"Celery!"

"Yep. See these leaves?" He bent and lovingly ran his hand along a line of green fronds sticking out of the ground. They looked amazingly healthy for early November.

"Don't they freeze, Seth?"

"Oh, yes. I generally kick a little straw over 'em this time of year. But a spot of frost improves a parsnip. Sweetens 'em right up. I don't suppose you knew that." His pale blue eyes twinkled as she shook her head. She wasn't fond of parsnips, frost or no frost. He seemed delighted to be telling her something she didn't know.

"Come in for tea, miss. I've got something to show ya." Seth planted his spade deeply and left it standing there. "Come in! Come in!" He waved her toward his shack.

Hannah hesitated, remembering the last time she'd had tea, then thought, *Oh, what the heck—we're both lonely.* And she followed him in.

The shack was no more than six or seven feet wide—a corridor, really—and maybe twelve feet long. A cot at the far end, with a frayed curtain in front of it, which he hastily pulled shut as she entered, was obviously Seth's bedroom. The front of the shack, near the door, had a wooden table and one chair, no doubt Seth's own handiwork, and a pot-bellied stove, which threw out considerable heat. There was no electricity. No lights, beyond candles and an oil lamp. No books, no magazines. No personal items, no photographs. The few pictures on the wall—literally pasted to the boards—had been cut from calendars and magazines.

"Here, sit, miss!" Seth pushed the chair toward her and rolled an empty wooden barrel on its edge to the other side of the table for himself. When Hannah had been there before, the barrel had contained an injured skunk, which Seth had been nursing back to health. There was no sign of the skunk now.

Hannah sat down and watched her host as he busied himself making tea. He wasn't an old man, probably no more than fifty. But he was worn-looking, thin and threadbare. She knew he reused tea bags that he collected in the town restaurants and cafés, but she also knew that he kept a small canister of unused tea bags for guests. Seth poured boiling water into the two mugs he'd set out on the table. She was relieved to see he was taking the cracked one for himself.

Slowly he dipped a new tea bag into first one cup—hers—then the other. When the water in both mugs looked fairly brown, he removed the bag, let it drip for a few seconds, then carefully pegged it to a small line strung across a corner of the shack. He was saving it for another day.

"Milk or sugar, miss?"

Hannah shook her head. "No, this is just fine. And please don't cut the cake," she protested. "I can't stay long. I just had lunch anyway. I'm not a bit hungry."

"Well, if you say so," Seth said. "If you say so." He sat down and stared at her while she drank her tea. Pretty insipid stuff. One could only guess at how old the tea bags were. Or where he'd found them.

"You said you had something to show me," she reminded him.

Seth bolted up and went to his cot, where he rummaged under the mattress and produced an envelope. "A letter!" he said, brandishing it.

"I see." Hannah took the envelope. It was a little tatty-looking and had obviously been much handled, but Seth hadn't opened it. The letter was from the Town of Glory, addressed to Mr. Seth Wilbee.

"Aren't you going to open it? Maybe it's important," Hannah said, laughing. The intense look on Seth's face stopped her.

"You go ahead, miss. You open it," he said with a shrug that didn't quite manage nonchalance. He leaned forward and took a great slurp of his tea. His eyes never left her face.

Hannah opened the envelope carefully. There was one sheet inside. "Here—" She started to hand it over to him, but he gripped her wrist and pushed her hand with the letter in it back to her side of the table.

"No! No, you go ahead. You tell me what it says." His eyes still focused intently on hers. It was as though he was trying to tell her something without putting it into words. She suddenly realized: Seth Wilbee couldn't read.

"Okay," she said, hoping her voice didn't betray her surprise. The poor man! She quickly scanned the letter, her heart sinking, then read its contents aloud to him. The town was informing him that his shack would have to be removed from municipal property immediately, that the town was planning to landscape the riverbank to integrate it into a walking and bicycle path connecting the town square to the municipal park farther upstream. He had until the middle of December to relocate.

Hannah watched his pale eyes fill with tears and his big gnarled hands begin to tremble as he attempted to hold his tea mug steady. "Oh, my," he said finally. Sadly. "Oh, my."

There were worse things, Hannah decided, than having a stubborn red tint that would not wash out of your hair and a parrot with a bad mouth.

That was Wednesday.

On Thursday, just as Hannah finished drafting a letter on Seth's behalf, asking the town to give the harmless homeless man more time to relocate, the telephone rang, and Joan squawked in protest, as she usually did. Hannah got up from her dining table to answer it.

"Hannah Parrish?"

Hannah's heart leaped. She knew immediately who it was. But she hadn't told him her last name....

"Y-yes. Speaking."

"It's Jack. From last Friday? Jack Gamble."

CHAPTER FIVE

"JACK!" HANNAH CLUTCHED the phone in one hand, trying to shush Joan with wild gestures. The parrot ignored her.

"Happy to hear from me?" He sounded pleased. "What's that in the background—a radio?"

"No." She looked behind her. "It's a...a parrot. How did you get my number? Oh—of course, I'm pleased to hear from you."

"You are?" There was a brief silence. Joan, mercifully, had shut up. "I went to see your sister this morning, early. Before she went to work. She told me you were staying in Glory, that you were house-sitting for a friend."

House-sitting?

"She said you'd be there for a while, she didn't know how long. I thought, hey, that's good news. Because guess where I am?"

"I...I have no idea, Jack," she said weakly. *House-sitting?* She'd kill Emily!

"Glory. Yeah, no kidding!" he said, although she hadn't spoken. "I guess we never got a chance to learn much about each other on Friday. I didn't mention it, but I've given up prospecting and I'm taking over my uncle's farm. You know, once from a small town, always from small town?'' He laughed.

"Sure. I guess so," Hannah murmured unconvincingly. She must be coming across like an idiot. He had to be wondering why he'd bothered calling.

"My uncle's place. Ira Chesley, east of town, toward Vulcan. Maybe you've heard of him?''

She had. Ira Chesley lived near the Longquists on the Gallant farm. Phoebe Longquist had been one of the library's high-school volunteers. But there was no way she was getting into *that*—why a house sitter would know of a scruffy old bachelor farmer like Ira Chesley. *House sitter?* "It's great to hear from you, Jack," she went on, gathering all her resources. "Really great. I'm so glad you called." It was true; she was delighted to hear from him. But...then what?

"I thought maybe we could see each other again," he said, rushing a little. Was he nervous? Impossible! "I'd like to take you out, maybe tomorrow if you don't have any other plans. Dinner? A buddy told me about a nice place in High River we could try. Japanese. What do you think?''

Hannah realized she was being awfully quiet. She had to say something—anything. Another chance with Jack? This was just *too* lucky. "I'd love that. Shall I meet you somewhere? My car's fixed."

"No, I'll pick you up at your place. Emily gave me the address. She's a nice girl, Hannah. Very helpful.''

After Jack had hung up, promising to collect her at six the next evening, Hannah dialed her sister's cell phone. Very helpful, was she? Very helpful, indeed!

"BUT, HANNY, HE WAS so drop-dead gorgeous, I couldn't believe that—"

"That he'd be interested in me," Hannah interjected grimly.

"No, no! I just was worried that—you know, that he'd wonder what a cool girl like you was doing in a boring apartment like that out there in Hicksville and, well, maybe put two and two together—"

"I *want* him to put two and two together! Now you've got me in deeper, Em. I could have come clean about last Friday. Laughed it off as a Halloween thing. Now it just seems like we're a couple of liars." Hannah practically wept. She knew Emily was just trying to help her, but some help! And it wasn't as though *Emily's* life was on the line here.

"Oh, I'm so sorry, Hannah. I really wanted to help, that's all. Honest." Emily sniffed. She sounded suitably chastened. Hannah forgave her, as she always did.

"Now maybe you can tell me how I'm going to get out of this one, since you're so darn smart," Hannah returned grumpily, feeling a little better. At least Emily was contrite.

But was she really?

"Oh, I've had some super ideas, Hanny," she rushed on. "I'll gather up a bunch of stuff from some of my friends, some really funky clothes, and I'll drive out and you can try them all on. Something's bound to work. You want to convey, let's see, cool, class, funky—''

"Emily," Hannah interrupted. "I don't think you get it. This isn't a part in some play, you know. All I want to convey is me. *Me!* Hannah Parrish. No matter how boring and ordinary. If I'm too ordinary for him, then he's not my kind of guy. Maybe it's just not meant to be."

"Don't say that, Hannah! You've got this great chance with a super guy. Who would've guessed he'd actually come over to my place? He's persistent, too! You must've really made an impression. I nearly died when I opened the door this morning..." Off she went on her own train of thought, and Hannah tuned out. All she could think about was what a mess she was in—again. Only this time it wasn't *entirely* her own fault.

There was just one thing to do. Hannah felt her heart squeeze in regret. That was to wear the borrowed clothes Emily came up with—she certainly wasn't buying any more with her own money—pull off this dinner with the drop-dead gorgeous Jack Gamble and then stop answering her phone.

After that, maybe she could look for another job in a different town.

THE HOUSE-SITTING GIG was in a nice area of town, Jack thought. It wasn't where the fancy folk lived, up on Buffalo Hill, and it wasn't the seedy side of town, down on Painter's Flats. It was close to the town center, within walking distance of the town amenities—the library, the clinic, the town hall, Main

Street. A fairly nondescript, stucco, two-story walk-up apartment building, postwar construction. He was pretty sure it was the only actual apartment building in Glory.

The unit she was staying in was at the back, over-looking the parking lot and playing fields beyond. There was a girls' soccer game in progress. Jack took a big breath and knocked. He felt foolish now, stopping to pick up some flowers on the way. The stems felt crumpled in his hand.

But he'd thought this over carefully. He'd decided he was being hasty last week in Saul's barbershop. He had to face the facts—he liked party gals. Glamour babes. This idea of settling down with a quiet little Glory girl might not be such a good idea, after all. Meeting Hannah Parrish last week had helped him change his mind. She didn't strike him as the usual glamour girl, anyway. There was more to her. A lot more.

And then to find out she was here in town! Right under his nose! Jack knocked again. This time there was a hell of a racket inside, some kind of squawk-ing. Well, she'd said there was a parrot on the prem-ises, or at least he *thought* that was what she'd said yesterday.

"Oh! You're early." Hannah looked gorgeous. Tight black velvet pants, some kind of long flashy-looking tunic, dangly silver earrings, those wild boots she'd had on last week...

He glanced at his watch. "Only five minutes early. Here—these are for you." He thrust the bouquet at her. She seemed taken aback.

"For me?" She flashed him a beautiful smile and reached for the flowers. Then she moved inside. "Won't you come in for a minute? I'll just put these in some water—"

"Jacko! Take off, eh? Atta girl! Take off, eh?"

She took his arm as he came into the small vestibule of the apartment. "Oh, don't mind her. It's just Joan, my—er, my friend's parrot. She can be really cranky sometimes."

"I see that. Or, rather, hear that." Jack took full measure of the apartment as he stepped inside. Hannah disappeared into the kitchen. He made a face at the bird.

The parrot squawked and began to twirl madly on its wooden perch, croaking out the same line over and over again. "Take off, eh? Take off! Jacko!" A black cat sat on top of a china hutch in the dining room and stared down at him.

"How did that bird know my name?"

"Oh, she calls every man Jacko. A previous owner taught her to talk." Hannah called from the kitchen. Jack moved a little farther into the living room.

Other than the weird pets, the place was very nice. Cozy. Inviting. Nicely furnished. A calm peaceful place, sort of the way he'd like the farmhouse to be done up once the cleaners were through with it. Ira Chesley had lived in bachelor squalor, which Jack abhorred. He'd hired a crew of cleaners to come in from Vulcan, and they were finishing up on the weekend.

"Thanks so much for the flowers!" She glanced at him as he came back to stand at the entrance to the kitchen. "It's very thoughtful of you." She seemed genuinely pleased, and he was glad now that he'd brought them. He watched as she stood on tiptoe and reached into a high cupboard for a glass vase, noting with appreciation the sleek line of the velvet over her bottom, her long legs—

"Nice place here," he said, turning around. No need for her to catch him leering. "How long's your friend away?"

"Friend? Oh…oh, a while. I'm not sure. She's on a…a tour of some kind. In Europe."

"I suppose it isn't that easy to get away when you've got a cranky parrot."

Hannah laughed. It occurred to him again that she had a delightful laugh, very musical and low. Sexy.

"No, you're right there." She clipped each stem of the mixed bouquet—lilies, carnations, mums, whatever—and inserted it into the vase, rearranging a couple of blooms before she was satisfied.

"Don't you work?"

She looked startled, even alarmed. The scissors clattered to the counter. He frowned. "Oh, yes, I do. But I'm on holiday right now."

"I see." He thrust his hands into the pockets of his new trousers. He'd spent a bundle on clothes last weekend, both for social occasions and for work. His bush garb of jeans and the all-weather jackets he wore for prospecting wouldn't do now that he was back in civilization.

"There!" She smiled up at him. "Lovely. You can set this on the dining-room table and I'll just grab my coat."

He carried the flowers into the living-dining area. Very pleasant, he thought again. Coral walls, comfortable-looking furniture, polished end tables. Everything neat and tidy. There was an oval needlework frame standing by a chair, with a partly completed piece of work on it. Looked like the friend was a real homebody. Jack had a flash of regret. She seemed the kind of woman he'd thought might one day be for him.

Until he'd met Hannah.

He placed the vase in the center of the dining table, a square antique-looking piece of furniture with four chairs pulled up, all with seats in a striped plum fabric. Classy. He noticed a manila folder on the table, neatly marked, "Town of Glory—Seth Wilbee."

"Well?" She appeared with a wrap over her arm, some slinky sexy thing. Purple and blue, all kinds of colors. It looked terrific with that long reddish hair. He'd remembered it as being more vivid last week. It seemed more auburn now. And curlier. "Ready whenever you are."

She acted a bit nervous and Jack wondered why as he followed her out of the apartment. She locked the door carefully and didn't say anything when he took her arm. "You like Japanese food?" he asked, realizing he hadn't really checked her preference.

"Oh, yes. Anything," she answered, with a breathless laugh. Maybe she was just glad to be going out. Glory hadn't impressed him as a very exciting town. He didn't think much had changed since the years he'd spent summers here with his uncle Ira. When he was a kid, he hadn't noticed. Now he still didn't care, because he wasn't looking for excitement. Not since he'd made the decision to settle down, to get married, to start farming, to live a whole different life.

"What happened to your car?" She sounded surprised. His shiny nearly new Dodge pickup was parked at the curb.

"I sold it. Picked this up in Calgary the other day. Not new, but a little more useful now that I'm a farmer. I hope you don't mind riding in a truck?" Probably most of her dates drove some kind of flashy up-to-date vehicle. He felt a twinge of nostalgia for the Mustang he'd sold.

"Heavens no! You should see my old clunker." She laughed and got into the passenger side and Jack closed the door.

Heavens no. He hadn't heard that expression in a long long time. Now, if only the restaurant was decent. Jack wasn't particularly keen on foreign food, but he figured it was just the kind of trendy thing a woman like Hannah would enjoy.

He glanced at her. She'd buckled her seat belt and was looking out the window with interest. A lot of houses still had Halloween decorations up.

Jack took a deep breath. Maybe he was crazy. Maybe he should've left well enough alone. Maybe he shouldn't have gone back to her sister's like that, to track her down. But...he knew he wasn't crazy. If he hadn't made the effort, he'd always wonder. It was better this way, to find out if his instincts about Hannah Parrish were right.

If they were...well, he'd have to decide what to do next.

CHAPTER SIX

"WHY FARMING? I like taking chances." He flashed her a winning smile that had her smiling back. "Planting a crop in the spring and hoping to make money off it in the fall is risky," he went on.

"What about your uncle?" Hannah said, leaning forward. "Will he be coming back?" They'd had to wait a little before they could be seated in the small restaurant and were enjoying a drink before dinner. Enjoying? Well, Jack was having a beer, a Japanese brand. He was probably enjoying it. In a panic, Hannah had ordered something called a "sidecar" off the cocktail menu, and it was disgusting. She rarely touched anything but sherry or a glass of wine with dinner.

"He's at the Crowfoot, extended care. Healed up fairly well, but he's weak. An old man." Jack shook his head and frowned. She felt her heart go out to him. He obviously had a great deal of affection for Ira Chesley. "He'll need more care than I can provide if I bring him home to Glory. His house is a mess. What my aunt Minnie would have called a typical bachelor's place." Jack laughed and took a sip of his beer, the devil-may-care look back on his face. "I've hired cleaners, but I need someone to fix it up. I'm no decorator. You know anyone in that line of work?''

Hannah would've loved to take on a job like that. She adored decorating. But how could she offer when he thought she was only a house sitter, someone who'd been accidentally plunked in Glory for a few weeks? She admired the way he felt about his uncle, a rather dour, grumpy old man—at least, that was how he seemed to her. Most guys wouldn't dream of assuming that kind of responsibility for an elderly uncle.

''You want to come out and take a look at the joint? Maybe give me some ideas?''

''Your farmhouse? Sure! I'd love to.'' Hannah made an effort to hold back her enthusiasm. She reminded herself that this evening was the only time she'd be spending with Jack. She couldn't keep this up. Nails, hair, clothes—all lies. Plus, she'd decided that the red rinse was finally showing signs of fading. Soon she'd be back to her usual brown. Eight shampoos! What a laugh. More like eighteen.

''Another one?'' He held up his drink. The waitress was headed their way.

''No.'' She shook her head.

''Didn't like it, huh?'' he said with a curious glance at her nearly full glass.

''No. Sorry—I'm not much of a drinker.'' She shook her head again. Maybe that wasn't what Emily or one of her friends would have admitted. But she wasn't her sophisticated younger sister. Not by a long shot. And there was a limit to how much she could pretend.

She watched as Jack talked to the waitress. He was easygoing, familiar, friendly. Emily was right. Jack was a handsome guy. He had on a dark-blue crewneck—could it be cashmere?—a snazzy sports jacket and charcoal trousers. Everything looked new. Earlier, Hannah had noticed he was wearing an old Rolex. The really classy kind. Stainless steel. Not that modern Rolexes weren't classy, but, well, there was something about that forties and fifties style that never got old.

Sometimes she felt she should have been born then. She definitely did not suit a new millennium with her interests: cooking, needlework, watercolor painting, animals, gardening, old three-hanky black-and-white movies, books. She liked ballroom dancing, too, but she'd never met a man, apart from her father, who was any good at it.

"Hannah?"

She was startled at the sudden warm feel of his hand on hers. "Y-yes?"

"We can go in now." He held her gaze for a few seconds and Hannah felt her blood *swoosh*. She caught her breath. His smile painted a picture for her, and it was an X-rated picture. She was in way over her head. Really, how desperate *was* she to allow herself be swept along in something like this? Well, she'd had the option of coming clean. On the phone. And she hadn't, had she?

He took her hand as they followed the hostess into the small dining room. Hannah felt very conspicuous. The place was sparely but beautifully furnished with smooth wood furniture of birch or beech and lots of subdued lighting. The sound of water trickling came from a small pond installed near the door. She could see the flash of goldfish and wondered if the copper pennies she saw glittering on the bottom harmed the fish.

Even though they'd had to wait, the place wasn't that busy, less than a third occupied. Maybe they were short-staffed, Hannah thought as she accepted the large menu handed her by a smiling Japanese woman. There was some tinkly kind of music playing quietly in the background, faintly annoying.

"I've never been here before," Jack confided, leaning forward. "I've heard it's decent grub."

He didn't look that hopeful. Hannah smiled. She'd never had Japanese food before, either.

The menu was a mystery. She'd heard of sushi, but wasn't entirely sure what it was. Neither of them knew what *sunomono* was, and the cryptic English translation beneath the Japanese wasn't really helpful. *Gyoza?*

Jack solved their quandary by suggesting that the server decide for them, bringing dinner for two— including something called tempura.

"If we hate it," he said, reaching forward to take her hands in his again, "we'll just go out to McDonald's."

Hannah gave a noncommittal nod. She wasn't comfortable with him holding her hands, although she didn't pull away. He seemed very physical. In a way, she liked that. She'd gone out with Bruce Twist three times, and he'd never even tried to kiss her. Maybe after the episode on her sister's doorstep last

Friday, Jack had decided they were past the "first date" stage. Which meant—what?

"So, tell me about yourself," he said, sending Hannah's pulse into a skitter. "What kind of work do you do? Where'd you grow up? Is Emily your only sister?"

No point panicking. She was twenty-eight; she could handle this. Hannah decided to be truthful but offer no details. "Emily's my only sibling. We grew up right here in Alberta in a small town called Tamarack. I have a degree in library science."

"A librarian!" He seemed surprised. "Really? A *librarian?*"

"Yes." This conversation could be dangerous. "Tell me about your farming plans," she added quickly. "And yourself. What are you going to, you know, plant? Grow? Whatever you call it." Might as well keep the conversation on him. Less risky.

"Ira's raised crops all these years, hay and grain, but I want to try something different. At least with part of the farm. Maybe you could help me..." He squeezed her hand slightly, and then, to her dismay, she felt him slide his thumb gently along her palm. *Omigod.* The sensation zinged down to the soles of her feet and back again.

"Oh?" She gently withdrew her hand, pretending she needed to scratch her other wrist. "In what way?"

"Research. I want to raise game for the restaurant trade. Deer or elk. It's a booming market. I've already talked to suppliers about acquiring some breeding stock. In fact, on Monday I'm meeting with someone in Calgary and—''

''Deer?'' An image of Bambi calling for his mother swam into her mind. ''Oh, Jack, surely not!''

''Or elk. Even wild boars—they're catching on.'' He shrugged. ''It's a big investment, though. You've got to have good high fences for deer and elk. And disease is always a concern, with a local wild population. What do you think?''

His eyes were intent on her, as though her opinion really mattered. Thank goodness she was on holiday for the next two weeks! That was all she needed— Jack Gamble strolling into the town library and asking for reference materials.

''I don't think you should be raising deer,'' she said firmly. ''It's just not...not right.'' She still saw Bambi crying his big brown eyes out in front of her.

''Too cute?'' His eyes crinkled at the corners.

''Yes. Forget deer.''

''Okay. Wild pigs?'' He made a face at her, leaning toward her and squiggling his hands over his ears, and Hannah burst out laughing. ''Come on, they can be cute, too. See?''

''Jack! Stop it!''

He growled and snarled and snuffled like a demented pig, and Hannah felt all the tension she'd been holding simply dissolve. She glanced around the room to see if anyone had noticed his antics. He suddenly stopped and slipped his hand around hers so that their fingers were entwined on the tabletop. ''Okay, let's talk about something else,'' he said suddenly serious. ''Your friend.''

"My friend?" Hannah frowned.

Just then the server arrived with a steaming pot of tea, which gave Hannah a chance to regain her composure. Jack released her hand and she sat back in her chair, feeling a little flustered.

"Yeah, the friend you're house-sitting for? I'm curious about her." The server poured the tea and left. "What's her name?"

That friend. "Why?" Hannah really didn't want to get drawn into making up even more stuff about the friend Emily had invented.

"Oh, I just wondered what her name was. What kind of tea is this, do you think?" He picked up his bowl and examined the amber liquid closely.

"Mmm, jasmine?" she asked, inhaling, closing her eyes for a second or two, madly racking her brain. She'd never dreamed he'd ask this many questions about the so-called house-sitting job.

"Jasmine? That's her name?"

"Uh-huh. Jasmine Kelly." That came straight out of nowhere.

"You know what?" He leaned forward. "The amazing thing is, if I hadn't met you first, I'd be seriously interested in someone like her—no kidding. She married, by the way?"

Hannah sputtered her tea. "Married?" she gasped. "No. Why?"

"I'm almost embarrassed to say," he answered with a grin. He looked around. "Listen, do you want a drink now or something with your dinner later? Wine? Sake? We can tell the waitress as soon as we see her. They serve it warmed, I'm told."

Hannah felt reckless. After all, chances were that after this evening, she'd never see Jack Gamble again. Especially considering the way things were going. Her guard was down, since that giggle over the wild pigs. She was bound to make a major mistake; why not live a little first? "Oh, sure. Let's try the sake."

"Okay." Jack smiled. "Yeah, I made my mind up when I decided to take over the farm that it's time I got married." He grinned and played with his chopsticks, bouncing them lightly against the side of his plate. "It's no hardship. I *want* to get married. Wife, kids, all that. I've spent too many years by myself in the bush, and I'm ready for a big change in my life."

Married. Hannah had clenched her hands under the table and was staring at him. "Oh?"

"And I decided the right woman for me was someone just like your friend seems to be. You know, domestic? She's got a great apartment. I'll bet she's a good cook, likes kids, honest as the day is long, good-humored—she has to be, look at those crazy animals she's got. A real treasure for some lucky guy. Am I right?"

Hannah swallowed. She couldn't speak. A horrifying prospect had just opened up in her mind. Jack was looking for…someone like her!

"This is a tough confession to make, but I've always been a sucker for flashy good-looking women with, uh, well, you know. Appeal. Like you." His eyes were very warm on her. Very admiring. She was sure he'd been going to say something like "big tits."

"But I'm not—"

"You are," he interrupted. "You're a terrific-looking woman. Beautiful. Sexy. That hair! I love it. I've always had a soft spot for redheads. The way you dress—cool, classy. I mean, any guy in this room..." He glanced around quickly. There were two elderly couples dining on the other side of the room and a truck-driver type reading a newspaper and slurping down noodles nearby. "Well maybe not in *this* room," he corrected himself with a grin. "Seriously, any red-blooded guy would notice you right away. And he'd wish he was in my shoes."

Hannah felt herself stiffen. She'd never heard such garbage. "Don't you think that's kind of...superficial?"

"It is," he admitted, shaking his head, as though they were talking about someone else, not him. "I admit it." He put his hand on his heart. "It's totally superficial, and that's why I'm ashamed of myself. Still, I'm a guy." He raised one eyebrow in boyish appeal. "It's the way guys are. But I had myself convinced I could ignore all that and go to a small town like Glory, find some nice quiet Glory girl and ask her to marry me. Just like that!" He snapped his fingers and shook his head again, apparently amused at his own naiveté, then he sat back, gazing at her. "Can you believe it?"

"I—I don't know what to think," she murmured. That was the understatement of the century. Her tea bowl was empty, and she poured herself some more. Green tea, it was, not jasmine. Her mind was whirling, and she felt a bit sick.

"I realized when I met you that I was fooling my-self. Hannah, I know you're going to think this makes no sense, but the minute I met you, I knew you were different. You were gorgeous, sexy, all that stuff, but you were a lot more than that. I could tell. And then, I couldn't stop thinking about you all the time I was in Calgary this week. I had to see you again. That's why I went back to your sister's and—"

"And she told you all about me," Hannah said quietly. *All the lies.* She felt tears rising and she blinked them back, afraid her eyelashes would fall off. She'd only worn false eyelashes twice in her life—tonight and last Friday—and she didn't have a clue what they'd do under pressure. She rummaged in her purse and found a tissue and dabbed at her eyes.

"Allergies?" he asked, concerned.

"No," she said, tucking the tissue back in her handbag. "Just something in my eye."

She'd never met a man who talked the way Jack did. He was open and honest and liked to laugh. He told jokes with a skill she could only envy. Much as she loved books, words had never come easy to her. She'd labored over the exact phrasing of the letter she'd sent to the municipality on Seth Wilbee's be-half, pleading for an extension of his order to move. Next week she intended to go to the open council meeting to speak up for the poor man.

She felt vaguely depressed. Where was their meal? "Next thing you're going to say, I suppose, is that you fell for me right then and there. Or something like that.'' Some line! She'd hoped he wasn't like that. How many women did he try that on? *I've always had a soft spot for redheads/blondes/brunettes.* She sniffed. She wanted to blow her nose, badly. A bimbo, that was what he thought she was.

''But it's true, Hannah. I did.'' His voice was very deep and he looked more serious than he had all night. If he was acting, he was good at it. ''I wasn't going to say anything, not yet. It's only our second date, right? But it *is* true. I saw you in the hotel lobby and something inside me just went *Bingo,* this is it, Jack. This is the one for you— What's the matter?''

Hannah felt blindly for her handbag, which she'd set down somewhere near her feet. ''I—I have to go, uh, do something. I'll be back in a minute.'' She stood up, jarring the table and making the dishes rattle. If only she could reach the ladies' room before she burst into tears.

Jack Gamble. The man of her dreams. And he'd said he'd be interested in her *friend,* if he wasn't so darn interested in her.

He'd said she was exactly his type. *Beautiful. Gorgeous. Sexy.* Line or not, no one had ever called her those things before. And after this evening, no one ever would again.

Except maybe Joan. What kind of life was that— depending on a bird for compliments?

CHAPTER SEVEN

JACK STARED after her. There was nothing wrong with her eye. It was him; it had to be him. He'd come on too strong, dammit. He hadn't meant to say all that about her being the one for him. And doing his dumb pig impression—was that any way to impress a lady? There was just something about Hannah. She made him do things. Say things. Confessions he wouldn't have told his best friend—or barber. And he'd only seen her twice, known her less than a week! Less than a day, when it came right down to it.

"Your wife? She will be back?" The server looked worried as she began to place the serving dishes on the table.

"In a few minutes. Hey, this looks good." Jack made an effort to be enthusiastic. The last thing he wanted at the moment was a meal he didn't recognize. He wished he hadn't tried for a big impression and had just taken her to a local steak house, which would have been his preference. But right now he didn't give a damn about food, Japanese or otherwise. He wanted to follow Hannah, make her tell him what the problem was, comfort her, apologize, promise her anything, if he could just start over and this time not put his size-twelve caulked boot in his mouth.

"We have some sushi and California rolls for you. Also *sunomono*—cold noodle salad with rice vinegar..." Man, *that* sounded terrific, Jack thought glumly.

"And fish—*yuan zuke*." She beamed at him, but her dark eyes still looked worried.

"Thank you. My, er, my wife will be back soon. Some sake, too, please?"

The server hurried off again.

My wife. He liked the sound of it. *My wife.*

Jack shook his head and took a deep breath. He was dreaming—again. He glanced over his shoulder. Hannah was coming back.

"You okay?" he asked as she took her seat across from him. Her eyes were bright and her cheeks were red. She'd combed her hair and put on fresh lipstick.

"Fine. This looks delicious!" She seemed determined to disregard their earlier conversation. Who was he to argue?

"Great. Sushi?" He held the platter out to her and managed to manipulate his chopsticks well enough to unload two interesting-looking bite-size pieces of rice and something else onto her plate.

They both dipped and ate at the same time. Hannah chewed slowly. Jack wasn't sure what he'd just eaten, but it was definitely raw. Fish? Shrimp?

She smiled slightly and swallowed. "It's not cooked," she announced, frowning. Then after a few seconds she shrugged and reached for another piece. "Not bad, though."

Jack had to agree. Whatever it was, it was tasty. He had the feeling that any meal he shared with her would be perfect.

She drank a lot of the sake in the tiny stoneware cups provided. Jack stopped at one small cup, since he was driving. They didn't talk much after the rest of the meal arrived. He concentrated on handling his chopsticks and not slopping food all over himself. Hannah was quiet, which worried him. This date didn't seem to be going very well, and it had started out with such promise.

Finally Hannah seemed to come to some kind of decision. He had no idea what she'd been mulling over; he was just relieved she wanted to talk to him again.

"So," she began, with a big smile. Her eyes sparkled and Jack wasn't sure how much had to do with the sake she'd drunk and how much had to do with his scintillating company. "Let's start over. I am a librarian, I'm not married, I like animals and I'm not what you think I am. I don't want to talk about myself any more than that. Okay? Now, tell me everything about Jack Gamble."

She wasn't what he thought she was? What was that supposed to mean? What did she *think* he thought she was? Okay, he could play the game.

"I'm a geologist. I grew up pretty much an orphan, mostly in Saskatchewan. My dad abandoned our family when I was just a baby. No memory of him. My mom died when I was eight. I have no siblings. I was raised mainly by relatives, including Ira Chesley. I studied hard, became a geologist then turned to prospecting. Now I'm going to be a farmer. I've dated plenty of women, but I've never been serious about one—" he refrained from adding *until now* "—but I'd like to get married soon. You know that. That's me. What do you think of this stuff?" He held up a clump of bamboo shoots between his chopsticks.

She giggled. It suited her. "I like it. I keep losing my veggies." Her earrings jangled as she leaned forward to peer into the bubbling cauldron of broth. Jack saw a piece of chicken drift by and lunged for it.

"Aha!" He held it high, dangling and dripping over the table, and she laughed. Then he moved it toward her, and she opened her mouth to accept his offering. Jack felt his heart lurch against his breastbone.

She giggled again, her cheeks red, swallowed, then dug into the pot and offered him something pale and steaming. He didn't even look at it. "You know what? I think that was octopus!" she said, her eyes dancing.

He chewed slowly and swallowed. "You know what? I don't care."

Their eyes met. Hannah's smile faded slightly and her green eyes glowed, and Jack made himself a solemn vow: Things were back on track, he had no idea how or why, but he wasn't screwing up again.

He'd been right last Friday. Hannah Parrish *was* the woman for him.

HANNAH FELT DIZZY as she stood up to put on her wrap. She hoped it wasn't the raw fish. The entire meal had been unusual and delicious. Jack took her elbow after he paid the bill, and they went out into the cold dark night. She leaned against him. Jack Gamble. Warm, solid-feeling. Good-natured. Funny. The stars were bright and white overhead. She shivered.

"Cold?" He squeezed her shoulders.

"Mmm. Not really," she mumbled. "That sake really warmed me up. Like hot chocolate."

"Well, not quite hot chocolate," he said with a wry smile.

She smiled too. She was happy exactly where she was—right in this exact spot in the universe, after a wonderful meal, after a terrific time with a man she'd never dreamed she'd see again. Right here in High River, Alberta. It was a forty-minute drive to Glory but she didn't care if they had to walk back. And then? She'd made up her mind that she was confessing everything when they got back to her apartment. If she wasn't such a coward, she'd do it now.

"Jack?" She stopped halfway to his pickup. He turned to her, an inquiring look on his face. "Kiss me, Jack!"

She threw both arms around him, letting her wrap slide to the ground and offered him her face, eyes closed. The streetlight shining behind him made her squeeze her eyes tighter. She heard the low rumble of his laughter.

"Hey, babe! I'd be glad to." She felt his mouth touch hers. Just as she'd remembered! Her knees went weak, her legs wonky. Just like Friday on the doorstep of her sister's house. Hannah clung to him, putting heart and soul into this one sweet experience. After Jack took her home and she told him the truth... Well, that would be it. She could never face a man she'd lied to the way she'd lied since last Friday. Once, maybe. After all, it had been Halloween that first time. But there was no excuse for what she'd done today—this evening. No matter what Emily said.

"Oh, baby!" Jack muttered into her hair. She felt his arms hard around her. "You're so special. You're such a warm wonderful sexy woman!"

With a groan he kissed her again. Hannah's knees gave way and she clung to him, giggling helplessly. "Oh, for heaven's sake, I slipped! Is it icy?"

Jack laughed, too, and when she got her footing again, he picked up her wrap, draped it around her shoulders and, after one last kiss, helped her into the passenger side of the truck. He practically had to lift her up, the running board seemed so high. Higher than when she'd gotten into it earlier, Hannah thought. Everything seemed so...so *strange*.

"Home?"

"Yes." She nodded. "Joan will be wondering where I am. And Mr. Spitz."

"Mr. Spitz, huh? Is this a man in your life I should know about?"

"Mr. Spitz is the cat."

She heard his chuckle and the hum of the engine as he started it. She felt very tired. It couldn't be that late—no more than ten o'clock. That was what happened when you lived the boring life she did. Bed by ten, up at seven, half an hour for breakfast, ten minutes to read the paper, a fifteen-minute walk to work, washing on Monday, shopping on Tuesday...

Hannah wasn't sure what they discussed on the way to Glory, but she vaguely recalled Jack talking about his prospecting days up north. Then he was gently shaking her awake. They were parked in front of her apartment.

She'd fallen asleep in the truck! Just like some twelve-year-old being driven home from Grandma's house.

FOR A FEW MOMENTS Jack just gazed at the sleeping Hannah in the light from the street lamp. She was a mystery—strong, sexy, but also vulnerable and innocent somehow. Her eyes shut, her lips slightly parted, the strap of her bag tucked into one relaxed hand. The long painted fingernails, the hammered silver earrings, the slinky shawl. It didn't add up, and yet, in some weird way, it did.

"Hannah?" He hated to wake her. He would've preferred to take her to his place—well, not now, but when it was all fixed up—and tuck her into bed beside him.

His wife? He could see it. He'd better not let anything like a marrriage proposal slip out of his big mouth. Not yet. Hannah was carrying around something that was bothering her. Maybe it had to do with this house-sitting gig. Maybe it had to do with being stuck in boring old Glory for her holidays. Hannah a farmer's wife? Could he be so lucky? Not likely. Jack felt cold shudders run through his body.

He clenched his jaw and touched her arm again. "Hannah? We're home."

"Home?" She opened her eyes and stared deep into his soul. Then she sat up groggily and blinked. "Heavens. I must have fallen asleep. Oh, I'm so sorry, Jack, you must think I'm awful…"

"Not awful, babe. Just tired, that's all. Come on, I'll take you in."

He walked around the truck to the passenger side. The big date was over. Then he had another twenty-minute drive out to his cold dark dingy farmhouse.

But not right away. She insisted he come inside for a coffee. That struck him as a pretty old-fashioned offer, but he realized she wasn't quite herself. He knew she'd had quite a bit of sake to drink. Coffee was probably a good idea.

"Hiya, gorgeous!" The parrot woke up, untucking its head from under its wing.

"Oh, Joan…" Hannah tossed her wrap in the direction of a chair and missed, then walked toward the parrot and pulled a dark cloth down over the cage. "I'm sorry. I forgot to cover you up." The parrot muttered sleepily—Jack was sure he heard a soft "blimey, fiddlesticks!"—and then was silent.

Hannah seemed really distressed. Fidgety. Had it bothered her *that* much that she'd forgotten to cover the bird? Or that she'd fallen asleep in his truck? Sure, it wasn't the usual ending to a date, but then, so far everything about their relationship had been unusual, to say the least. Right from the start, when she'd dropped the contents of her purse in the lobby of the St. Regis.

"How about I make the coffee?" Jack suggested. "You sit down and I'll be with you in a jiffy."

She laughed and began to rub her eyes, then quickly stopped and sat down on the sofa.

"What's so funny?"

"You," she said, looking up. "Jiffy. I haven't heard anyone say that in ages."

"Must be a Saskatchewan word," he said. "Where's your coffee?"

"The fridge." She looked disconsolate again; he hoped the coffee would help, but maybe that was expecting too much of caffeine.

"Listen, you feeling okay, Hannah?" he ventured as the coffee machine began gurgling.

"Me? Of...of course. Why do you ask?"

"You drank quite a lot of wine with dinner."

"I did not! I didn't even like it that much!" She looked upset. As though he'd accused her of something serious.

"You did, Hannah. I drank one cup and you drank the rest. Hey, it's okay." He held up both hands in mock surrender. "Happens from time to time to the best of us." He ducked back into the kitchen to bring out a couple of mugs of coffee. Did she take cream or sugar? He couldn't remember.

"This all right?" He set the coffee down in front of her.

"Fine." She hadn't even looked at it. She twisted the hem of the embroidered tunic she was wearing, one foot tucked up under her as she sat on the sofa. He wanted to sit down beside her, but he wasn't sure of her in this mood. It reminded him of the episode in the restaurant. He settled into an upholstered chair to one side of the sofa.

He was about to make some light remark, but thought better of it and raised the steaming coffee to his mouth. Yuck. One percent milk wasn't his idea of coffee cream.

"Jack," she began, looking worriedly at him, "I have something to tell you. Something important."

"Uh-huh?" He gazed at her across the top of his mug. "What's that, Hannah? You're married? You're a drag queen? You deal drugs?"

"This is serious. I'm…I'm not who you think I am." She seemed on the verge of bursting into tears. She still hadn't touched her coffee.

"Yeah. You said something like that in the restaurant. What do you mean? You're not Hannah Parrish?" He smiled.

"I am. I *am* Hannah Parrish," she said emphatically, nodding her head. "I'm just not what I seem to be. It's all a great big lie. I'm not house-sitting. This is really *my* apartment, this is *my* parrot and that cat's *my* cat and…and all the stuff in here is mine. It's so hard to explain."

Jack stared at her. "Come on, Hannah. What are you talking about?"

"It's true!" She got up, then got down on her knees and peered under the skirt of the sofa. "I can prove it. Watch this. Mr. Spitz?" She looked earnestly up at Jack. Her eyes were overbright, yet distant. She'd definitely had too much rice wine. Maybe she'd been more nervous with him than he'd realized; he should have kept an eye on her. But why was she talking like this? "It's my cat. He adores me. I rescued him from the pound. Watch. He-e-ere, Mr. Spitz!"

There was a heavy thump in the vicinity of the dining room, and Jack turned around. The cat had leaped onto the dining-room table from the china cabinet. As he watched, the cat jumped onto a chair, then onto the floor.

"Come, kitty!" Hannah called. "Lapsies!" She patted her lap enticingly from her position back on the sofa.

The cat didn't even glance at her. With its tail held high, it walked directly away from her into the hall-way and turned into an open doorway, probably a bedroom, and disappeared.

Jack took another gulp of his coffee and scorched his tongue. No way was he checking out Hannah's reaction to the cat's defection.

"He's never done that before," she muttered, sounding bewildered. Jack wanted to laugh. He also wanted to go over and pull her into his arms and tell her that he didn't care who she thought she was or what was going on, that he liked her just the way she was.

"Hey, it doesn't matter. Drink your coffee."

"This *is* my place." She waved one arm around.

"What about your friend, Jasmine Kelly?"

"There is no Jasmine Kelly. I made it all up!" She twisted her hands again in the tunic hem. "I did! Don't you believe me?"

"Nope." Jack drained his coffee and stood. "I think you're a little mixed-up. You had a bit too much sake tonight and maybe it didn't agree with you. And you fell asleep in my truck. You're disoriented—''

"But Jack! Look here, these aren't my clothes!" To his dismay, she started removing her earrings and plucking at the tunic. "This is my sister's top. These are her friend's earrings. This isn't even my hair!" She grabbed a handful of her hair. "Red! I don't have red hair, I have ordinary mousy-brown hair."

Her hair looked red to him. Jack reached for her hand and patted it gently. "Come on, honey. I'll wait until you're changed and ready for bed, then I'll turn out all the lights and make sure your door is locked. You get a good night's sleep, you'll feel a hundred percent better in the morning. Promise."

"I feel fine! There's nothing wrong with me! You're patronizing me! Why don't you believe me?"

"Because this isn't you talking, Hannah. This is preposterous. You *do* have red hair," he explained patiently, raising his hand to finger a lock of her glorious hair. "And why would you make up all that stuff about house-sitting? Why would your sister? Come on—"

"But I'm telling you the truth! This person you think is me isn't me at all." Her eyes were wide. He wanted nothing more than to kiss this crazy, wonderful woman. Put her mind on a different track altogether.

She suddenly threw the silver earrings across the room. One bounced off the parrot's cage and brought a squawk of protest from the snoozing bird. "These aren't mine!" She looked furious. She started to pull off the tunic and Jack whirled around so that his back was to her.

"Whoa! Settle down here, Hannah. Don't get undressed. Please. We hardly know each other. Down the hall and into your bedroom. That's a good girl." He flinched as he heard her stalk down the hallway, tossing a decidedly unladylike epithet over her shoulder.

A door slammed. Jack waited ten minutes. There was no further sound from her bedroom. Finally he decided he'd better check on her, make sure she was okay. She was asleep in her bed, a handmade old-fashioned quilt tucked up under her chin. He could see the sleeves of a rose-sprigged cotton nightgown, decidedly a Jasmine Kelly touch. Her Hannah Parrish clothes were puddled in the middle of the floor. Jack paused, then quickly bent and placed a chaste kiss on her cheek. Jasmine? Hannah? It was time for him to go.

"Sweet dreams, princess," he whispered, "whoever you are."

CHAPTER EIGHT

HANNAH AWOKE to the sound of her telephone ringing and the bright light of midmorning streaming through her uncurtained windows. She *never* went to bed without closing the curtains.

She made her way to the bathroom, the events of the previous evening slowly dropping into place in her horrified mind. She flicked on the bathroom light and screamed. Whatever was on her face fell to the floor, and she hopped back, trying to balance on one foot, any foot, so long as it wasn't near the thing.

One-half of a set of false eyelashes lay harmlessly at her feet. Hannah sank onto the side of the bathtub, torn between relief and hysterical laughter. What was happening to her? She'd tried to tell Jack about the stupid trick she and Emily had played on him, and he hadn't believed a word. She'd gone to bed without cleansing her face and still wearing false eyelashes! One had come off in the night and attacked her— Hannah began to giggle. Thank heavens Jack hadn't spent the night. She could just see herself waking up beside him, all love-dazed and with big black eyelashes stuck to her cheek. He'd leap out of bed and start running and never stop.

Maybe that was what he was doing this morning. Running. She couldn't blame him.

All the laughter drizzled to a stop inside her. She'd blown it. She'd blown it big time. First she'd gone and drunk too much wine—no, *first* she'd gone along with Emily's crazy idea. But how could she blame her sister? All she'd had to do was say no. The truth was, she'd wanted desperately to see Jack again. The truth was she'd hoped against hope that something would happen—*something*—that would make things all right again. It hadn't.

Instead, she'd tried to explain the deception to him, and he had flat out not believed her. He thought she was being silly, making it up, for who-knew-what reason. That she'd drunk too much sake. He still thought she was cool, sophisticated, sexy Hannah Parrish. Sophisticated, sure—he should have heard her screaming at the "spider" on the bathroom floor.

Hannah washed her face and removed the false lashes from her other eye, dropping both into the trash. End of that. She stepped into the shower and vigorously shampooed her hair. Then, when she'd rinsed, she shampooed again. How many times was that? She'd lost count, but at least the red was fading noticeably. She felt sick every time she thought about what she'd done. It was so unlike her; she'd never done anything so deliberately false in her life. Even if he'd believed her last night, would he have forgiven her? *Honest as the day is long,* he'd said. That was what he wanted in a woman.

A simple trick designed to amuse her sister Emily

had turned into something that was affecting her entire life. That wasn't an exaggeration; she liked Jack.
More than liked him. She really thought they might
have had a chance together—

Then Hannah froze, suds running down her
shocked face. *It was worse....*

He'd told her he wanted to marry someone like
Jasmine Kelly, the friend she was supposedly house-
sitting for. She'd told him there was no friend, that
she was the one who lived in the apartment! Hannah
moaned and turned off the water. He must think she
was trying to pretend there was no Jasmine Kelly
because she—Hannah—was interested in him. He
must think she was so desperate, so shameless, so
needy, that she'd make up anything, be anything, do
anything, to impress a man. To impress Jack Gamble.
He was running, all right. As far and as fast as he
could. Wouldn't she do the same if she was in his
position?

Hannah stumbled back into the hall and into her
bedroom. She heard Joan squawk and the phone trill
again, but she ignored both. She flopped onto her bed
and covered her face with the pillow.

And she'd thought things were bad before!

The phone rang a third time and Hannah still ignored it. If it was Emily, she didn't want to talk to
her; if it was Jack, she didn't want to talk to him.
She didn't want to talk to anyone but Joan and
maybe Mrs. Putty. Even Mr. Spitz had better stay out
of her way today.

HANNAH SPENT the next two days working hard on
the presentation she wanted to make at the Wednes-

day-evening open meeting in the municipal-council chambers. Once a month the town council held casual sessions where the public could speak on issues of interest without having to go on a formal agenda. Hannah intended to ask for a stay of proceedings against the order to move Seth Wilbee. She hoped the town would simply forget the whole issue, but barring that, she wanted them to let Seth stay until spring, when he could possibly find a new location. Or have the time to build another shack.

On Monday she packed up all the clothing and jewelry Emily had so thoughtfully collected for her and took it back to Calgary to dump on her doorstep. If Emily had been home, Hannah would have relented and pushed the doorbell to say hello. She missed her sister and usually talked to her at least once a week. Their parents were retired and always traveling; the latest letter Hannah had received had been postmarked somewhere in Africa. Namibia? Nigeria? But luckily she knew Emily was at work. Hannah had no desire to be grilled about Jack, and she knew Emily would do more than grill her. She'd roast her if she knew the latest!

Then Hannah drove to the Southcentre Mall to check out a teaching-supply store that her friend Ella Searle had recommended. She was looking for literacy material. Seth Wilbee was going to learn to read his own mail before the winter was through, or her name wasn't Hannah Parrish.

"ELK, YOU SAY?" There was silence of nearly a minute as the old man in the hospital recliner chair considered Jack's proposal. "You'll want to check with the town, son. Maybe they'd put in a plug for you with the Ag Department. Venture like that takes money. Big money. I got some you can use."

"Never mind, Uncle Ira. I've got money," Jack said, patting his uncle's liver-spotted hand. The old man looked so frail it was hard to imagine him farming all by himself these last years, out in all kinds of weather.

"How's the dogs?"

"Fine. Angus Tump is keeping an eye on them. I told you that. He comes in around suppertime just to make sure everything's okay." Ira's ragtag collection of no-good hounds was his pride and joy. Every time Jack visited, Ira asked about the dogs.

"Angus, eh? He's a good man—he'll take care of them all right," the old man murmured. He glanced at the wall clock. Was it his suppertime? Was he anxious for Jack to leave already?

"How about you? What does the doc say?" Jack was trying to be cheerful. He was shocked at how much feebler Ira seemed, even in the week since he'd seen him.

"Elk, eh?" The old bachelor repeated, ignoring Jack's query about his health. Ira definitely seemed taken with the notion of Jack's raising elk or deer. The wild-boar idea had never been a serious one, despite what Jack had told Hannah. "They take real good care of me here, boy. I got company. Decent grub couple times a day served up. I was only—" his pale eyes wandered toward Jack's "—I was only worried about the dogs, y'see?"

The man in the next bed had the television on, and Jack noticed that his uncle's attention kept drifting to the screen. An infomercial—someone demonstrating a food dehydrator or something equally useful. Time to leave. He stood.

"Well, I'll check in on you after I hear back from the fellow in Regina—"

"Eh?" His uncle's gaze wandered to Jack again. He seemed suddenly agitated. He held out his hand. "Listen. You get yourself married, y'hear? You get yourself a wife, now you got a farm and some prospects. Don't...don't make the mistake I did. Don't delay—"

"What mistake, Uncle Ira?" This was the first Jack had heard about any woman in Ira Chesley's life.

"I wanted to marry Gladys Petrie, my sister's friend. Gladys was sweet on me, too. I had plans back then. Big plans. I went out to Alberta and got the farm going and one thing and another, and by the time I went back to fetch Gladys, back in Maple Creek, it was too late. She'd married someone else. She got tired of waiting."

Jack didn't know what to say. He was astounded at his uncle's story. Poor old duff! Jack reached for his hand. "Well, don't worry about me, Uncle Ira. I've got my eye on someone right now."

"That's the thinking. Don't delay, son!" The old man squeezed his fingers. He still had considerable strength in his hands, despite the apparent frailty. "Don't delay."

"I won't," Jack said, mainly to placate him. "I'll

stop in and see you next week, all right?'' Jack shrugged on his coat and smiled at a pretty nurse who came by to pick up his uncle's chart. When he looked at the old man, he was surprised to see him wink.

''They've got nice scenery in here, eh?'' He winked again and gave Jack a faint smile. ''TV's good, too. Lots of channels.'' His uncle watched him go toward the door. He was already glancing back at the infomercial before Jack had left the room.

Get married. Check with the town. Buy groceries. Call Ira's doctor. Hire a painter. Pay Angus Tump. Call Hannah again. Why wasn't she answering her phone? *Call the elk fellow in Regina. Check on the price of fencing. Get a haircut?* Nope. Too soon.

Get married.

Now why did that particular item keep jumping to the top of his list?

CHAPTER NINE

THE MUNICIPAL CHAMBERS were packed. Hannah was surprised, but when she spoke to a few people, she realized two pressing issues accounted for the turnout: the selection of a town animal—most favored the gopher, but a small contingent insisted on calling the creature Richardson's ground squirrel, which infuriated the gopher supporters; and the theme for this year's Main Street Christmas display. The aging angels and stars used for a decade had finally been retired, and the town planned to acquire new streetlight and banner decorations.

Seth Wilbee wasn't there. He'd blanched when Hannah told him what she'd planned on his behalf and asked him to accompany her to the municipal hall. He didn't care for crowds, he said; they made him sweat. Hannah didn't press him. She hoped to be able to bring him good news after the meeting, and that would be the end of it.

She hadn't heard from Jack. He'd left a dozen messages the first two days, when she wasn't answering her phone or her door. But then today and yesterday, when she'd decided that she couldn't hide anymore, that she had to face up to the consequences of her foolishness, no matter how humiliating, there'd been nothing. Was he out of town? There was always the possibility that he'd decided she was seriously unbalanced, pretending to be Jasmine Kelly. Maybe he was counting his lucky stars.

The meeting started at a ridiculous time, half-past four. It was getting dark early these days, and the first snowfall in Glory—the first to stay, at least— had made the sidewalks slippery and dusted the landscape with white. It was a lovely time of year, though, Hannah's favorite: not too cold, yet brisk and dry. Perfect pre-Christmas weather. In the library the students were still enthusiastic about their projects, and she enjoyed helping them find what they were looking for, introducing them to the world of research and books.

Hannah walked to the municipal hall alone. She'd put a pot roast in a slow oven before she left the apartment and had fed Mr. Spitz and Joan early. She had no idea how long the meeting would go on, or if she'd even have a chance to speak. She wore her new snowboots with the zip-up fronts and her woolly tights, along with a corduroy skirt and a fleecy Icelandic sweater she'd knit several years before in one of her knitting phases. She'd knitted one for Emily, too, in blue and gray tones, and given it to her for Christmas that year. Over it all, she wore her navy wool pea coat and a red tam. The color in her hair had finally departed and she was back to her usual brown. Everything felt good about the change. Her only regret was that while she'd been playing the glamorous Hannah Parrish, she'd met a man she knew she could really care about—already did, impossible as it seemed—and had blown her opportunity by trying to deceive him further. All because she was scared to death he wouldn't like her as she really was. Which, in a way was true, no matter what he said about the "friend" she was house-sitting for. After all, he'd been attracted to *her*—Hannah—precisely because she appeared to be a glitzy glamour girl, hadn't he?

Hannah sighed. Life wasn't fair. But then, she'd never really expected it to be. She stopped at Seth's mailbox to pop in the beginner's workbook she'd bought at the teaching-store in Calgary. The first task was learning the alphabet. When Seth had finished with that workbook, Hannah had a stack of others. She was looking forward to the project; it took her mind off her own problems a little. The trouble was, she had too much time on her hands. She supposed that once she got back to work next week, she'd be fine.

Hannah recognized a lot of Glory townfolk in the crowd. She waved to Myra Schultz, the postmistress, and Honor Gallant, who was there with her sister-in-law, Nan. Ben Longquist, Nan's son, sat beside them, very handsome and grown-up these days. Hannah thought he must be in his early twenties now; he was attending university somewhere, she'd heard. She spotted a friend of Mrs. Putty's and waved. Mrs. Vandenbroek was an elderly widow who'd come to the community from Holland after the war and had settled in a big house on Alder Street, where she rented her upstairs flat to tenants.

The clerk called the buzzing crowd to order. The

first item regarded the selection of a town animal. The nearby town of Tamarack had recently chosen the mountain lion, to the chagrin of some Glory folk who felt a gopher would be too unimpressive in comparison. But the sentiment seemed to be generally in favor of the lively prairie rodent that had once populated bustling gopher "towns" of interlinked burrows in the prairie sod. These days, after decades of poisoning and trapping, the animal was rarely seen outside of such safe areas as the busy gopher settlement on the grounds of the Royal Tyrell Museum of Paleontology at Drumheller. Glory had a long-established gopher population in the riverside park, thus the support for electing it town animal. Still, it was true: the actual name of what had always been called a gopher was Richardson's ground squirrel.

"Who the heck's this Richardson, anyway?" complained one member of the public. "Everybody knows a gopher's a gopher!"

"If I may speak to that, Your Worship," began a small bespectacled man wearing a vest and striped tie, addressing the mayor. This was Norman Weber, who worked at the liquor store. He nervously pushed back his glasses and referred to a piece of paper in his hand. "The true and proper name for what is popularly known as a gopher is Richardson's ground squirrel," he read. He looked at the mayor. "Now, do we want the town of Glory to be a laughingstock because we don't call our town animal by its proper name?"

The poor man was drowned out by a chorus of "Aw, sit down" and "Who cares?" Hannah tried not to smile; a lot of people took this very seriously. Clearly, the gopher people were in the majority. No way she was suggesting *spermophilii richardsonii,* the Latin name, just to be really accurate!

The debate continued, with the clerk finally calling a halt to discussion and opening the floor to suggestions about the festive season's street decorations. The next half hour was spent arguing the merits of Santas and reindeers over candy canes and snowmen. By six she wondered if she'd have a chance to speak at all. Usually these meetings were fairly short. A little later, though, the call came from the town clerk, ''Any more business?'' and she put up her hand.

''Hannah Parrish!''

She left her coat and purse at her seat and walked to the end of the aisle so she could speak into the microphone. She pulled her sweater down neatly and cleared her throat. To her great embarrassment, she heard a wolf whistle from the corner of the room, where a group of skateboarders had taken seats. A general chuckle followed. The teens, according to the man next to her, were there to ask the town for a skateboard park in the new riverside development.

''I'm here to speak on behalf of Seth Wilbee, who, as many of you know, has a small dwelling on the riverbank in the vicinity of the proposed park.'' There was a murmur from the crowd. Hannah didn't know whether to be encouraged by that or not. Seth Wilbee was tolerated in the community, but he wasn't claimed as a friend by anyone she knew. She was sure town children were just as wary of the loner who lived in the riverbank shack as she had been of Mrs. Birch, the "old witch" of her own childhood.

Hannah continued, relating how she'd visited him and discovered he'd been ordered to move his shack immediately. She had decided right from the start to keep Seth's secret but pointed out to the mayor and councillors that since construction wouldn't start until spring, perhaps Mr. Wilbee could be given an extension on the order, so he'd have more time to find a suitable dwelling place.

"Yeah, like a cave!" shouted someone.

"Or a barrel!" shouted another. Some chuckled and others booed the speakers.

The mayor, the butcher from the IGA, asked the council if there were any serious objections to giving Mr. Wilbee an extension. No one had any objections, although one councillor, a real-estate agent, stood and lectured the crowd on the dangers of "indigents, mendicants and dilettantes" taking over the streets of Glory. No one was quite sure what he meant, but Hannah did not think it augured well for the young and generally unpopular skateboard crowd.

"Ruth Putty!" the town clerk called out. Hannah was surprised. She hadn't known her neighbor was there.

The plump elderly woman made her way to the microphone, and took it from Hannah. Mrs. Putty was very red and out of breath.

"I just want to say that although I wish Seth Wilbee would go into a home where he'd be off our streets and well looked after, I know he won't because he's too darn stubborn." The crowd murmured in agreement. "But I want to put in a word here for my neighbor, Hannah Parrish. We live in the same apartment building, and I've known Hannah for several years. She's a dear young thing, a real asset at our town library and a wonderful friend to me. I know she keeps an eye on Seth and even takes the old fool homemade cookies and such." The crowd laughed.

"Now she's going to bat for him against the town and even teaching him to read! How about that? I think we should have a round of applause for our librarian, Miss Hannah Parrish. She's a fine example to all our young people!" Mrs. Putty glared in the direction of the skateboarders, who sent up a good-tempered jeer.

The crowd burst into applause, much to Hannah's dismay. Mrs. Putty grabbed her and kissed her cheek, then went huffing and puffing back to her seat. Hannah followed, blushing. Just before she sat down, she glanced behind her, smiling at her many applauding supporters. Then she froze.

Staring at her from the back of the room was one person she'd never thought she'd see in this room. It was Jack Gamble, dressed in jeans and a windbreaker, and he looked as shocked and surprised as she was.

CHAPTER TEN

JACK WAS WAITING for her on the steps of her apartment building when Hannah arrived home. It had started to snow again, and she wasn't sure she'd have noticed him right away. But a quick rap on the window above the doorway, the living-room window belonging to Mrs. Putty, left no doubt in her mind. When she looked up, Mrs. Putty made violent gestures pointing down, toward the door. Evidently she'd seen Jack and wanted to make sure Hannah didn't miss him.

How *could* she miss him? He looked as wonderful as ever—no, even more so—dressed in casual working clothes. She glanced down the street and noticed his pickup parked down the block a little, out of the loading zone. He watched her approach, making no move to come toward her.

She felt self-conscious. But then she lifted her chin and met his gaze straight on. She liked who she was. She'd always liked who she was—plain Hannah Parrish. She decided to ignore him. After all, she had no idea why he was here. Why hadn't he acknowledged her at the town hall? She'd looked for him in the crowd as the meeting broke up, but he'd left. Then she'd been delayed talking to various people, and after that, had decided to stop at Seth's place to tell him it seemed very likely the town would give him a reprieve. Seth's pale eyes had watered dangerously, and he'd held her gloved hands in his large gnarled ones and thanked her again and again. She'd noticed the open workbook on his wooden table, with a coal-oil lantern burning over it. The dotted lines of *a*'s were already traced in pencil.

Hannah clutched her purse and the bag Seth had given her more tightly as she saw Jack step out from under the portico and move toward her.

"What took you so long?" he asked, his voice warm.

They were under the streetlight, well within Mrs. Putty's view. Hannah looked stubbornly up at him, her lips pressed firmly together. She decided to ignore his question. "I saw you at the meeting."

"Yes." Jack moved a little closer and smiled at her. "Hannah Parrish, isn't it? The town librarian? This is where she lives and her neighbor's name is Ruth Putty and she's known her for several years?"

Hannah knew her cheeks were a furious red. Mrs. Putty had set the facts out very clearly at the meeting, and Jack hadn't missed a thing. She nodded. She didn't quite trust her voice.

"And Hannah Parrish has a parrot named Joan and a very independent cat called Mr. Spitz?" he went on, one eyebrow raised, a slight smile on his face.

Hannah nodded and dug in her pocket for her key. She was feeling a little better. At least Jack wasn't angry. He touched her arm and she turned to him.

"Hannah!" He framed her face in his hands. "Forgive me?"

"For what?" she asked, her breath painful in her lungs.

"For not believing you. When you tried to tell me the truth." He bent down and brushed her lips with his and Hannah felt her knees jiggle. He always had this effect on her!

"I—I can't say I blame you, Jack," she replied quietly. Even thinking of it now, her foolish deception made her voice quaver and her eyes burn. "It was all so stupid. I'm so sorry. I can't begin to explain—"

"Emily told me," he broke in. "She told me the whole story. When you didn't answer your phone, I nearly went mad. You didn't answer your door. I thought something had happened to you. I—"

"Oh, Jack!" Hannah dropped her purse and the paper bag Seth had given her. "Kiss me!"

Jack did, with enthusiasm. Hannah gave herself up to his embrace. This was where she belonged. *Oh, thank you, Emily, thank you.*

"Hannah, honey," Jack murmured, his face against her tam. "Is it too early in our relationship to say that I really, *really* like you? Exactly the way you are?"

"No," Hannah said, smiling into his jacket. She realized her face was wet with tears, tears of joy. Mrs. Putty was certainly getting an eyeful.

"Okay, then." He held her away from him so he could look at her. "I really, *really* like you, Hannah Parrish!"

"And I really, *really* like you, Jack. I do."

"Good. I wanted to hear that." He held her tighter and dropped a kiss on her nose. He pulled off her tam and buried his face in her hair. She heard his muffled laugh.

"What's so funny?" She barely trusted her voice.

"Your hair. It's a glorious brown. And it's so curly." He smiled down at her, twisting one tendril of her hair around his finger. "Did I ever tell you I'm very partial to brunettes?"

"Oh, Jack!"

He bent and kissed her again. Hannah opened her eyes to see her neighbor give her a thumbs-up before drawing her curtains—rather reluctantly, Hannah thought with a smile.

"Have you had supper?" she asked when she caught her breath.

"No," he said with a huge grin. "Are you inviting me?"

"Yes, I am," she said. She wondered if she looked as giddy as she felt. *Another chance with Jack!*

"Let me guess what you're serving. Meat loaf?"

"No." She smiled.

"Baked ham, noodles and string beans?"

"No." She giggled.

"But you do have something in the oven, right? For after the meeting. Because you're an organized, careful, domestic kind of person, right? Not to mention sexy as all get-out."

She nodded, eyes dancing. "Give up?"

He took her key and opened the front door of her building. "Last guess—pot roast?"

"Right!"

"Hannah Parrish, you are the woman of my dreams." He held the door for her. "Would you consider this too early for me to mention the possibility of you becoming a farmer's wife someday?"

She felt her heart melt all over again. "No, I wouldn't," she said softly.

"Oh, baby!" Jack swooped her into his arms and kissed her again. Hannah was glad they were out of sight of her interested neighbor.

"Although, I have to admit," Hannah managed, her heart beating furiously, "it would depend a lot on who the farmer was."

Jack let out a whoop of laughter and released her, and Hannah glanced down at the stuff she'd dropped. He bent and picked up her purse and the paper bag, brushing off the snow.

"What's in this?"

"Oh, just some vegetables Seth gave me."

"Turnips? Yuck, I hate turnips."

Hannah peered in the bag. "No, parsnips. Seth says they're a very misunderstood vegetable."

"They go with pot roast?"

"Maybe," she teased. She just couldn't stop smiling. "You like parsnips?"

"Not really. Why?" Jack looked bewildered.

Hannah laughed and stood on tiptoe and kissed him on the chin. "You will. Trust me. Seth says they're always sweeter after a frost. *Always.*"

Promise Me Picket Fence
Janice Kay Johnson

ELK SPRINGS, OREGON

Have you ever been to Elk Springs? You won't find it on a map, but it's out there in Central Oregon, a once old-fashioned town surrounded by high desert ranching country. These past ten years, Elk Springs has been transformed by a new ski resort on Juanita Butte outside town.

New and old met when Scott McNeil, a man who helped build that ski resort, married Meg Patton, who was born and grew up in Elk Springs, then brought her son back to raise him in her hometown. You're about to meet Scott's brother, by the way. Kevin McNeil has come to Elk Springs to live and work— although his restless nature has him assuming he won't stay.

Oh, while you're in town, stick your head in the new public safety building that houses the police department. If anything epitomizes change in this community, it's the Elk Springs P.D., run for a quarter century by hard-nosed Chief Ed Patton, who didn't know the meaning of mercy. Longtime residents are pretty sure he's rolling over in his grave now that a woman, his own daughter, Renee Patton, wears the badge! Those same residents will tell you that, along with her two sisters—both also in law enforcement—Renee does a fine job of keeping the peace in Elk Springs.

So enjoy your visit and come again.

Janice Kay Johnson

Other Elk Springs books by Janice Kay Johnson

HARLEQUIN SUPERROMANCE

CHAPTER ONE

THE CANNON BOOMED, white smoke puffing from its mouth. Blue-coated Yankee cavalry cantered through the forest, flashes of gleaming chestnut coat or gold braid glinting between branches. Closer, on the grassy hillside, Rebel and Yankee infantrymen maneuvered, making forays and being driven back by the sharp crack of rifle fire. Wounded fell as the watching crowd gasped. Bodies littered the landscape.

His stern gaze fixed on the hillside skirmish, a Confederate colonel strode past the split-rail fence where Melanie Parker leaned. His gray frock coat had a curved breast with two seven-button rows and elaborate gold braid on the sleeves and trim on collar and cuffs. Blue trim ran up his trouser legs. His graying head was covered by an officer's kepi, a kind of slouch cap.

Melanie watched his progress with pardonable pride. She had made his uniform, from inner pockets to decorative braid. In fact, half the uniforms on this field had come from her sewing machine.

The Civil War reenactors were a passionate bunch, she'd discovered. Every tiny detail had to be right, for these men and women were out here to educate, as well as have fun. She had become something of an expert on Rebel and Yankee uniforms both, from the pullover white muslin shirt with removable collar to the Confederate rank insignia on the coat sleeves. She'd sewed many of the gowns worn by camp followers, too. Melanie had something of an obsession herself for historical accuracy.

Today's reenactment of an obscure battle was being staged primarily for children. Scouting troops from all over central Oregon, both boys and girls, had gathered in the state park outside Elk Springs to watch, learn and participate. Melanie was here as leader of her daughter Angie's troop.

Except for a few stolen moments of pleasure taken in her handiwork, she was too busy keeping tabs on the girls to follow the strategy on the battlefield. Somebody *always* had to go to the portable toilets a quarter of a mile away. The booths selling 1860s-era keepsakes, clothing and candy enticed eight-year-old girls with allowance money tucked in their pockets. Melanie had spent the entire day thinking, *Now, where is Jennifer? Oh. Good. Well, then, what about Rainy? And Sarah. She's missing, too, isn't she?* Melanie did not envy the troop leaders with younger children.

A buzz passed through the crowd, a ripple she scarcely noticed as she counted noses for the four hundred and eighty-eighth time.

"Melanie." A regional Scout leader paused, her expression harassed and even a little anxious. "You haven't seen a wandering four-year-old, have you? A boy in green corduroy overalls?"

"Are you kidding?" Melanie waved a hand and raised her voice. "Angie and Rachel, where do you think you're going?" She switched her attention back to the leader. "Is this kid really lost?"

"Nobody has seen him in the past hour. Or more." She shook her head. "His dad has a group of older boys." She nodded vaguely toward the encampment. "*He* thought his son was with his wife, *she* thought he was with the dad. You know how that goes."

No, actually, Melanie didn't. Angie's dad had never been interested in taking her places. In fact, she hadn't even seen him in almost two years.

But Melanie nodded. "I'll keep an eye out."

"Right."

No small boy in green overalls darted through the crowd or tried to duck under the split-rail fence to join the battle. Eventually Melanie and other Scout leaders organized their kids to hunt through the crowd and down by the lake.

The battle on the hillside dwindled in spirit, and the wounded rose to fight another day. Cavalry officers hunted through the fringe of the woods for the child.

Somebody pointed out the boy's mother, who raced along the riverbank, calling his name frantically, voice rising to a near scream. "Brandon! Brandon, come to Mommy!"

"We need to send the kids home," a senior Boy Scout leader decided, and the others concurred. Melanie corralled her girls by her Bronco, but Sarah's mother hurried across the parking lot.

"Aren't you in the volunteer search-and-rescue group? Let me take the girls. You might be needed here. Angie can come home with Sarah."

As they piled into the Dodge Caravan, Melanie counted noses one last time and then hugged her daughter and thanked Sarah's mother. "You'll see that they all get home? Bless you. I'll hope I'm not needed in the end."

An ardent hiker, she had joined the search-and-rescue group this past summer and had only been called out once, when a hiker got separated from his party in the Deschutes National Forest. His cell phone saved the day, which had taken some of the romance out of the rescue of a man with a sprained ankle, in Melanie's private opinion.

As the group gathered, she said, "We're sure this little boy wasn't…well…"

"Taken?" the ranger who headed the group finished for her, his jaw set grimly. "No. We can't be. But there was virtually no automobile traffic out of here in the past few hours. Remember, pretty much the whole audience was Scout troops. Unless we have some sicko leader who dragged the kid off…"

Nobody wanted to think about that.

"The kid is a wanderer, apparently. Couple months ago, he got up before his parents one morning and set off down the street. They found him a mile away. So that's the likeliest possibility." He looked around. "Other questions? No? Okay. Tom, you take your group and do a sweep along the riverbank." He continued to give orders, and groups of eight or ten split off to follow them.

Melanie had become aware of a man she didn't know standing quietly nearby. He stood out from the crowd by virtue of his height, his lean powerful body and short-cropped but noticeably wavy auburn hair. In the late-afternoon sunlight, that hair was almost as red as the sweat-slick neck of the bay mare hitched to the nearby fence.

"Kevin, you handle the woods beyond the concession area. Go several miles, the kid has been missing for almost three hours now, but keep it slow. His mother says this is nap time, and he may have found a place to curl up."

The big auburn-haired man in jeans and dusty hiking boots said in a deep easy voice, "You got it. Okay." Clear gray eyes met Melanie's for an oddly startling moment before moving on. "You eight— no, nine, are with me."

As they hurried across the beaten-down grass that had formed the parking lot, he gave orders: Fan out, but stay within sight and shouting distance of one another. He took the center himself. Melanie had the impression no one else knew him, either, but his air of command was so natural no one argued. Somehow, as they entered the ponderosa pines, Melanie found herself beside him.

The woods weren't dense, nothing like the Pacific Northwest coastal forests or the Florida Everglades. Here, reddish dust rose in tiny puffs with each footfall, and the scent of pine was sharp. If the ground had been level, finding one little boy would have been easy. As it was, however, the hill rising steeply from the Deschutes River was cut by narrow ravines with trickles of water that, in spring and early summer, would have been torrents. Every dip of ground had to be investigated, every clump of madrona or even long grass. Thank goodness this was late September and not August, when the heat would have had all of them dripping with sweat.

Melanie heaved herself up a clump of crumbling aged lava. Why couldn't Brandon Marsh have been wearing red or even royal blue? Why green?

A big tanned hand was suddenly right under her nose. She blinked and looked up into those unnerving gray eyes.

"Oh. Thank you," she said breathlessly, and let his hand engulf hers. Kevin, whose last name she didn't know, hoisted her up the last rise. Discombobulated by sensations she hadn't felt in a long time—the skitter of nerves in her palm, the warmth that traveled easily up her arm and down to her belly—she stumbled and bumped into him.

He was every bit as solid as he looked.

She jumped back and teetered on the brink. Steadying herself, Melanie mumbled, "I'm sorry. If I'd known what I was going to be doing today, I'd have worn my boots."

"Your shoes look sturdy." He still held her hand, as though he didn't trust her not to tumble back the way she'd come.

She couldn't imagine why.

"I almost wore canvas slip-ons," she admitted. As if he would care.

A smile touched his sexy mouth. "We haven't met. I'm Kevin McNeil."

"Melanie Parker. I had a troop of girls here today. My daughter's troop."

"Ah." He let go of her hand. After a small silence he asked, sounding overly casual, "Was your husband here to take her home?"

"Um? Oh, I don't have…" Could it be? Was he hoping she *didn't* have a husband? "I mean, I'm divorced. One of the other mothers took charge of the girls."

He made a pleased sound that sent a pleasant frisson tiptoeing up her spine. "Well, Melanie, we'd better keep moving."

"I can't imagine a four-year-old boy climbed up here."

"I can't, either." A grimace tugged his mouth. "This kid sounds like an adventurer, though. Let's hope…"

She knew what he hoped: that four-year-old Brandon *had* ventured into the woods and not onto a slippery rock in the river. She was glad not to be in the group that had followed the Deschutes downstream.

He headed toward a giant fallen ponderosa riddled with insect holes, Melanie toward a lava outcrop. No small boy snoozed in a cranny. Looking up, she spotted the man searching on her other side. They exchanged waves and a few shouted words.

The trees grew larger as the ground leveled, their rough boles sufficient to hide a child. She kept glancing to her left, where Kevin McNeil moved quietly through the woods, never a branch popping under his feet. He walked lightly, with a contained grace, no extraneous swing of the arms or bob of his head. A natural woodsman. It was easy to imagine him in buckskins and moccasins.

Several times, in the slow progress through the woods, Kevin came near enough for them to talk briefly.

"Not very many women in the search-and-rescue group," he commented once.

"I don't mountain-climb," she said somewhat defensively, "but I've always loved hiking, so I thought I could help in this kind of search even if I'm not strong enough to carry an injured man."

"I didn't mean that as criticism."

"But you did feel you needed to help me over a rough bit."

She'd have sworn his eyes darkened even as his voice deepened. "Needed? No. It just seemed like a good excuse."

He was flirting with her, the mother of an eight-year-old. She didn't have the experience often.

"Oh," she said inanely.

Obviously she didn't have the experience often enough, Melanie thought ruefully.

She was immediately annoyed at herself for worrying about something so frivolous when a child was missing.

A brief smile touched Kevin McNeil's eyes and mouth, but he turned away when a shout came from his left.

"Well, will you look at that?" he murmured.

She looked, and felt a burst of elation. John Clooney, who owned Elk Springs's major furniture store and who had been part of the group, was striding toward them with a sleepy boy cradled in his arms.

Shaking his auburn head in wonderment, Kevin put his whistle to his mouth and blew three short sharp blasts, the signal to gather. Then he took the walkie-talkie from his belt and spoke briefly into it.

In the distance Melanie heard other whistles.

"Hello, Brandon," Kevin said, when John had reached them. "Your mommy has been looking for you."

The boy buried his face shyly in John's chest. The adults laughed. When the whole party had gathered, they started down, taking turns carrying Brandon, who woke up and began to enjoy himself, bouncing on the men's shoulders and chattering.

"That," Kevin said to Melanie, "is one kid who needs to be kept on a leash. I've never approved of leading a child around like a dog, but there's an exception to every rule."

She had been very aware that he was right beside her in the descent. "Thank God my daughter's timid!" she exclaimed. "The worst she ever did was hide inside a clothing rack at the Emporium."

"What's she like?" he asked, matching his steps to hers. "Does she look like her mother?"

"A little." Angie's hair was a shade darker, her brown eyes a shade lighter, but she had Melanie's round face and snub nose. "Although she's going to be taller. Like her father. Right now, she's skinny, shy and sweet. Angie is the kind who stands up for a classmate when other kids are making fun of him. She has a good heart."

"Something tells me she gets that from you, too."

Flustered, Melanie stopped and let others pass on the narrow trail. "You're flirting with me."

"You noticed." For the first time, his lean tanned face looked wary. "You're not flirting back."

"I'm a mom! I don't know how." Now she felt incredibly stupid.

"But you're not married."

Someone else brushed past them. Melanie shook her head.

"Engaged?" When she shook her head again, he said, "Seeing someone?"

"No." Now she sounded as shy as her daughter.

"Ah." He had a way of investing that drawn-out sound with a rumble of satisfaction that brought warmth to her cheeks. "Well, then, Melanie Parker, would you have dinner with me some night?"

"But...I don't know you."

"I was hoping to remedy that." He took pity on her. "I've just started teaching at the community college. My brother is general manager at the Juanita Butte ski area. Scott McNeil?"

She'd read his name in the newspaper.

"I'm respectable," he promised, in that velvet-deep voice he used when he was looking straight into her eyes.

She did sometimes dream of finding a man she could love, of remarrying, of perhaps even having another child. But the odds had never seemed very good, given that she was thirty now and the good men her age in Elk Springs were generally married.

And she was not leaving Elk Springs, no matter

what. She'd decided that some time ago. She'd had a lifetime of wandering. This was home. Angie would grow up in the rambling old house Melanie had inherited when Nana died. She would never have to tearfully leave her friends behind or walk into a new school midterm, facing a roomful of mocking strangers. Angie, Melanie had vowed four years ago when she'd come home to Elk Springs for good, would always know where she belonged.

But Kevin McNeil was apparently single, incredibly sexy and established right here in Elk Springs. Dreams did come true, a small inner voice whispered.

"Okay." She sounded gruff rather than sultry, but her throat seemed to be constricting her vocal chords. "Yes. I'd like to have dinner with you."

"Good." His smile was slightly crooked, almost tender and heart-stoppingly sexy. "Now that we have that out of the way, let's go watch a reunion."

CHAPTER TWO

"WELL, WELL, WELL." Kevin rotated on his heels, gazing in wonder at the racks and heaps of fantastic, colorful costumes that filled the room like Aladdin's cave.

"You didn't ask what I did for a living." Melanie watched him from the doorway.

When he'd seen the sign outside her old house, the one arching above the white picket fence that bounded her yard, he'd asked to see some of the costumes. Somehow, he hadn't pictured such...profusion. Or the exquisite detail that made these garments light-years from the cheap Halloween costumes sold to kids for trick-or-treating.

"I couldn't picture what you did for a living." Something physical, he had guessed, despite her pale silky skin, a delicious contrast to her warm brown hair. But she was slim and fit and moved well. Besides, not that many women joined the search-and-rescue group. She might own a nursery or work for the county parks or make cabinets. "But I wouldn't have guessed something so..."

She folded her arms. "Outlandish?"

"Unusual," he corrected, eyeing an elaborate green velvet dress that might have been Elizabethan in style. With her smooth long hair and tall slender figure, Melanie would look gorgeous in it.

Unusual wasn't the first word that had come to mind, however. It was *domestic,* and this bothered him. The women he'd been involved with were biologists, park rangers, oil geologists. They were outdoorswomen, with lives often as nomadic as his.

But what difference did it make? he asked himself. He and Melanie Parker didn't have a relationship; they were going on one date. The future wasn't an issue.

She looked around now, too, her expression reminiscent, even bemused. "It started small. The granddaughter of one of Nana's friends was getting married. She complained about how mundane all the wedding dresses she saw were. She didn't want to look like every other bride, she said. I asked what she wanted to look like. She ended up with a Renaissance theme. Her dress was white and gold and absolutely glorious, if I do say so myself. The bridesmaids all wore deep-blue silk over gold embroidered underskirts, the bodices really low cut…" Unselfconsciously, she gestured at her own bosom, making all too vivid the picture she drew. "Slashed finestrella sleeves…" She blinked, apparently realizing she had probably lost him. "Anyway, the dresses were a hit. I'd been job-hunting, but I was asked to make the gowns for another wedding and then another. Eventually I branched out into other types of costumes. Now I rent, as well as sell. Obviously—" she touched an exotic Gypsy-style dress hanging beside her ''—this is my busy time of year. Usually more of these costumes are packed away.''

Kevin hadn't dressed up for Halloween in twenty years. Yet interestingly, most of these costumes were in adult sizes.

''What will *you* be for Halloween?'' he asked, tilting his head.

''Me?'' Melanie wrinkled her nose. ''A seamstress trapped behind my sewing machine making last-minute alterations. Somebody is sure to show up at the last possible second saying his costume doesn't fit.'' Her pursed lips barely hid her sudden merriment. ''Now, *you*…why, I think you have the legs to be a Regency dandy. Or maybe you'd prefer a seventeenth-century French getup with bloomer breeches fastened below the knees with garters. Striped breeches. Say, red and gold. Crimson tights work well below that. They accentuate the calves—''

Kevin recoiled. ''In your dreams.''

She pretended to look thoughtful, a smile playing around her generous mouth. ''I've never made chain mail, but I could try, if that's more your thing…''

He grinned. ''I can't say my tastes have ever been that kinky, but if that's what you're into…''

Melanie gave a startled giggle. She slapped her fingers to her lips. ''Oh, dear. I sound like Angie.'' Her pretty brown eyes reproved him. ''Maybe we should go.''

He rubbed a hand over the jaw he'd shaved only half an hour before. ''Maybe so. Although I'm beginning to wish we were going to a costume ball. So

I could see you in that dress.'' He nodded toward the green velvet number.

She glanced down at herself. What she was actually wearing was a short black skirt, black tights and a V-neck snug-fitting sweater the color of a ripe plum. She looked Bohemian, a young poet ready to go to a coffeehouse for deep and lengthy discussions about politics and art and love.

Hell, Kevin thought, forget the Elizabethan getup; he kind of liked her the way she was, hair swishing over her shoulder in a ponytail that had started atop her head and was already sliding down from its own weight. The other day, when he should have been focused on nothing but finding a four-year-old in green corduroy, his head had kept turning until he spotted Melanie Parker with that leggy distinctive walk. Bands of late-afternoon sunlight had broken between the pines above, awakening a quiet glow in her hair that had been tumbling from its confines then, too. It had looked like heavy silk.

He could hardly wait to slide his fingers into it and feel the thick strands slip like water between them.

A date, he reminded himself. This was only a date.

''We aren't going anyplace fancy, are we?'' she asked, sounding anxious.

''No need for velvet tonight.'' He crossed the room to her and touched her chin, lifting it until their eyes met. ''I like what you're wearing.'' Especially the way the skirt revealed those legs that went on forever.

Definitely a downside to the floor-length gowns of past centuries.

He took her to Mario's, a local pizza joint his brother had introduced him to the first week he was in Elk Springs. A thick yeasty crust and distinctive mix of cheeses made their pizza one of a kind. The place was big, barnlike, with private booths and candlelight. Comfortable, but atmospheric enough for an evening out.

Melanie didn't introduce him to her daughter and he didn't ask where the girl was. They chatted about nothing special on the short drive, then argued amiably over which pizza toppings to order before finally sitting down with a pitcher of beer. She barely sipped at hers, Kevin noticed.

Seeing his glance, Melanie made a face. "I get tipsy easily. Then I don't know how to shut up."

"Let secrets slip out, do you?" he asked, amused.

"Maybe."

"Tell me one now," he challenged her. "Or at least, something significant about you."

She didn't disappoint him. Her chin came up and she said, "I don't intend to ever leave Elk Springs. I've traveled all my life and now I'm staying put."

His reaction to her confident announcement was a peculiar mix. He'd never imagined staying in one place forever. The idea made him…edgy. Claustrophobic. He also felt admiration and even envy at her certainty—*he* didn't quite know what he was going to do with the rest of his life. And finally, a kind of panic rippled at the edges of his awareness. What was he doing here with her, a woman who lived behind a white picket fence, that universal symbol of domesticity?

"What kind of travel?" he asked. "Tell me."

While they waited for their pizza, she talked about her childhood as an Air Force brat. Her father had been transferred frequently, dragging his family along. Base housing was almost indistinguishable from place to place, but friends were always left behind.

"Florida, Germany, Japan, California, Washington—we never stayed more than three years anywhere. My daydreams were always of a real home. Marrying a boy I'd known since kindergarten." She grimaced. "So guess who I married?"

"A fighter pilot?" he hazarded.

"A baseball player."

He almost laughed, her answer was so unexpected.

"Minor league. Of course, we just knew he was going to make the big time, and then we'd have it all. For the moment, I'd travel with him and we'd live in crummy rental housing, but once he was a Yankee or a Blue Jay or an Angel, we'd buy a house and start a family, and I could join him sometimes on road trips, just for fun. The only thing is, he didn't make it that far. He got called up and then sent down again and then got traded. One town after another. We lived in lousy apartments and mobile homes, and half the time he was gone. I got pregnant by accident, and once Angie was born, it was harder. Ryan wasn't ready to be a father, he admitted." Pain finally showed on her gentle face. "Then I found out he was seeing other women when the team was on the road. There I was, trying hard to make a home, and he didn't want one."

As if by instinct, Kevin's hand covered hers on the table. "What did you do?"

"I came home to Elk Springs," Melanie said simply. "My grandmother lived here, in that house. My whole life, she was here. We'd visit, sometimes, for two weeks, or later I'd even stay all summer." She wasn't seeing him again, her gaze poignantly fixed on the past. "I had my own bedroom, upstairs under the eaves, with flowered wallpaper she let me pick out myself. It's Angie's bedroom now. Oh, how I wanted to stay and go to school in Elk Springs, but my parents wouldn't let me." Her voice ached with longing. "After my divorce, though, Nana welcomed Angie and me with open arms. She encouraged me to go into business for myself." Melanie's eyes met his again, the sadness in them telling him the end to this story. "She died last winter and left me the house."

"And you're never leaving it."

"That's right." She sounded utterly composed. "I want my daughter to grow up in one place, with friendships that span more than a year or two. I love what I do for a living, being able to walk at night without worrying, knowing the people in every business I frequent. I like to plant perennials and bulbs and know I'll see them come up in the spring. Hawaii in the winter might be nice—for two weeks. Then give me home." She smiled. "I think that's our number they're calling. Then it's your turn."

"My turn?" He slid out of the booth.

"Your secret."

His secret. Damn. Did he tell her about the bullet

he'd taken in his gut? Or the revelation he'd had afterward as he slowly recovered in a hospital bed?

Kevin grabbed the pizza and two plates, bringing them back to the table. He tried to figure out what to say to her as he dished up thick slices and swore when strands of cheese wrapped around his fingers.

Be honest about the changes in his life? Admit he was feeling his way like a man in the woods on a pitch-black night? One who knew which way to go, or thought he did, if he hadn't been turned around completely, or if the moon cloaked in clouds wasn't really behind him, instead of ahead?

Or stick to what he did know?

"Tell me something significant about you," she said, after enjoying her first bite.

"When I was growing up, I never wanted a home." *Scare her off, why don't you?* he thought, seeing her startlement. "My father loved the wilderness," he explained. "We camped, hiked, backpacked, cross-country skied. Every minute when he wasn't working, we headed into the backcountry. Scott loved the out-of-doors, too, but once he discovered alpine skiing, that was it for him. Me?" Kevin shrugged. "I liked the silence and the loneliness of the forest or the canyons. When you cross-country ski, the only sound is the swish of your own skis on the snow, the plop of a heavy clump falling from a branch. I like being in places where I'm the only human for miles. I dreamed of manning one of those lonely fire lookouts or testing the water in salmon-spawning streams in the Olympic Mountains."

"Then why did you become a college professor?" she asked tentatively.

"I've been in the National Park Service the past fifteen years. But it's changed." While they ate he talked about the crowds who were ruining the great wilderness areas saved as national parks; about the vandalism and the crime and the increasing role park rangers had as law-enforcement officers. "The pay is no great shakes," he concluded, "the housing is similar to what you described on military bases, the transfers got old... I found myself trying to restore meadows trampled by millions of feet, instead of interpreting the pristine wilderness for eager visitors. I woke up one day—" *in a hospital bed* "—and realized the job wasn't for me anymore. Scott told me about an opening here in Elk Springs, at the community college, teaching forestry and park management, and I grabbed it. He loves Elk Springs, it looked like a nice town on my visits, and if I hanker for the backcountry, there's plenty of it within an easy drive." He gestured, a slice of pizza in his hand. "So here I am."

"Then you've never taught?"

"I was primarily a naturalist with the Park Service, which means I spent the greater part of my career leading groups on nature walks, designing interpretive centers or hikes, writing handouts and so on. All teaching, in a way."

Melanie was easy to talk to. He admitted to his cowardice on the day he'd walked into his first classroom. But now he found the teaching stimulating. A few kids were taking one of his classes because it met some requirement and they thought it would be a no-brainer. Those were discovering their mistake. The other kids were excited. Many had grown up in Elk Springs or Bend or Medford, and they'd spent their youths hiking in these mountains or rock-hunting in the high-desert country. They wanted to know how to protect the wilderness, how to log responsibly, how to follow a career in the park or forest services.

The evening passed with incredible speed. Usually closemouthed, Kevin realized he'd talked away a good deal of it. When he wasn't talking but listening, he was captivated by Melanie's face. The delicate line of her cheeks, her small nose, the widow's peak her brown hair formed on her graceful forehead. All fascinated him and somehow added up to an utterly feminine face, which was also strong. He could see the will beneath the softness.

He had always had an image of women who were homebodies, whose greatest dreams were to sew and raise children, and they were nothing like Melanie Parker. As the end of the evening neared, Kevin found that his resistance to seriously seeing a woman like her was crumbling with nary a whimper.

Big deal. Another date. Another few dates. He wasn't asking her to marry him, was he?

And dammit, he had decided in that hospital bed to change his life, to settle down. Okay, he hadn't thought as far ahead as marriage or children or a white picket fence, but would it be so bad? He'd left the Park Service—although technically he was on leave and hadn't resigned. Maybe Elk Springs would become his permanent home. Maybe he'd met Melanie Parker for a reason.

"You're staring," she said.

He hadn't even realized she'd quit talking. "I'm sorry. I was thinking—" why not admit it? "—about kissing you good-night. Come on." He slid from the booth and held out his hand for hers. "Let's go."

Pink rose in her cheeks, but after only the tiniest hesitation she laid her hand in his and scooted out. Neither had brought coats, although the nights were starting to get cold.

Unfortunately downtown Elk Springs was bustling. People emerged from restaurants, and the gallery across the street had something going on. Music, light and voices poured from it. Kevin had a moment of frustration and even irritation. If he and Melanie were backpacking, they could be lying on their sleeping bags right now staring up at a sky spangled vividly with stars, not washed out by electric lights. Maybe the coals of a small fire would glow beside them. Didn't these people in town ever long for solitude, silence, a pure experience of the earth as it had been created?

Melanie saw his face and tugged at his hand. "Let's walk down by the river."

"Sure." His bad mood passed as quickly as it had come. He wasn't used to crowds anymore. He would adjust. Melanie might be just the person to help him.

A block away, they left behind the busy sidewalks and soon found the city park on the banks of the Deschutes in front of them. He'd have liked to throw rocks and break the lights illuminating the parking lot, but at least the grassy bank of the river was dark, the whisper of the river current more powerful than the now-muted voices behind them.

"This is more like it." The tension eased. "At last I can kiss you."

"You can only do it in the dark?" Gentle humor infused her words. "Does my face scare you?"

He framed it with his hands. His voice became husky. "Your face is exquisite. The tiny dimple that forms next to your mouth when you smile has been driving me crazy."

"Oh," she murmured, sounding shy. Her hands stole up to flatten on his chest. "I like your face, too."

"Well, kissing is a good way to seal our mutual admiration. And…express it more fully."

"Yes." Melanie spoke gravely. "I suspect that's true."

His head bent; his mouth paused a hairbreadth from hers. "I'm glad we agree."

She rose onto tiptoe and their lips touched, a soft tentative brush, then met again to linger. Exhilaration and desire crashed through him, but he resisted the powerful urge to yank her up against him. Nipping, sampling, he told himself to take it slow. She didn't strike him as a woman who would easily indulge in an affair. A husband went with a home. Until he knew he wanted to be any such thing, he had to be careful.

But moving away was one of the hardest things he'd ever done. "That," he said, in a voice only a little gritty, ''was the perfect cap to a wonderful evening.''

''It was nice, wasn't it?''

''Can we do it again tomorrow night?''

''I'm afraid not. I can't leave Angie too often.'' She hesitated. ''But she has a soccer game tomorrow afternoon. Would you like to come?''

I have a child, she might as well have said. He recognized the gauntlet: *Are you serious, or aren't you?*

Kevin took a deep breath and said, ''When and where?''

CHAPTER THREE

THE FOOTBALL SPIRALED through the floodlit sky and dropped neatly between the goalposts. The crowd in the stands, wearing parkas and gloves against the cold night, erupted to their feet to scream their approval. On the sidelines, the elk trumpeted his triumph and dipped his antlers in challenge to the team from Medford on the other side of the field.

Melanie smiled. The antlers had been a neat trick. She was rather proud of her elaborate construction of wire and plaster-cast material wrapped in brown cotton velvet. The head, too, she thought rivaled Northwest Coast Indian masks; she'd even used some cedar in a bow to the tradition. Now, if only the high-school kids took good care of the costume...

"Nice work," Kevin said from beside her. His gaze was following hers. "The kid playing the elk is having a helluva good time."

"He's Tiffany Schaefer's boyfriend—she's the baby-sitter I use most regularly. I understand that having a mascot for the high-school football and basketball teams was his idea. Obviously he's a bit of a ham."

"And that's Tiffany?" Kevin nodded toward the pyramid of cheerleaders, topped by a petite blonde.

Angie bounced on Melanie's other side. "She's really pretty, isn't she?"

Melanie didn't envy Tiffany's older sister, who was raising her. Tiffany was great with children, but sometimes impulsive. She was also ravishingly beautiful, a combination that would make any guardian nervous.

"Here we go," Kevin murmured as the Elks kicked off. The seconds were ticking down; that last field goal had put the home team ahead by six. Only a touchdown could beat them now.

Melanie had never attended an Elk Springs High School football game before, but the draw of seeing Tiffany in action, as well as the debut of the mascot, had been irresistible. When she had mentioned to Kevin that she and Angie were going, he'd promptly said, "Do you want company? Did I tell you I was the quarterback in high school?"

Angie, predictably, was bored and cold. She was far more interested in the antics of the cheerleaders than the action on the field, which she didn't understand. "How come he threw the ball away?" she would ask. "Why does the other team have it now? Why doesn't he get up and keep running?"

Kevin tried to explain, but Angie didn't really want to know what a "down" was. She wanted the game to be over so they could go for pizza, which Kevin had promised.

Medford made the mistake of trying to move the ball on the ground. Fourth down, three yards to go. The crowd stayed breathlessly on their feet, Melanie and Kevin among them. Linemen smashed into each other; bodies piled up. The ball came squirting out and, with a bellow, a stocky Elk Springs linebacker threw himself on it. The game was over.

Joining the mob filing out of the stadium, Melanie had to stop half a dozen times to talk to people she knew. It gave her great satisfaction every time someone called out her name. She loved that this was the kind of small town where she met friends, acquaintances and customers everywhere she went. Who would want to live constantly among strangers when you could have this sense of community?

Of course, she had to introduce Kevin over and over. He was relaxed and friendly, seeming not to mind the curiosity in people's eyes. As they crossed the parking lot, however, and Angie ran ahead to his four-by-four, he murmured, "Don't you date?"

"Not often," Melanie admitted. "Why?"

"I haven't been sized up that way since the first time I asked a girl to go steady. And that was in fifth grade."

"Nosiness is a human condition."

Being able to introduce him had added a delightful fillip to the evening, she had to admit, if only to herself. She could hardly believe she'd been so lucky as to have Kevin interested in her. Of course, she'd dreamed she might meet the right man and remarry someday. But Elk Springs wasn't loaded with possibilities. Then he'd appeared that day at the park, a newcomer in town. If they fell in love—Melanie didn't want to admit that she might already be half-way there—if they got so far, he would surely be willing to stay in Elk Springs. Why not? His brother was here, he seemed to be enjoying teaching at the community college, and as he'd said himself, central Oregon was perfect for a lover of the outdoors.

Some mornings Melanie had to pinch herself to make sure her happiness was real. This was their fifth date. Better yet, he was willing to do *real* things. For example, he'd not only attended Angie's soccer game, he'd volunteered to be the assistant coach for the rest of the year.

"I'm free afternoons," he'd said that day when the coach asked for volunteers. "Sure, I've played the game." Deftly stealing the ball from one of the girls, he'd started bumping it on his knee.

"Will you show us how to do that?" Angie had piped up.

Angie, predictably, thought the sun rose and set with Kevin. That part worried Melanie a little. She *had* only dated him five times. What if they *didn't* fall in love? Was Angie counting too much on Kevin always being around?

At the pizza parlor—more generic than Mario's, and also more to the taste of eight-year-old girls— most of the diners had been at the football game. The mood was jovial, the noise level high.

They grabbed a booth some teenagers had just left. Angie found friends and begged a pile of quarters off Kevin and her mom, after which she disappeared into the video-game room.

"You shouldn't have given her so many," Melanie said. "She won't give up next time she wants something from you."

"But I remember how frustrating it was when your

parents only doled out two quarters. They were gone in about thirty seconds, and then all you could do was stand around and watch other kids play.''

"Sometimes parents have to say no."

"Sure they do." He watched her with a small frown on his face, as if he sensed she was worried about more than the indulgence of a little money. "But was this one of them?"

"No," she conceded. "I suppose not."

His big hand gripped hers with the strength she loved. "She's a great kid. I like her."

But she *loves* you, Melanie thought. She couldn't say that, either. Wasn't even sure she wanted to. What was wrong with her? Ten minutes ago she'd been incredibly, idiotically happy. Now she was brooding about the future.

For once, why couldn't she just enjoy herself? Fall in love. Get her heart broken. It happened. She and Angie would survive. She'd be crazy not to take the risk. Especially considering how perfect Kevin was for her.

"I know you do," she said, giving his hand a squeeze. "She thinks you're great, too."

"You want to go hiking this weekend?" He grinned. "You know all the best places to go, right?"

Melanie immediately thought of a lake she'd always loved, nestled on the flanks of Juanita Butte. Five miles in, the walk was too long for Angie, so Melanie hadn't been in a long time. But maybe Angie could spend the day with a friend.

And maybe, just maybe, this late in the season the

trail and the shores of the pristine mountain lake would be nearly deserted. She and Kevin could be truly alone.

Not *that* alone! she chided herself instantly.

Of course, he saw her blush, she knew he did, but she only said briskly, "Deal."

His grin was positively wicked. "Alone at last," he murmured, and she blushed again.

He'd definitely read her mind.

"SO...LET'S TALK about logging. How do we balance the need for lumber and jobs with our responsibility for protecting the environment? Should the national forests *be* logged? Or is the Forest Service doing nothing but selling out the public interest? What about these timber trades? Let's talk."

Kevin leaned comfortably against the windowsill in his classroom. Twenty-five students in this forestry class. Five or six would be truly vocal, another few might chime in with a remark or two. The others he'd have to poke and prod.

Which he was discovering he was pretty good at. Sometimes he could even fire them up enough to fuel a good argument. They'd been studying logging practices, the new federal formulas for how much timber could be taken, the dismal financial picture for mills and logging communities. Now he wanted to know what they thought, where their convictions lay.

Tim Naber, who always had something to say, leaned forward in his chair. The kind with a small attached writing surface, it looked too small for his large frame. "The Forest Service panders to loggers. Their first obligation should be to save the public lands for future generations. Hell—I mean, heck— they're selling timber for practically nothing, anyway! They should at least be getting a fair price. No landowner would sell trees for what our government takes."

"You're right." Kevin spread his hands and looked around. "What do the rest of you think?"

"We're a government by the people for the people." The kid who spoke up was one who rarely participated. Now his cheeks were flushed with anger. "We restrict logging too severely and we're hurting people. Whole communities are living on welfare. Are owls more important?"

"Yeah," another kid agreed. "And if we sell the timber for as much as private landowners, more loggers will go out of business, and lumber will get so expensive people won't be able to afford to build houses. Like, is that what we want?"

The discussion—okay, argument—ranged freely after that, with Kevin occasionally refereeing. By the time he had to say, "Okay, let's stop here," he was pleased both with the fiery exchanges and the informed level of the entire discussion.

He'd made the decision from the beginning to encourage not only dispassionate analysis but also moral involvement in decision-making. Management of forests was no longer by the numbers. The issues were complex, and what was right or wrong was far from clear. He was getting these kids to think—and to see one another's viewpoints.

Teaching was proving more satisfying than he'd expected. Lying in that hospital bed after getting shot at Mount Rainier National Park, Kevin had known it was time for a change. But in truth, he'd grabbed this opportunity more to give himself a chance to reflect than to become a career college professor. Being shut in a classroom day in and day out—the idea had been anathema to him once upon a time.

He didn't have to decide yet what to do with the rest of his life—it was only October, he was committed to the college through May—but he was starting to think there were worse ways to make a living.

Whether or not he wanted to do it in Elk Springs…hell, he didn't know. He didn't even know if there was a permanent job here for him.

What he *did* know was that he should have told Melanie Parker some of this. He hadn't said, ''My teaching position is temporary.'' He hadn't admitted that he felt like an eighteen-year-old kid again, on the brink of a world full of possibilities but unsure which one to grab. No, not *again*—when he *was* eighteen, he'd known what he wanted to do with his life. He'd still be doing the same thing if he could have held on to the ideal: protecting the wilderness he loved, teaching others to do the same. But his disillusionment and frustration had been growing for years, coming to a head the day he'd ordered some drunken idiots to pack up the party they'd been holding in a fragile meadow, only to have one of them pull out a gun and shoot him.

He could still remember vividly the moment he fell, face smacking into a patch of late snow, the scent of rich earth and avalanche lilies in his nostrils. He'd heard the ensuing excited discussion, the thud of feet as they fled. He'd be dead if a mountain guide hadn't heard the gunshot and come to investigate.

Kevin didn't want to be cop. He didn't want to share his wilderness with drunks or with lazy folks who didn't bother to get out of their RVs or even with nice families who came to see nature's wonders but didn't respect them.

It was time to get into another line of business.

Okay, fine. But he should have admitted to some of his uncertainty about the future to Melanie. He'd been kissing her, when they had the chance, like a man who meant it. Not like one who was going to walk away as soon as he figured out his route.

She was adding to his confusion, because he was starting to think he didn't want to leave her behind. He was making himself go slowly, be sure. It would be easy to get caught up in this new life, think he was ready to make it permanent and then wake up one morning and realize a small town and a wedding ring and a stepdaughter were hemming him in unbearably.

But dammit, he liked the kid, and he liked her mother even more. Melanie insisted she wasn't ever leaving Elk Springs, but then, she'd been speaking as a single mother, not as a wife.

Whoa! he thought, locking the classroom door behind him. *Let's not get hasty here. Wife—that was a strong word.*

Too strong.

But he did enjoy thinking about her: the tiny dimple beside her mouth, her low throaty chuckle, the tenderness in her eyes when she talked about her daughter. His body tightened when he just pictured her leggy walk, the swing of hips, the graceful line of her neck and the heavy silk of that hair. He wanted her fiercely, and would have had her by now if she'd been anything but what she was: a woman who was made for marriage and motherhood, not hot sex that was…well, not meaningless—he hoped he'd never had such a thing—but not a symbol of commitment, either.

Walking across the campus to his office, appreciating the bright fallen leaves and the crisp autumn air, he figured life was good. Unsettled, maybe, but how many men his age could see so many possibilities waiting to be grabbed?

Maybe the experience was wasted on teenagers.

CHAPTER FOUR

"YOU'RE BEAUTIFUL," Kevin said, staring.

Pleasure spread in a warm tide all the way to Melanie's fingers and toes as he looked his fill. It was only the dress, she tried to tell herself. But the glow in his eyes made her suspect he was imagining her with the dress *off*, not admiring the heavy folds of velvet or the fit of the stiff bodice.

Well, maybe the fit of the bodice.

More warmth eddied. She couldn't blame the long-sleeved gown for making her feel overheated.

"Thank you, kind sir." Melanie dipped in a curtsy. "You make a handsome pirate."

He did look rather dashing in snug black pants and knee-high boots, a red scarf knotted on his head and a white shirt open at the throat with billowing sleeves cuffed at the wrist. He had refused the ubiquitous black eye patch.

"I want to be able to see you," he'd said simply.

Someone had wanted to rent the green velvet Elizabethan gown. The someone was a good customer, a doctor's wife whose daughter had just announced her engagement. Melanie should have been trying to please her.

But she'd heard herself saying, "I'm sorry, I'm

afraid that one..." *Is already reserved,* she'd been about to say, but what if the doctor's wife appeared at the same Halloween party Kevin was taking Melanie to? She'd swallowed and admitted, "I'm holding on to that dress for myself. The man I'm dating especially admired it." She waited for annoyance to spread across Linda Colvin's face.

Instead, her client had smiled with delight. "Really? You're dating? It must be serious." She'd moved a heap of garments from a chair and plopped down. "Tell all."

Melanie wasn't about to tell all to anyone, but she did admit that she was dating Scott McNeil's brother.

Tonight she hadn't invited Kevin over until after she'd accompanied Angie and three friends trick-or-treating in their neighborhood. That was another thing Melanie liked about Elk Springs—the fact that children could still safely accept candy from people they didn't know. It just seemed as if nobody in town was really a stranger. She could stop a woman on the street and in the course of chatting discover that she had a child in Angie's class at school or had been a bridesmaid in a wedding for which Melanie had made the gowns. Melanie knew at least by reputation many of the neighbors, even if she hadn't personally met them. At the wonderful Queen Anne house two blocks down, for example, lived Jack Murray, the county sheriff, who had recently married a woman who also hired Tiffany Schaefer to baby-sit. Circles of overlapping acquaintances—the very thing that made Elk Springs home.

"I've never met your brother," she said on the way out to the car.

"Scott is a good guy." Kevin opened the car door for her and bowed gallantly. "His wife is a cop. Did I say that? Half the people who'll be here tonight are probably cops, too."

Melanie adjusted her skirts and latched her seat belt, thinking what an anachronism she was, a sixteenth-century woman in a twenty-first-century vehicle.

When the costumed Kevin had joined her, somehow also looking appropriate behind the wheel of the manly vehicle, she asked, "What do a bunch of police officers talk about when they get together socially?"

"Nervous?"

"Maybe a little," she admitted.

"Don't be. They get grisly once in a while, but half the time you find the women talking recipes and children and the men sports or politics. Scott's adopted daughter must be close to Angie's age, plus, he has a toddler."

The driveway leading to Scott McNeil's modern cedar-sided home up the mountain highway was lined with paper lanterns in ghostly white with bats flitting as the candles flickered. A dozen or more jack-o'-lanterns crowded the front steps, and eerie music spilled out.

Melanie found her worries about fitting in squelched immediately. Scott looked enough like Kevin to be his twin; both men were broad-shouldered, athletic, tanned and auburn-haired. They slapped each other on the back in the affectionate way of men, and Kevin introduced Melanie to Scott's wife, Meg, and her sisters, Abby and Renee. All three were blond, elegant, attractive women with ready smiles and vintage gowns. Abby was a flapper, Renee a Gibson girl and Meg a Second World War woman of means.

"Ooh!" Abby exclaimed when she set eyes on Melanie. "I thought I looked good until I saw you. Wow. What a dress."

"Thank you." Melanie explained what she did for a living and discovered—of course—that the three sisters had heard of her. Renee, in fact, was good friends with Linda Colvin, the doctor's wife.

"We went to high school together, believe it or not," she said. "In fact, Linda's here somewhere…" She glanced over her shoulder toward the living room.

Melanie gave silent thanks that she hadn't lied about why she couldn't rent the Elizabethan gown. Honesty was indeed the best policy, she thought.

Further conversation revealed that Meg and Scott's adopted daughter, Emily, was in Angie's class. After that, conversation was a breeze.

In fact, Melanie ended up having a wonderful time. She liked everyone she met. The finger food was divine, the dancing, which spilled out onto a huge back deck, despite the chilly night, was fun, and Kevin was flatteringly attentive. It was with regret that Melanie realized the party was breaking up.

She'd been listening to Kevin tell stories about his days in the Park Service: about smoke-jumping, dangerous mountain rescues and nights spent tucked on precipitous ledges. All were entertaining, some funny, some suspenseful.

At the last minute one of the men who'd been listening said something that bothered Melanie enough she knew she'd have to think about it later.

"Don't tell me you're going to be happy shut in a classroom nine months of the year!" he said, shaking his head. "Sounds like the life."

Kevin laughed and demurred, but with some anxiety Melanie studied his face and would have sworn she saw regret there.

Surely only a reminiscent kind, she told herself quickly, a momentary sadness for times gone by. He wouldn't have quit his job as a park ranger and moved to Elk Springs if he wasn't ready to settle down. Would he?

As Kevin ushered her out the door, his hand firmly planted on the small of her back, Abby called after Melanie, "Can I come by your place and see it?" She smiled flirtatiously at her husband, a dark handsome man who was also a cop. "If you have more outfits like the one you're wearing, I may dress up more often."

Lieutenant Ben Shea smiled at his wife with an expression that made Melanie's heart skip a beat. Had anybody ever looked at her like that?

"You do that, honey," he said. "All I ask is, not too many buttons."

Abby elbowed him. Laughing, Kevin and Melanie made it out the door. The air had a real bite, and she saw her breath in the porchlight. A parka would have clashed with her dress, but she wished she had one now.

"Brr," she said. "I can feel winter hovering."

"Nine months of winter, three months of summer. Isn't that what they say about Elk Springs?"

She hurried to the defense of her home. "We have a spring. Sort of. And an autumn."

"Uh-huh."

She poked him and he laughed again, a deep comfortable sound. Then he wrapped his arm around her shoulders and murmured in her ear, "I'm tempted to insult your beloved town just to see you get fired up."

Was she that bad? "I get fired up about other things," she said defensively, then wished she could snatch the words back.

His voice became a sexy rumble. "Oh, I'm counting on it."

"I didn't mean..."

"I know you didn't." He opened the door of his four-by-four. "Hop in, milady."

She let him give her a boost and rather enjoyed the way his hand lingered on her hip. His hand often lingered, she'd noticed, as it had on the small of her back earlier. In fact, most of the evening he had kept a hand on her arm or back. Either he was someone who liked to touch, or he was very very attracted to her. She rather hoped it was the latter.

He went around and got in on the driver's side, but instead of belting himself in, he reached for her. "I've been wanting to kiss you all night," he said huskily, and bent his head.

Melanie met his mouth eagerly. She loved the feel of his hand cupping her head, his fingers working in her hair, his grip on her arm. His knuckles brushed the side of her breast, and she sighed.

A groan vibrated in his chest and the kiss deepened, his mouth suddenly hard and demanding. His tongue touched hers, and she was the one to moan. His hand flattened on her breast; she pushed against him, frustrated by the hard bodice of the dress.

His laugh against her mouth was ragged. "How the hell did people make love in those days?"

Breathlessly, she said, "I'm not sure they wore underwear."

"Ah." Briefly his hand flexed on her thigh. "Interesting idea."

Very. She imagined him throwing her skirts up, dropping to his knees... A spasm deep in her belly almost made her moan again.

Headlights flashed in the rearview mirror, and Kevin swore, pulling back. "My sense of timing..." he muttered.

"It's okay. I... The baby-sitter..." She straightened her skirts, fought to steady her voice, couldn't help shrinking away. "I really should get home."

She was a coward. He would have suggested she go home with him—she knew he would have. She *wanted* to. But give her thirty seconds to think, and what did she do? Chicken out, of course. Women on the movie screen and in books made love anywhere and everywhere all the time. Heck, probably real women did, too, the ones she saw at the grocery or the stationery store. If they met a man and were attracted, they had sex with him. It wasn't as if Angie would ever know, Melanie thought miserably, and she was entitled to a life, wasn't she?

But she just couldn't do something like that so casually. She needed to be very sure.

She needed to know she loved him.

In silence, Kevin started the engine and put the vehicle into gear. Some of the Halloween lanterns had flickered out, while others burned low, wisps of mysterious light on each side of the wooded lane. Melanie stared fiercely out the window and tried not to cry.

What if he asked, *Will you come home with me?* Would she really tell him no?

Not, she admitted to herself, if he once looked at her the way Ben Shea had at his wife Abby, with such passion and tenderness and intensity. With such...love.

Oh, no, she thought, her stomach lurching. She couldn't be in love. Not already! Not when Kevin had said nothing to suggest he was thinking about wedding bells and forever.

His voice, edged with something indefinable, broke the silence about the time he made the turn onto the mountain highway. "Hey. I didn't mean to get carried away. I'm sorry if I upset you."

"No. Oh, no!" she exclaimed. "I, um, enjoyed... I mean..."

"Enjoyed is good." His hand reached over and clasped hers, warm and strong. "I did, too." After a moment he asked, "Did you have fun tonight?"

"I had a wonderful time!" She hesitated. "You're quite a storyteller."

"In other words, I dominated the conversation," he said ruefully.

"Oh, no! Everyone enjoyed your stories. You know they did. You kept talking because people kept asking questions." Very casually she added, "Do you miss such an adventurous life?"

"Miss it?" He shot her a look she couldn't interpret with only the light from the dashboard. "Remind me sometime to tell you about my last day as a park ranger. That part I don't miss. Sure, I have moments where I feel…restless. But, you know, those were the exciting bits I was talking about tonight. Most of what I did was considerably more mundane. The nature walk for families is not exactly a stroll on the wild side."

"No," she said cautiously, "I suppose not. No regrets, then?"

"Regrets are for old men." He sounded almost arrogant. "I still have the chance to choose what I want to do with my life."

And what he had chosen was to live in Elk Springs. Relief loosened tension she'd hardly known she was feeling. She'd been silly; she could have told funny stories about her days as a minor-league baseball player's wife, too, but that didn't mean she wanted to go back.

"I like your attitude," she decided. "Most people are so…settled by our age. It must be exciting to change careers."

"I've noticed," his voice became a notch huskier,

"that my personal life seems to be changing in a big way, too. You have something to do with that, you know."

Her heart squeezed. Did he mean...? Was he hinting...? He must be!

"I can't comment," she said lightly, "since I don't know what your life was like before you met me."

His hand found hers again. "One hell of a lot emptier."

"Oh." Her heart was drumming. "Kevin—"

"Home sweet home." He pulled up to the curb in front of her house and turned off the engine. The baby-sitter pulled back the curtain and peered out. Sounding regretful, Kevin said, "Looks to me like you're eagerly awaited. And that we'll have to continue this discussion another day."

Another day? Could she bear to wait?

Did she have a choice?

"I was lucky to get Tiffany tonight. I had to bribe her, big time. She's probably hoping to slip out with her boyfriend and egg a few houses before dawn."

He laughed, and the moment was lost.

To be recaptured, Melanie reminded herself.

Soon.

CHAPTER FIVE

WEARING AN IMPRESSIVE stovepipe hat and a black wool suit—borrowed from a family of Civil War reenactors—a very short Abraham Lincoln walked onto the stage, cleared his throat and waited for the audience to quit whispering. Voice unexpectedly gruff for an eight-year-old, he declared, ''Four square and seven years ago, our fathers bought forth on this continent, a new nation, con...conceived in liberty, and dedicated to the pop station that all men are created equal.''

Beside Melanie, Kevin covered his mouth and cleared his throat. She knew very well that he was disguising a laugh. She was glad he'd made the effort. Eight-year-olds were so very earnest.

After a strong start, the young Abraham Lincoln struggled with the remainder of the Gettysburg Address, his voice faltering, his wide desperate gaze occasionally turning to the wings of the stage for a cue. But at last he finished in triumph, ''...and that government of the people, by the people, for the people, shall not perish from the earth!''

Enthusiastic applause evoked a pleased smile and a deep bow from the boy, who was immediately succeeded on the stage by an equally short Elizabeth

Cady Stanton, performed by Angie Parker. Her severe Quaker-style gown had been created by her mother, just as Lincoln's suit was.

In a huge rush, she whisked through her speech. "Resolved, that it is the duty of the women of this country to secure to themselves their sacred right to the elective franchise," she concluded, curtsied and dashed from the stage.

"Definitely a star," Kevin whispered.

"Well, I don't know about that..." Melanie whispered back, pleased despite herself.

One historical character after another appeared on the stage in a grand cavalcade that Melanie rather enjoyed. She kept sneaking glances at Kevin to see if he was bored, but if he was, he hid it. Not that she would feel guilty if he was—he'd invited himself when Angie had proudly told him of her role in the school performance.

Afterward the kids came from backstage, still in their costumes, to receive their parents' congratulations. Kevin swept Angie into an extravagant hug. "Kiddo, you were fabulous."

"I talked too fast, didn't I?" Her anxious gaze sought her mother. "I practiced talking really really slow, and then I could hear myself going fast. Was it awful?"

"Kevin's right." Melanie hugged her, too. "You were great. Only a little bit fast."

"Really?" The big brown eyes, so much like her father's, searched Melanie's face.

"Really," Melanie said firmly. "In fact, the whole

performance was wonderful. I want to tell Mrs. Jensen so while you're changing."

Her daughter shuffled her feet. "Well, um, a bunch of the girls are spending the night at Chelsea's. Can I, too?" she pleaded.

An instinctive protest rose to Melanie's tongue. With Angie away for the night, she wouldn't have the excuse of having to get home for the baby-sitter or not being able to ask Kevin in. She would have to tell the truth: *I'm not ready*. Or, *I need to know you love me.*

Or, was it possible she'd realize she *was* ready?

She stole a glance his way and saw he was waiting for her answer as much as her daughter was. His eyes had darkened, become intent; although he hadn't moved and was seemingly relaxed, she *felt* the difference, as if his sudden tension crackled through the air.

Melanie drew a deep breath. "Of course you can, Angie. If—" she held up one hand "—it's okay with Chelsea's mother and this isn't something you girls have cooked up without asking."

But, no. She didn't get off so easily.

Chelsea's mom, a laid-back woman who worked at the U.S. Forest Service office, agreed that she'd let Chelsea invite up to five other girls. "They won't be any problem, I promise. On the way home, we'll rent a video, and I'll order a pizza later, in case they get hungry. I can run Angie home around lunchtime, if that's okay," she added.

"I don't need my toothbrush or anything," Angie assured her mother. "I can just sleep in my T-shirt."

It felt like a conspiracy. Melanie might have been suspicious if she'd thought there was the slightest chance Kevin knew Chelsea's mom. But, in trying to get the girls organized and out to her van, she hardly seemed to notice him.

Left with him in the gymnasium as the crowd eddied out, Melanie said, "Well."

He waited.

"I've been deserted."

His narrowed eyes focused on her mouth. "Not by me."

"I noticed," she admitted.

"Shall we go?"

"Oh." Of course. They had no reason to wait. "Sure."

Outside, under the yellow sodium lamps in the school parking lot, Melanie couldn't think of a thing to say. She waited while Kevin unlocked the four-by-four.

"It feels like snow," she surprised herself by announcing.

"It does," he agreed. "Where does Chelsea live? Will Angie be able to get home tomorrow if six inches falls?"

What a nice man, she thought warmly. The last thing he must want was for her to dash across the parking lot and tell Angie, who was even now squeezing into Chelsea's van, that she couldn't spend the night, after all. Yet he was suggesting that very thing, if need be.

"Angie could walk if she had to," Melanie said. "It's not that far, and she loves the snow."

"Ah." He waited while she got in, then circled to the driver's side. "I've never asked whether you're a skier," he said as he settled behind the wheel.

Grateful to have a topic—any topic—that wasn't emotionally loaded, Melanie chattered all the way to her house about the skiing lessons she'd had when her father was stationed in Germany, including her crush on her instructor and the resulting improvement in her grasp of German.

"I thought I'd completely forgotten how to ski when I moved back here, but do you know, it must be like riding a bicycle, because it came back easily. Although I'm no more than intermediate! The Olympic team won't be recruiting me."

He parked in her driveway and turned off the engine. Melanie tried to think of something else to say about her skiing ability and failed.

After a prolonged silence, Kevin said, "Shall I wish you good-night?"

Crunch time. "I..." She bit her lip. "Would you like to come in?"

So often, it seemed, important things were said when she couldn't see his face well enough to make out his expression. "You don't have to ask me." He sounded grave.

"I...want to." Suddenly she knew she meant it. She was still nervous, but she understood now that her heart didn't lack certainty. Her problem was that she felt like a teenager on the brink of her first time. It had been so long; would she know what to do? Would Kevin think her breasts were small? Would *she* please or disappoint him? Would she be disap-

pointed, and discover she'd built up a mere crush into
the love of the century? "That is," she finished, a
different kind of uncertainty overtaking her, "if *you*
want to."

"Oh, yeah." His voice took on a rough cast. "I
want to."

On the way up to the porch, she wondered with
belated social anxiety what drinks she had available
to offer him. The occasion seemed to call for wine.
Hadn't her parents left a bottle on their last visit?
She had a corkscrew; she knew she did.

Her fingers were shaking as she unlocked the front
door and let them in. His felt remarkably steady
when he reached up to unzip her parka and slip it
off her shoulders.

Now she could see his face, and the hot glow in
his eyes made her tremble.

She was going to offer him...something. Herself.
No. A drink.

He tossed their parkas onto the back of the couch.
Eyes never leaving hers, he took a step nearer,
wrapped his hand around the back of her head and
bent to kiss her.

All thought vanished. She only felt. The heat of
his mouth, the thrust of his tongue, the strength of
his hand, the solid wall of his body. Kissing him back
felt like the most natural thing she'd ever done.
Groaning, he gripped her hips and pulled her tightly
against him. She wound an ankle around his, tugged
at his hair when he tried to lift his mouth from hers.
They were both panting for breath when he nipped
at her neck.

"My bedroom…"

He yanked her turtleneck over her head. Pins fell and her hair tumbled to her shoulders. He growled something prayerful and buried his fingers in it. "Beautiful."

She was struggling to get his shirt off. She had it up to his armpits when she saw the livid scar on his flat belly. Her hands stilled, and he froze at the same moment.

"What happened?" She sounded as shocked as she felt. She touched it lightly. "You never said. This looks new!"

"Not that new. It's been almost six months. I was shot."

Melanie let his shirt fall. "But…what happened?" she repeated, feeling dense. He'd been shot only six months ago and never said?

He let out a sound. "I'm sorry. I should have told you. I did say something once."

"You said something?"

"When you asked if I missed my old life. I said I'd tell you sometime about my last day as a park ranger."

She remembered the casual way he'd said it, as if something absurd, not dead serious, had happened that last day.

Kevin reached for her. "I don't like to think about it."

Melanie backed up a step, feeling the need for distance. "You must have realized I'd see the scar."

"It's nothing I'm hiding." He frowned, but more as if irritated at himself than at her. "It's why I left the Park Service. No, not why. Just the last straw. I'm a naturalist, not a cop, but the public is destroying the parks. I came across a bunch of drunks partying somewhere they shouldn't have been, and when I asked them to pack it up, one of them pulled a gun and shot me. He's in prison now. I spent weeks in the hospital being fed by a tube, and I made the decision to get the hell out.''

"Because you were shot." She felt numb.

"Yeah..." He caught something in her tone. "No! Not because I was shot. Because my role was changing. Because it wasn't what I wanted to do anymore.''

"You suddenly decided you wanted to be a college professor.''

He eyed her warily. "The opportunity came along and I grabbed it. Dammit, Melanie, what's wrong? Why is the fact that I was shot such a big deal here?''

"Because you never told me!'' she flared. "Because you don't want to talk about it. Because life decisions made in the hospital after something like that happens may not be lasting ones.''

"What the hell does that mean?''

"It means—'' she hugged herself, conscious of her near-nakedness ''—that you might end up missing what you had.'' *It means that you might end up leaving Elk Springs. And me.* "Mostly, it bothers me that while I was telling you everything I consider important about myself, you didn't mention that a bullet prompted your arrival in town.''

Kevin swore. "Melanie, I love you.''

She should have been thrilled, not wondering

whether that was one of those things men said at such a moment. "Then—" she nodded at his stomach, covered by his shirt "—why didn't you say anything?"

"Male pride?" He let out a long breath and rubbed the back of his neck. "That, and—" he grimaced "—I guess I didn't want you to think just what you're thinking now. That this was impulsive. That I'll recover and realize I've made a mistake."

"You know, it never would have occurred to me...*then*." She imbued the one word with significance. "Now, I have to wonder if *you* aren't the one who's starting to think you were impulsive."

Kevin took a quick step toward her. "Melanie, this isn't what matters. It's how you feel about me, and how I feel about you."

"I guess—" she hugged herself harder "—that's what scares me."

Somehow his arms were around her again, his warmth enveloping her. "It scares you that I love you?"

"It scares me that you're who you are and not..."

His muscles tightened. "A local yokel who owns his own construction business?"

She went stiff in his embrace. "That's right. A man with roots."

"Which part matters to you?" He was suddenly angry, and could she blame him? "My roots? Or who I am?"

"You," she whispered, "of course. But..."

His jaw flexed. "But?"

"This." Her hands fluttered. She was trying very

hard to cover her cleavage, exposed by her laciest bra. "I'm sorry. I thought I was ready, but I'm not. This is my fault for...for..."

"Leading me on?" His laugh was harsh. "Don't be ridiculous. We both wanted to be here. But I suspect you're right. You're not the only one who needs to do some thinking."

Why did that hurt? She didn't let herself figure that out.

"It's just as well that...something stopped us."

"Yeah." He tossed her turtleneck to her. She clutched it to her bosom like a maidenly spinster. Kevin's voice softened marginally. "Good night, Melanie." He stepped forward, kissed her lightly on the mouth and left.

She wondered if she would hear from him again.

CHAPTER SIX

THE KNOCK on his office door brought Kevin's head up. He wrote "A—excellent" in red pen, his handwriting slashing across the top of the paper he'd just read. Others were spread across his desk.

"Come in," he called.

His visitor was unexpected. The president of the college, a vigorous sandy-haired man, opened the door. "Kevin. I'm glad to catch you. I have someone here I'd like you to meet."

At only forty, John Hunnisett was young to have the position. Formerly the director of admissions at a private university, he'd been brought in just this past year, word had it, to make major changes. Since the ski area had opened at Juanita Butte, Elk Springs had grown at a tumultuous rate, the college alongside the town. Hunnisett had recruited not just Kevin but other new faculty members aggressively, while some tenured professors were being eased out.

Kevin rose to his feet behind his desk. "John, good to see you."

A gray-haired, stocky man with shrewd eyes followed John Hunnisett into Kevin's spare office.

"Roger Sterling," he said, shaking Kevin's hand.

"I'm at the University of Oregon. I've heard good things about your teaching."

"Thank you," Kevin said warily. "Have a seat. What brings you here?"

Sterling sat, crossed his legs and said straight out, "We're discussing ways to offer four-year degrees from the university here in Elk Springs. For the moment, just in a few departments. As you know, we've already begun in Education. Another area that interests us is yours. Tell me how feasible you think it would be to expand the Forestry and Park Management programs into a four-year major."

The two men left half an hour later, their purpose accomplished. They wanted Kevin to design the program, become chairman of the department, consult on hiring colleagues. They wanted him to become tenured, instead of temporary.

They wanted to tie him down.

After their departure, he automatically graded another paper. "B—competent but could have been more thoughtful. See comments." It had taken all his concentration to make it through one five-page paper. He couldn't face another. Setting down his pen, he shoved back his chair.

He'd had only morning classes today; it was still barely one o'clock. Kevin felt a sudden desperate need to be out-of-doors. The walls were closing in.

Within an hour he left his vehicle at the trailhead to Puma Lake, swung a day pack over his shoulder and strode past the wooden sign that said "Puma Lake 2.3 miles." A good eight inches of snow had fallen up here this past week, but eager cross-country skiers, snowshoers and hikers had worn the snow from the trail. It climbed sharply between tall stands of ponderosa pines, then dropped over a ridge toward the lake, a chilly blue-gray under snow-heavy skies. His stride was that of a man accustomed to covering miles in a day. His breath came out in clouds, his arms swung freely.

As always, his thoughts untangled out here in the wilderness and solitude. Okay, he was being pushed to make a decision sooner than he'd expected to have to, but was that a bad thing? He should feel flattered that, after only one quarter of classes, feedback should be so good on his teaching. He had to work; he was finding he was good at this. So why not?

Now he had a solid future to offer Melanie, too. The other night, as she'd clutched that turtleneck to her breasts and stared at him with huge panicky eyes, he'd almost asked her to marry him. But what could he say? *I don't know where I'll be next year, but I want you with me?* Romantic, but not what she wanted to hear right now.

It would mean resigning from the National Park Service once and for all. Knowing he was on a leave of absence only had felt like a safety valve. He could recuperate, try a new life but know his old one was still open to him. He imagined himself sitting down to write that letter of resignation. Visiting one of the national parks that had been his old stomping grounds, driving in and paying his fee like all the tourists in their RVs, staying on the marked paths, seeing old friends and having nothing to say.

Reaching the lakeshore, he paused and listened to

the silence. How often would he find himself alone in a place like this again? Puma Lake would be surrounded by families picnicking most of the year. How often would he have the time to seek solitude?

Frowning, he set out again with his ground-eating stride to circle the small lake. He actually felt short of breath, which irritated him. He still hadn't recovered, had been too sedentary. He needed to add some miles to his daily run. Push himself.

Maybe it was too soon to make a decision. Sure, Melanie wanted to stay in Elk Springs, but if she loved him, she would go if that's where his heart led, wouldn't she? He could see how the school year went, how hemmed in and confined he felt.

He could ask Melanie to marry him and find out whether she had balked the other night because of fear about who he was—or because she didn't really love him.

Kevin drew a deep cold breath and blew it out in a frigid stream. His lungs seemed to expand now that he'd let himself off the hook. Not that long ago he'd been lying in a hospital bed. Melanie had accused him of doubting his own motives. Maybe she was right; maybe she wasn't.

He'd given himself a year to decide what he wanted for the future. *Take it,* he told himself. *Be sure.*

WHEN HE CALLED Melanie that night, he got only her answering machine. Kevin hung up without leaving a message. He wondered if she was screening her calls because she didn't want to hear from him, or whether she wasn't home. The idea that she might have gone out with another man made him grind his teeth.

Dammit, this was the trouble with dating a single mother. He couldn't come by in the evening for a serious talk—Angie would be around. Okay, how about after his last class tomorrow? No, he had several students scheduled for appointments, and by the time he was done with them, Angie would be home from school. Thursday at Angie's soccer practice. Hell, they'd decided not to hold practice this week, the weather was getting so cold. Sunday was the last game of the season.

He still hadn't made up his mind how to approach Melanie when fate intervened the next day. He was crossing the quad when he heard her name mentioned by a pair of coeds going in the opposite direction.

"…speaker today. Melanie Parker. She's bringing historical costumes. She's supposed to be really entertaining."

Kevin spun around and trailed the girls. "Excuse me," he said.

They turned to stare at him.

"I couldn't help overhearing your conversation. Melanie Parker is speaking on campus today?"

"Well, I don't think it's open." The coed flushed. "I guess you're not a student, are you?"

"No, I'm an instructor here."

"Well, she's talking to my class."

"And which class would that be?" He spoke with eroding patience.

"Oh. World History 102."

He extracted the remaining details from her. Time, building, classroom. He'd have to cancel one meeting, but to hell with it. Jason Bernard was trying to plea-bargain for a higher grade than he'd earned last quarter, but Kevin had already turned in his grades, and even if he hadn't, he wouldn't have changed Jason's.

At two o'clock, he strolled into the back of one of the auditorium-style classrooms, where the larger survey classes were held. Students were still settling into seats and whispering. Up front, Melanie was laying out garments, presumably so that she could reach them easily later. The moment he saw her, he felt pleasure and relief and frustration. Why did this one woman exert such a pull?

Her hands were slim, quick-moving, competent, her neck long and graceful. Her every move was sure, contained; she didn't toss her hair or laugh or fidget when nervous. She had a quality of…stillness, or perhaps, serenity.

Solved, Kevin thought wryly: the mystery of why she attracted him so greatly. In her very being, Melanie possessed the one quality he had spent his life seeking.

He made his way down the side of the auditorium until he found a pillar where he could lean inconspicuously but was close enough to see and hear her well.

She never did spot him as she gave a forty-five-minute presentation that held the students enthralled. Her point, not surprisingly, was that fashion reflected both culture and life on a nitty-gritty level. She stripped to a hideous undergarment, causing a stir in the auditorium, and had two girls from the front row manhandle her into a corset and tie it tightly enough to create the wisp of a waist Victorians sought. Then she showed how the corset and hoops affected her mobility, how, in essence, the garments forced her to behave with the propriety considered the ideal. The fingerless gloves often seen in photos were to keep hands warm in inadequately heated houses, she told them, describing how the lower classes who did have to work dressed.

Kevin found her talk as fascinating as the students apparently did. Creating Halloween costumes was the least of her skills, he saw. He imagined her taking her show on the road, perhaps filming educational videos, creating similar presentations on ancient Greece or Egypt or the Druids. It wouldn't matter so much then if she had a home base....

Kevin was honest enough with himself to recognize when he was being self-serving. Yeah, if she agreed to marry him and he went back to the Park Service or took up another essentially nomadic career, he and she could talk about ways she could refocus what she did. *But don't kid yourself,* he thought grimly; Melanie *likes* her life here. She was not going to jump at the idea of doing presentations around the country and announce that really she wanted to sell her house and hit the road.

He waited until the professor's offer to help her pack up had been refused, until the last students were exiting the auditorium. Then he stepped forward.

"You were great."

Melanie started, a pair of lace fingerless gloves dropping from her hands. "Oh! You were here?"

He couldn't tell if she was happy to see him or dismayed. "Saw the whole performance."

Pink suffusing her cheeks, she bent her head and went back to packing the Victorian garments into suitcases. "Do you think the students got anything out of it?"

"You brought history alive," Kevin said, meaning it. "They learned more today than they will the rest of the quarter."

She stole a glance at him. "Thank you," she said quietly.

"I wanted to talk to you. To apologize."

"Apologize?" Melanie didn't look up this time. "For what?"

"For not being honest." He moved restlessly, not liking the feeling of being in the wrong. "Without thinking it through, I knew you preferred the idea of my being settled here in Elk Springs, being a college instructor, instead of on temporary leave from the Park Service. So…there were things I didn't say."

She carefully folded a black gown. "That's what you're on? Temporary leave?"

Inwardly he cursed; he hadn't meant to tell her that way. Hadn't meant to imply that he was still considering going back.

"No. I mean, yes, but only in the bureaucratic sense. I didn't submit my resignation for all the reasons you mentioned the other night. I wanted to be sure I wasn't making the decision impulsively. I gave myself a year to think about the future."

"And this is that year."

"Yeah. I didn't expect to meet someone like you, certainly not right away."

"Someone like me?" She sounded distinctly cool.

Hell, he was going about this all wrong. "I didn't expect to fall in love."

She stopped what she was doing at last and met his eyes. "Are you so sure that's what you've done?"

Anger sparked. "Have I given you that much reason to doubt me?"

"No," Melanie said, "of course not. You've been nice to Angie."

A door at the top of the auditorium opened. Kevin cast a frustrated glance up, but no one had come in.

Feeling pressured, he forged on. "I want you to marry me. Will you?"

"Oh, Kevin." Terrible sadness sounded in her voice. "I wish you hadn't asked. Not now."

"Why not?" His tone was aggressive. Talons of fear tore at his chest from the inside.

"You know why. I swore I'd raise Angie here in Elk Springs, give her the life I didn't have. I married someone once who wasn't...wasn't settled. How can I make the same mistake again, just because I'm..." She stopped.

"Because you're what?"

"Falling in love," she said in a low voice.

Relief didn't join his other emotions. He knew better. Instead, he swore. "You love me, I love you, but you won't marry me."

"I can't!" she cried, eyes brimming with tears. "Love isn't the only thing that matters, you know!"

"I thought it was the most important," he said bitterly.

Grief formed lines on her face, killing the serenity he so admired. "I made a vow."

"And you'll hurt both of us to keep it." He squeezed his eyes shut. "Think about what you're doing, Melanie. Just think."

Hands at her sides, she stared at him. "I will," she whispered. "How can I help it?"

He left her there, unmoving, although students had begun to filter in from the top of the auditorium. His anger and frustration were too great for him to give a damn that she might be left in an awkward position.

They were even too great for him to admit that he'd blown it, that he shouldn't have asked. Not like that, not then.

So why in hell had he done it? Someone else looking in might suggest he'd sabotaged his chances on purpose.

He swore softly as he stalked outside.

Had part of him *wanted* the answer he'd gotten?

CHAPTER SEVEN

SHE'D KNOWN he was too stubborn a man to leave things alone. Melanie preferred to think that way— of him as stubborn—than to believe he loved her too deeply to accept her refusal.

A lead weight had lain on her chest since he'd proposed. He was everything—almost—that she had dreamed of finding. Kind, tender, patient, sexy, even good with her daughter.

Everything but honest, a glowing kernel of anger reminded her. Everything but the settled resident of Elk Springs he'd led her to believe he was.

She'd told him from the beginning what she was determined to have for herself and for Angie, and instead of being similarly honest, he'd lied by omission. He had *made* her fall in love with him, knowing the whole while that he had more in common with her ex-husband than he did with her ideal. If he was hurt, he deserved to be, she told herself.

Her own hurt…well, perhaps she deserved it, too, for being so blind to the many hints Kevin had dropped, for her foolish trust.

The very next day she was cutting out an Edwardian-style gown from pale peach silk when the doorbell to her business entrance rang. Instantly, in her bones, she knew it was him. She was very tempted not to answer it. Pull in her head like a turtle.

But he'd be back of course. Why not get it over with? She refused to think that she might be hoping he could change her mind, that he would announce he'd bought a house, resigned from the Park Service, that he would do anything, be anything, if only she would be his. She wouldn't believe it if he *did* say all that. People didn't change so easily.

When she opened the door, Kevin stood on the small side porch, hands shoved in the pockets of his parka, his russet hair disheveled. Behind him, the sky was gray and cold, promising snow that had yet to fall this winter in Elk Springs.

She'd known it would be him, and yet still she felt a ripple of purely sexual response to his presence.

"Can we talk?" he asked, creases seemingly worn overnight between his brows. "Don't say no. Please. I just need to understand."

Wordlessly Melanie stood aside, letting him pass her, his big body so close she smelled aftershave and the chill of the air.

He walked to her sewing table and touched the silk. "Beautiful," he murmured, then turned to face her. "Like you."

"I'm far from beautiful," Melanie said uncomfortably. "I'm…rather ordinary."

"Not to me." His voice had the texture of sandpaper. "Tell me why you won't take a chance on me."

"I told you." She didn't move from her stance by the door. Her hands were squeezed together painfully. "From the very beginning I told you. I've spent my whole life never belonging anywhere. I will not live that way again, and I won't do that to Angie."

"Your childhood was so unhappy?" Kevin asked in that same voice, the one that would have scraped her palms if she could have grasped it.

"Unhappy?" Strangely, she felt taken aback. "Not entirely. Of course not. But I hated the moves—"

He interrupted. "Were your parents happy? Did they love each other? You?"

"I...yes," she whispered, then repeated more strongly. "Yes. They were excited about a transfer. A new place. Sacramento? They talked about day trips to gold-rush ghost towns and the Sierra Mountains. Germany? The Alps, the Rhine, beer fests." The child in her still resented the sparkle in her mother's voice as she'd tried to coax her eldest daughter to share their anticipation. Yet the adult Melanie couldn't help reluctantly seeing Kevin's point: that perhaps she was blanking out the happy times and focusing entirely on her childish fear of the unknown, her certainty that she would never make a new friend. She continued, "I'm glad I saw the Alps and skied at Squaw Valley. But I would have traded all our adventures for the chance to grow up feeling secure, knowing I'd have a best friend to whisper with at school, that if I got lost..." She stopped, knowing how nonsensical that sounded. "Knowing I *wouldn't* get lost just walking home."

Of course, he heard what she hadn't finished saying. "You did get lost."

"Yes. In… I don't remember where." She didn't want to remember, had never even asked her mother about the episode. "All I know is, nobody spoke English and a strange man was following me, and…" She had been terrified. "I had bad dreams for years."

A frown gathered on his brow. "You won't marry me because you had nightmares as a child about being lost in a strange place."

"No! That isn't why I won't marry you!" He was deliberately misunderstanding. "You lied to me. How can I marry a man I can't trust?"

Kevin swore. "Melanie, I will never lie to you again. I wouldn't do anything to hurt you."

"You already have," she said starkly.

"Give me a chance."

How she ached to do just that! To gamble that he would never lie again, would try to make her happy.

"A chance to do what?" she asked, just above a whisper. "Take me to dinner again? Or put a wedding ring on my finger?"

"Can we at least keep seeing each other?" He was begging and, typically for a man, was angry to have to be. "We don't need to make decisions about the future now."

"Which is certainly your preference." Hearing her own waspish voice, Melanie wished she could snatch back the spiteful remark, make it unsaid. That had been her anger speaking.

Kevin stalked toward her, his face darkening.

"Dammit, Melanie!" he said between clenched teeth. "Is considering a change of career in your thirties evidence of instability? Unreliability? You seem to have found your vocation rather late in life for you to be sneering at me."

"I didn't mean…" Melanie faltered.

"Didn't you?" he asked softly. "I suggest you watch yourself. You're going to stifle your daughter."

Her chin shot up in outrage. "Don't you dare criticize how I choose to raise my child."

Still in that silky voice, he said, "Is that what I would have gotten as her stepfather, too? Butt out?"

Actually she'd thought how wonderful it would be to have someone like him to consult, to offer another perspective, to lean on those days when parenting was so terribly lonely. But her temper wouldn't let her admit it.

"*If* I thought you were the man I wanted to marry, I would have trusted you to be Angie's father. So the point is moot, isn't it?"

He visibly flinched, a muscle jerking in his cheek.

Shame cooled her anger. "I'm sorry." She made herself say it. "That was cruel."

"I would have been good to Angie."

Her throat closed. "I know," she whispered.

Kevin reached out and gripped her arms. "I don't want to lose you, Melanie."

She felt as if she was saying goodbye to any chance of romance or marriage. The man she'd thought she wanted wouldn't be Kevin. Could she really promise forever to someone kind and steady, who liked to stay home evenings and watch football, who probably had a paunch and no curiosity about the world beyond the Elk Springs city limits? No. After Kevin...no.

She was weakening and knew it. Deliberately she remembered one apartment where she'd lived with Ryan. The cockroaches and the freezer that incessantly needed defrosting, and the neighbors who had angry visitors at strange hours. The elementary school down the street with graffiti-covered walls and no grass.

Or the last move, when she'd just painted the kitchen a soft lemon yellow and made curtains. But Ryan had come home, grinned triumphantly and announced, "I'm on my way up, baby!" and they'd had to pack everything they owned that night. The twelve-hour drive with Angie crying in the back seat and Melanie with no idea where they'd sleep that night or what the new apartment would look like.

Kevin saw both her weakening and her ultimate decision on her face, because he let out a low animal sound and pulled her to him. His kiss was desperate, hungry.

She melted into the kiss, grasping the front of his parka to hold on as her knees buckled. Anger and regret seemed to have burned away the restraint that had kept their kisses polite. Now his tongue forced its way into her mouth, and she tangled it with hers.

For one moment Kevin lifted his head. His eyes were nearly black, his skin seeming to be stretched taut across his cheekbones, his whole face blazing with intensity. "I need you," he said in a raw voice that made her tremble inside. "Don't do this to us, Melanie."

Her every nerve ending was alive. She could not seem to pull back from him, though the hard thrust of his body against her belly made his desire plain.

Heaven help her, but she needed him, too, if only this once. "I want you," she managed, though tremulously. "I can't marry you, but...I do want you."

Another guttural sound, and he'd lifted her onto the sewing table and laid her back on the peach silk. A pin pricked her, but it felt unimportant, nothing compared to the hands lifting her shirt and unfastening her bra to free her breasts. Nothing compared to the hard smooth wall of his chest beneath her palms as she slid them under his sweater. Nothing compared to his hot urgent mouth, to the way her thighs parted to urge him closer.

His mouth on her breast was another sensation of such clarity that she wondered dizzily if she had ever really felt sexual need before. Her back arched and she made muffled sounds that should have embarrassed her. *She* was the one tugging at his buckle, trying frantically to free him from his jeans, though he still wore his parka.

Perhaps he had more presence of mind than she did, because he pulled back long enough to shed some clothes and to peel her jeans from her legs. For a moment she was chilled and her knees clenched together; what was she doing, desperately trying to couple with a man on her cutting table? On top of a precious bolt of shot silk?

But the moment he ripped his sweater over his

head and she saw his bare chest and shoulders, pale red-gold hair shimmering against an expanse of tanned skin, muscles moving smoothly beneath, the rush of sexual heat seared her inhibitions. Once he put his mouth against her calf, kissed and nipped and then trailed it higher, she lost any last ability to resist.

With a moan, she parted her legs again, silk fisted in her hands at her sides, and begged him to...no, not kiss her *there,* not this time. This time, she wanted him inside her.

He must have been carrying condoms, because suddenly he was putting one on with shaking hands. Then he rose over her, blocking out the world. Her fingernails bit into his shoulders as he thrust, a long slide that stretched her in ways she'd forgotten, or never experienced, she didn't know. She only knew that having him buried inside her was painful and exquisite, and she didn't want him to leave, even to pull back. He smothered her protests with kisses and pulled away only to surge deep inside her again. And again and again, until her body convulsed in pleasure so intense she understood at last why this moment was called ''the little death.''

She held Kevin as he moved a final time, as he groaned and she felt the ripples deep inside her. For a timeless moment, Melanie floated in a blissful sea of physical satisfaction, of tenderness, of love.

And then another pin pricked her hip, and this time she felt it, so sharp she knew it had drawn blood.

Just as she knew nothing had changed. She couldn't let it—not for her sake, and not for Angie's.

But for just a few more minutes she could revel

in his weight on her, his warmth, the slam of his heartbeat, the way he murmured her name. For just a few more minutes she could pretend that this was the first time.

Not the only time.

CHAPTER EIGHT

HIS CROSS-COUNTRY SKIS whispered on the snow. His rasp of breath was the only sound in a world cloaked in white. No, not entirely. To one side, a whirr made him turn his head in time to glimpse a flash of brilliant blue wings against the white and deep-green backdrop.

Scott had recommended this trail, a long easy rise to a ridge where, he promised, Kevin would see the valley and the town of Elk Springs spread out below him. Kevin had canceled his morning classes and counted on being alone.

His muscles ached pleasantly, his lungs expanded to take in deep drafts of cold air. Another sound, and he saw the brown rump of a deer bounding away at the sight of him. This was where he was happiest— alone, in the woods. His mother used to shake her head and swear he would have been one of those unshaven mountain men if he'd been born in another century. He'd thought she might be right. He had never needed other people in the way even Scott had.

The idea of "other people" skimmed Kevin's mind, took form and face, a tumble of dark hair, passion-clouded eyes, soft mouth, breasts as white as snow. Kevin gritted his teeth and tried to wall her out. In this solitude he could unclutter his mind, understand what was most important to him.

Of course he instantly saw Melanie again, this time as she told him with quiet finality that no matter what had just happened, she still couldn't marry him. She didn't even know if it was a good idea to keep seeing him.

"It hurts," she had said, in a small husky voice that cracked. "I'm so tempted to let myself love you and forget what it might mean. Maybe Ryan and I would have stayed happy if I hadn't hated our life so much. Maybe I soured our marriage with my unhappiness. I won't go through that again. I won't, Kevin. Don't ask me."

Trying to leave the memory behind, he skied faster, planting the poles with vicious stabs, driving himself in a near sprint. He wanted to be angry, contemptuous of a woman who wouldn't take risks. But how could he? They'd had great sex. Okay. Otherwise, all he was offering her was an open-ended future that must read to her like a rerun of her first marriage. He'd said it himself: Park Service housing was often pretty seedy. It was usually miles from the nearest town, making a long bus ride for schoolchildren. Friendships evaporated the moment you were reassigned.

It was the perfect life for a man who craved solitude, shunned commitment, cared more about the health of an acre of forest than why his neighbor suddenly looked hungover every morning and why only one car was now parked in their driveway.

It was the worst possible life for a woman who

craved community, longed for ties of friendship and family, wanted neighbors who knew one another's business.

They were what they were. Clearly not meant for each other.

Kevin was racing now, muscles burning, his breath near sobs. He was where he loved to be. This was all he needed. Anguish filled his chest. Slamming pulse, lungs frantically snatching at oxygen. Heart breaking.

He burst from the trees. A last steep crest covered with new-fallen snow lay before him, a sky as huge and achingly blue as any he'd ever seen arching above it. Making a crosshatch with his skis, leaving behind V prints, he climbed with scarcely broken stride. *This* was what he needed. All he needed. All he'd ever wanted.

With a harsh cry he topped the ridge and saw the spectacular sweep of country beyond. The high desert land, dusted with snow far below him, stretched as far as his eye could see, broken only by the meandering Deschutes River and the new—in geologic terms—lava cones that made the soil rust red.

And by the town sprawled below the forested foothills. Elk Springs.

His gaze didn't hunt for the horizon or study the petite lava cones that looked like scoops of ice cream dumped on the flat landscape. He was too busy seeking out familiar landmarks. His gaze didn't pause at the community-college grounds above town, the high school on the other side, the redbrick public-safety building where his brother's wife was chief of police.

There, that stretch of green, was where he and Melanie had walked along the river at night, where he had kissed her. He couldn't make out individual houses, but he found her neighborhood, her street.

Always before, when he drove into town—any town—for groceries, on the way back to the park he would leave behind with relief the last stoplight. He'd shake his head and wonder why anyone would want to live there.

Today, for the first time in his life, he looked down on a town and saw home. He stared until his eyes burned and he had to blink hard.

Would living in that old house with Melanie be so bad? She had a big yard with bird feeders and a tire swing—he remembered with fondness a tire swing his father had hung from an old elm that had probably long since been felled by disease. He had always wanted a dog, something that wasn't possible when you worked in the national parks. He had a feeling Angie would back him on that one.

He could commit to setting up the four-year program at the college. Kevin admitted to himself that he was getting a kick out of teaching. And he'd always enjoyed the challenge of planning new displays or programs. When this one was up and running like clockwork...well, that was years away. Maybe he'd still be content. Maybe Melanie would be willing to consider a move then, when Angie was grown or nearly so.

Leaning on his poles, Kevin bowed his head. His solitude and the wilderness weren't enough anymore.

Every time he went hiking or cross-country skiing, he wished Melanie was with him.

And Angie. He wanted to be a father to the kid, the kind of father she'd never had. He could tell she had liked it when he helped coach her soccer team. She'd never given any sign of resenting him.

Lifting his head, Kevin looked down at Elk Springs, spread beneath him like a topographic map he could touch. His heart swelling in his chest, he wished he was there and not at a dreamlike distance looking on.

Right this minute it seemed to him that was what he'd spent a lifetime doing: looking on as other people lived. Maybe that was what his discontentment this past couple of years had been about. Not the abuse of the wilderness by the great American public, but his own loneliness. Maybe he hadn't wanted to know why his neighbor was hungover, hadn't wanted to talk about the wife who had gone for good, because if he looked too closely, he'd see himself: someone who came home to an empty soulless house at night, who preferred a canopy of stars because it had a glory his own life lacked.

Maybe he'd come to Elk Springs looking for more than space to think, a clearing to rest his head at night for a while. Maybe he'd been looking for home.

Why hadn't he realized sooner that he had found exactly what he needed and wanted most?

With sudden decision, Kevin swung his skis back the way he'd come and shoved off, crouching to take advantage of the steep downward slope. He hadn't quite figured out how to convince Melanie of his change of heart—but he couldn't wait to start trying.

MELANIE CLANGED the lid back onto the garbage can. She could have hand-washed the crumpled stained silk—but she didn't want to. Discarding it felt symbolic, as if she had put into the garbage can her own foolishness, as well as a bolt of fabric.

Hurrying back into the house she'd thought was still empty, she bumped right into Angie.

"Oomph!" Holding her daughter up, Melanie staggered against a kitchen chair. "Oh, my gracious! I'm sorry! Are you all right?"

Angie blinked. "I think so."

"You're home from school." Brilliant.

"It's three-thirty," the eight-year-old pointed out with irrefutable logic.

"Is it really?" Her gaze went to the clock on the stove. "The day's flown." *Liar, liar, pants on fire.* Actually the day had crept on hands and knees. She had started cutting out the Edwardian dress for a customer, using a lemon-yellow silk, instead. Her concentration had been so poor she'd made several mistakes that wasted fabric and twice stabbed herself with pins, bleeding on the silk, besides. It was a relief to call it quits.

Angie dropped her book bag on a chair and headed for the refrigerator. "Is Kevin coming to dinner?" she asked, taking out the milk. "He hasn't been here all week."

Put on the spot, Melanie was tempted to hedge. She'd been trying in vain to think of some way of broaching the subject. Or perhaps she simply hadn't wanted to put into words a failure as great as her marriage.

Instead, she said honestly, "I'm...not sure I'll be seeing him again."

Angie spun around. Milk splattered. "Why not?"

"You're spilling," Melanie said automatically. "And I decided not to keep seeing him because he probably won't be in Elk Springs next year, anyway."

Tears welled up in Angie's eyes. "Doesn't he want to take us with him?"

"Take us...?" Melanie's breath whooshed out and she went to her daughter, gently taking the milk from her. "Oh, honey." Melanie tried to enfold her in a hug.

Angie jerked back, glaring through her tears. "I thought you'd marry him! I thought he'd be my dad!"

Melanie swallowed, a lump in her throat. "Kevin's job means he moves a lot. Every couple of years. You know he was a park ranger, and he's thinking of going back to that. If he does, he'll always be living out in the middle of nowhere. You'd have long bus rides to school and maybe no friends your age as neighbors, and I'd have to give up my business."

"So?" Pain and rebellion in every line of her thin body, Angie evaded another attempt to hug her. "He told me all about the places he's been. They're so cool! I want to leave Elk Springs. I *hate* Elk Springs."

"You don't mean that."

"I do mean it! I do! I want to go with Kevin!"
Bursting into tears, Angie ran from the room.

Melanie stood in the middle of the kitchen, listening to her daughter's feet thunder up the stairs. She
felt more inadequate than she ever had in her life,
even when she'd realized that Ryan didn't want the
home she was trying to make.

Sinking into a straight-backed kitchen chair, she
buried her face in her hands. Why hadn't she fore-
seen this? Angie had never really had a father. Of
course she'd fallen in love with Kevin! How could
she help it, when he had always been willing to in-
clude her, always treated her like an equal, had even
done something as special as helping coach her soccer team.

Angie just didn't understand what they would both
be giving up if her mom married Kevin. She didn't
remember much from before the divorce. Always
feeling rootless—she had no idea what that was like.
How important it was to know where you belonged.

Melanie knew she should let her daughter cry, wait
until a cooler moment. Her own tears crowded her
eyelids, as they had all day. But she couldn't let Angie mourn by herself upstairs, while she sat here at
the kitchen table feeling more alone than she had in
years. Alone and scared and hollow.

Using a paper towel to scrub away the dampness
on her cheeks, she went slowly upstairs. She let her
hand slide along the banister. When, as a child, she
visited Nana, she'd often slid down the banister. She
suspected Angie did, too. The walnut was polished

from a hundred years of hands and bottoms, wearing it to a fine patina.

Family photographs hung along the staircase. At the bottom, Nana's parents, posing with a Model T Ford, her mother wrapped in fur, little guessing what the Great Depression would bring. Nana as a girl, eyes big and solemn, and as a young woman with her first teaching job.

The years passed as Melanie climbed, the silky wood trailing beneath her fingertips.

Granddad, fine in his wedding suit. A few steps up hung the photo of him in front of his first store. Then the two together, bowed by the years, but proud in front of this house, bought in the early years of their marriage. Their daughter, baby pictures to wedding pictures. Melanie herself, as well as her much younger sister. And finally, Angie.

This house was their history, Melanie thought sadly. Her daughter's and hers. So why tonight did Nana seem to look back at her with reproach? Why was it so obvious that the photographs could be hung anywhere, that she, Melanie, took her memories and her heritage with her wherever she went?

She knocked on the door to Angie's bedroom. A small voice said, "Go away."

"Please." Melanie bit her lip. "Can we talk?"

She took the silence for assent and opened the door. Angie had flung herself down on her four-poster, face in her pillow.

Melanie sat beside her and gently rubbed her back. "Maybe I made the wrong choice," she said sadly, "but I've told you before how much I hated moving. I never had a friend longer than three years, until I came home to Elk Springs. I didn't want that for you.''

"But he could be my dad.'' Angie said through her tears. "I'm good at making friends. I wouldn't mind new friends.''

"This house…''

With sudden passion, Angie rolled over, her body stiff. "You always said people are what's important. Not things.''

Melanie's tears began to fall, hot and slow. "I did, didn't I?''

"I guess you can't marry him just so he can be my dad. Not if you don't want to.''

Oh, but she did want to!

"My work…''

Her daughter squeezed her hand and said, voice tentative, "Couldn't you keep making clothes and sell them somewhere? Or…or keep renting them, like you do now, but have someone else do it?''

Could she afford to pay overhead on a shop that wasn't connected to her house? And someone's salary? And who could she trust long-distance?

Suddenly she was thinking. It might be possible. Or what if she started a catalog, something she'd given passing thought to. Might there be other Park Service wives who'd be interested in working for her?

"I like walking to the bakery on Saturday mornings.'' Knowing how dumb that sounded, she said it, anyway.

"We don't every week.''

"But we *can*.''

Her daughter's forehead crinkled. "Wouldn't you like to walk somewhere different?"

No. That was the trouble. She wanted the familiar, not the new. She hadn't an adventurous bone in her body. But...*might* she be willing to walk somewhere different, to take the chance that it would become familiar, if the right person was beside her?

The answer was so obvious she knew her foolishness wasn't safely stowed with the ruined silk in the garbage can.

People *were* what mattered. Love was what bound her to her daughter and her parents and grandparents and their parents before them. This house...had been a refuge. She did love it, but it couldn't hold her, make her laugh, dry her tears, smile at her in the morning and bed her with passion at night. No house could give Angie what she needed.

Melanie *had* hated moving so often, both as a child and as a young wife. But would she have been so unhappy if Ryan had been different? If he had come home eagerly, played with his daughter, helped paint each new apartment? If instead of being impatient and irritated, wanting only to hang out with his new teammates, he had teased her and helped with the moves? If he had truly loved her, and she him?

If he had been Kevin?

"With Kevin," Melanie said softly to Angie, "I might like walking anywhere at all."

The dawning joy in her daughter's eyes matched her own. "Then...you changed your mind?"

Fear still gripped her heart, but a shaky smile showed itself. "Yes. Yes," she said wonderingly. "I think I have."

CHAPTER NINE

ANGIE HAD A FRIEND over, so Melanie didn't think much about the whispering and thumps she heard from other parts of the house. Once, when the door to her sewing room creaked, she called out, "Angie? What are you doing in there?"

"Showing Samantha some of the dresses." Wide-eyed, Angie had appeared in the doorway to the living room. "That's okay, isn't it, Mom?"

"Sure," she'd said absently. Her mind was on more than whether two eight-year-old girls would be careful with the costumes. She was trying to figure out how you called a man you had brutally rejected and said, *Gosh, I've changed my mind. Ask me again.*

She'd hurt him; Melanie knew she had. What if he'd changed his mind? She'd basically told him that she didn't love him enough to make any adjustment whatsoever in her life for his sake. Would it be any wonder if she'd killed his love?

Finally, heart pounding, Melanie picked up the phone and dialed his number. She owed him at least this much. Besides, for her own sake, as well as Angie's, she had to do something other than wait and hope.

As the telephone rang, her throat closed with terror. If he'd answered, her voice probably would have failed altogether. As it was, she listened to his voice message, took a deep breath and said, "This is Melanie. I, um, I've been thinking. I did say I would." She sounded timid, like somebody calling to ask for a loan. "Could we—" her voice squeaked "—well, could we talk again?"

She dropped the phone back into the cradle as if it were roasting hot and buried her face in her hands. She'd sounded like an idiot! Would he even bother to call her back? She should have gone over there, instead!

Which would have done no good since he obviously wasn't home.

Obviously? Heck, for all she knew, he'd been sitting there listening to her talk to his answering machine.

Melanie's hands muffled her whimper.

The house was awfully silent now. She could hear her own heartbeat. If the phone rang, it would scare her out of her skin. Melanie lifted her head and stared at it.

Would he call back? Come over? What if he did show up only to say, *Sorry, too little, too late?*

She realized five minutes had passed and she was still staring at the phone, as if willing life into it. *Do something!* she ordered herself.

Pay bills. That would do to keep her mind occupied, give new direction to her brooding. A cherry secretary desk, inherited from Nana along with the house, stood by the small-paned front windows. In the cubbies, Melanie kept bills, receipts, envelopes and stamps.

This month's check statement had arrived and was still unopened. She took out a calculator and soon discovered her checkbook was $2.49 off. In her favor, but she was determined to find the error, anyway. Doggedly she pursued it, but kept finding herself staring at the string of nonsensical numbers on the calculator. *Concentrate!* she told herself fiercely.

She almost managed, which might be why it took a moment for the murmur of voices in the hall to register. One of those voices was more of a…rumble. Distinctly masculine. And it said something like, "Thanks. Now go upstairs and don't come down until I call you. Promise?"

Melanie surfaced; her calculator read $1,973.73. Why, she didn't know. Her checking account rarely held that much money, and certainly didn't right now.

…don't come down until I call you?

Trembling, she swung in her chair to face the doorway. Through it strolled a Victorian gentleman in an elegant brocade smoking jacket, cravat and black trousers, with a pipe nonchalantly held between his teeth. A large handsome gentleman with russet hair and gray eyes.

"Kevin?" she said faintly.

He took the pipe from his mouth and said agreeably, "Indeed, my dear. But not the Kevin you know. This one is a fellow of means dressed to reflect his domestic contentment." He did a slow turn, as she had when showing students the garments. "He's pleased to be home, man of the house."

She gaped.

His expression changed. The pipe clattered to an end table. Voice hoarse, he said, "If you'll let him be."

"I made that jacket." As if it mattered.

"Jacket?" Kevin looked down at himself and gripped the lapels. "You mean, this bathrobe thing?"

"It's a smoking jacket."

"Oh." His face held heart-stopping vulnerability when he looked up. "Angie said it's what a father would wear at home. When he really belonged."

She still sat in the straight-backed Queen Anne chair. Her mind didn't seem to quite grasp the implications. "I just called you," she said stupidly. "Did you already get my message?"

"Message?"

"Wait!" Melanie remembered the door to her sewing room opening and closing, the whispers and shuffles. With near outrage, she asked, "You've been here all this time?"

"Well..." He shifted uneasily. "For twenty minutes or half an hour. It took us a while to find the right outfit. Angie wanted me to be a cowboy and lasso you. I had to convince her that wasn't the right message."

"*Angie* conspired with you?" Of course she had! Wasn't that what he'd been telling her?

"I'm afraid so," he said apologetically. "But I did ask her."

Melanie frowned. "She didn't call you?"

"No, I called her. Once I realized."

Finally they'd arrived at the heart of the matter. "Realized what?" she almost whispered.

"That Elk Springs *is* home now." His voice took on a rough urgency. "That you're what I've been looking for. You and Angie. I don't want to go back to the Park Service. I've been happier here these past months than I've been in years. Ever." He closed the few feet between them and dropped to one knee in front of her, seizing her hands in his. "Melanie, marry me. I won't uproot you. I swear."

Her fingers curled to grasp his. "But...you can."

There was a momentary silence as he studied her in perplexity. "Can what?"

"Uproot me." In a rush she said, "That's why I called you. To say that I did think, like I said I would. And I realized that I don't want to be left behind. If...if you really love me, I'll go anywhere with you."

"But you've told me how much you hated moving!"

"It wouldn't be my first choice," she admitted. "It was hard when I was a kid. I'd be dumped into a new school, and when I walked into class the first day, it always felt as if everyone was sneering. I was never wearing the right clothes or..." She stopped. "That doesn't matter. The thing is, I could have been happy with Ryan if he'd been different. If our marriage had been different. Mostly, I was unhappy with *him*. I was...like a girlfriend, not a wife. I was desperately trying to create a home everywhere we went,

and he didn't want one. The guys were all single."
She concluded simply, "He wanted to be one of
them."

Kevin's grip tightened. "He must have been
crazy."

"I've thought of ways I could continue working,"
Melanie continued on a flood of hope. "No matter
where we go."

"And Angie?"

"She makes friends easily." It was painful to admit the problem had always been hers, never her
child's. "Having a real father would mean more to
her than anything in the world."

Kevin squeezed his eyes shut and bowed his head
for a moment. Melanie's heart cramped. Had she said
something wrong? Was he having second thoughts
now?

But when he looked up, exultation blazed from his
eyes. "You have no idea what it means to me to
have you willing to give up every damned thing you
value to come with me."

She blinked back tears. "We can put the house up
for sale. Or…or keep it as a rental. Maybe someday…"

"Not someday." He let go of her hands to frame
her face, to brush his thumbs over her mouth.
"We're going to live here, sweetheart. The college
has asked me to stay on, to build a new program in
park management that will offer a four-year degree.
I've accepted. I could buy a house of my own,
but—" he glanced around "—this one looks appro-

priate for a college professor. If you don't mind sharing it.''

"You're doing this for me.'' That was all she could think. He was offering to give up everything *he* valued, for her. Hot tears welled in her eyes.

His fingertips caught the tears. Voice low and tender, Kevin said, "A selfish part of me wants to say yes. Let you think I've made a sacrifice. But the truth is, falling in love with you has made me understand a little sooner what I really want out of life.''

"And that is?'' She held her breath.

"You.'' His lips were against her cheek now, warm, seeking. "Angie. Friends. Family. Home.''

Their mouths met for a soft sweet kiss. Melanie's mind became hazy, but she had enough sanity to argue before it was too late.

"But…when you talked about your job and the places you've been…'' She groped for the right words and found them. "You had such passion.''

"Yeah, I did.'' He stood and pulled her up with him. "But I was also lonely. I didn't quit just because I got shot, Melanie. I wasn't lying when I told you I'd been unhappy before that. My job had changed, I didn't like the new direction, and… I guess I'd reached an age where I was looking around and noticing that everyone else had something I didn't. Home and family.'' He gave a short laugh. "Maybe it was Scott's letters that did it. The guy dove into the family thing from the high platform. He and Meg adopted a little girl, Meg had a teenage boy already, and then Meg got pregnant. Every letter he wrote was so damned happy, I could hardly stand it. Now I know—he had the right idea.''

Melanie felt as if she were in free fall. No, a parachute had caught her; she was floating now, not tumbling. ''Does that mean, um, that you might like to have other children?''

A sexy grin blazed on his face. ''Oh, I'm counting on it, sweetheart.'' His hands were wrapped around her waist, his thumbs grazing the underside of her breasts. ''Unless you have some objection.''

''No.'' Blast it, she was crying again. ''None,'' she blubbered.

He kissed her fiercely. Against her mouth, he said huskily, ''I wish we could start right now. But I'm not that sure my orders will be followed.''

''You mean, to stay upstairs?'' Through her tears, a giggle rose in her throat. ''I'm pretty sure I just heard a bump in the hall.''

''*What?*'' He swung around and roared, ''Angie Parker, you come out this minute!''

The doorway stayed empty for a moment. Then Angie edged into sight, head bowed, sneaking a peek up. ''I'm sorry,'' she said remorsefully. ''I just couldn't wait! But I did make Samantha stay up there.'' A tiny smile puckered the dimple in her cheek. ''Mommy said yes, didn't she?''

''Yep.'' His grin was as wide as a winter quilt. He flung his arm out. ''Whaddaya say, kiddo? Group hug?''

Angie ran to them. Melanie got tears in her eyes as the three of them closed their arms around one another.

"No." Over her daughter's head, Melanie met Kevin's gaze. The expression in his eyes was all she'd ever hoped to see. "Not a group hug," she finished softly. "A *family* hug."

HARLEQUIN®
SUPERROMANCE®

You are now entering

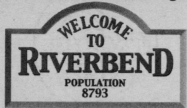

WELCOME TO
RIVERBEND
POPULATION
8793

Riverbend...the kind of place where everyone knows your name—and your business. Riverbend...home of the River Rats—a group of small-town sons and daughters who've been friends since high school.

The Rats are all grown up now. Living their lives and learning that some days are good and some days aren't—and that you can get through anything as long as you have your friends.

Starting in July 2000, Harlequin Superromance brings you Riverbend—six books about the River Rats and the Midwest town they live in.

BIRTHRIGHT by **Judith Arnold** (July 2000)
THAT SUMMER THING by **Pamela Bauer** (August 2000)
HOMECOMING by **Laura Abbot** (September 2000)
LAST-MINUTE MARRIAGE by **Marisa Carroll** (October 2000)
A CHRISTMAS LEGACY by **Kathryn Shay** (November 2000)

Available wherever Harlequin books are sold.

HARLEQUIN®
Makes any time special ™

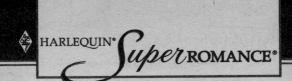

They spent a snowy night in each others'
arms. Now there's a baby
on the way....

SNOW BABY by Brenda Novak
(Superromance #939)

Chantel Miller has fallen for Dillon Broderick, the man
who held and comforted her during the blizzard. Then
she learns that her estranged sister is in love with him.
The sister whose affection Chantel's trying to regain. The
painful coincidence becomes even more devastating
when Chantel discovers she's pregnant.

On sale September 2000

Available wherever Harlequin books are sold.

**Don't miss
an exciting opportunity
to save on the purchase of
Harlequin and Silhouette books!**

Buy any two Harlequin or
Silhouette books and save
$10.00 off future Harlequin
and Silhouette purchases

OR

buy any three
Harlequin or Silhouette books
and save **$20.00 off** future
Harlequin and Silhouette purchases.

**Watch for details
coming in October 2000!**

PHQ400